MW01010572

I'm Still Here

By
Kathryn R. Biel

Chicka!,
I still owe you
a slice of cheescake!

I'M STILL HERE

Copyright © 2014 by Kathryn R. Biel

ISBN-10: 0-9913917-3-X
ISBN-13: 978-0-9913917-3-8

This book is a work of fiction. Names, characters, places and incidents are either products of the author's imagination or are used fictitiously, and any resemblance to actual persons, living or dead, business establishments, events or locales is purely coincidental.

All rights reserved.

No part of this book may be reproduced, scanned, or distributed in any printed or electronic form or by any electronic or mechanical means including information storage and retrieval systems, without permission in writing from the author. The only exception is by a reviewer, who may quote short excepts in a review. Please do not participate in or encourage piracy of copyrighted materials in violation with the author's rights. Purchase only authorized editions.

Cover design by Becky Monson.

Cover image via iStock photo by mammuth.

ACKNOWLEGDEMENTS

To my bestie, Michele Vagianelis. Yet another story that would not have been written without you. Oh, and make sure to thank JV for the spam email I supposedly sent to him that got this all started.

I had an incredible team of beta readers on this project. Without their collective insight, suggestions and encouragement, this book would be nowhere near what it is today: Jayne Denker, Tracy Krimmer, Heather McCoubrey, Jana Misho, Becky Monson, Susan Rys and Chrissy Wolfe.

And speaking of editors, this would be a hot mess without the critical eyes of Cahren Morris and Karen Pirozzi. I promise, someday, I will learn how to use a comma properly, as well as the difference between abject and object poverty.

I would still be floundering, trying to decide on a cover and a blurb if not for the great group over at ChickLitChatHQ.

My first friend in life, Julie Stewart (you will always be Julie Cheney to me!), thank you for giving me some insight about what it is like to be in a band. I wish you'd move back up here so I can go see you play again.

Meghan Francis, who is not only a talented soccer coach, but a gifted speech-language pathologist as well, thank you for answering my questions about aphasia. If there are any technical errors, I assure you that they were all mine in the making.

Becky Monson, cover designer extraordinaire—I'm totally crushing on this cover too.

Cheryl and Dean Schoeder, thank you for the use of your names. I'm sorry for what I did to them.

Without the support of my parents and husband, none of this would be possible. And now to that team, I've added my brother, Dan, who comes to my book events and asks insightful questions and my niece Lexi who helps me with my social media marketing. I'm so lucky to have all of you, as well as my biggest (smallest) supporters, Jake and Sophia.

KATHRYN R. BIEL

I never knew it was possible to miss someone you never met. Mike, the void you've left is immeasurable and I wish you were still here.

KATHRYN R. BIEL

DEDICATION

To my Tuesday night dance girls: No matter how I feel walking in the door, I know I'll feel better by the end of the night. It is my therapy through movement, and laughing until you cry doesn't hurt either. To Nicole, Jillian, Katie, Kaitlin, Dara, Jaimie, Megan and Kristen, thank you for listening, for your support, and most importantly, not laughing too hard at my dancing.

And to Margie and Charlene, who taught me how to dance in the first place.

CHAPTER ONE

I stepped on the sidewalk and walked with confidence. My hair was red and curly. My skin was flawless. My dress was tight, little and black. My car was, well shit, it was still a beat up, tired-looking, non-descript sedan (a 1992 Mercury Topaz, to be exact) with more rust than paint. I looked back over my shoulder. Yep, it was still there. It had not been magically replaced by a Porsche. I lost some (okay, all) of my bravado and my shoulders hunched for a minute. The confidence, fleeting as it was, was gone. I stopped and took a deep breath. I could do this. Aww, who the hell was I kidding? There was no way in hell I could do this. I turned around and walked as fast as my stilettos and tight LBD would let me, back to my POS mode of transportation. I jangled the key in the lock and jostled the door open. Bending and dipping so as not to flash my wares, I finally was inside my safe haven. With only three attempts at turning the engine over, I was off and sped away. I wanted to go home and hide in my bed for about six years. I decided that I needed some fortification if I was going to stay holed up for that long. I took the much familiar detour to the market to pick up some emergency supplies—a bag of Fritos and a box of Ho Hos.

What had I been thinking signing up for speed dating? It wasn't me. I wasn't that type of girl. I didn't do frivolous and flighty things like speed dating. I couldn't believe I let myself get talked into it. I didn't want to disappoint Jillian by saying no to her zany idea. I let her bully me into it. On the other hand, I was tired of being alone. I had been on my own for so long that the prospect of even possibly meeting someone held appeal.

1

Well, it wasn't going to be through speed dating, that was for sure.

As I was powering down the aisle towards the express check out, the heel snapped on my shoe. I stopped and stared, shoe in my hand like an alien life form. Really? Just my luck. I would say the universe was against me, if I believed in that sort of thing. 2013 was not turning out to be my year. Nope, not at all. I limped the rest of the way (why did the Ho Hos have to be in the back of the market?) to the check out, praying that no one noticed me. Of course, I was waaay overdressed for grocery shopping and had comfort food, as well as the heel from my shoe in my hand. Now I was lumbering through the store like Quasimoto, and I had the sneaking suspicion that my hair was growing larger by the minute. I'm fairly certain that I stuck out in the grocery store like a sore thumb, like the date-less loser on a Saturday night that I was. I made it to my car and kicked off my shoes as soon as I got inside. Good thing that I didn't need a pair of black heels anytime soon. I was on a restricted budget, and shoe shopping was not high on the list of essentials. Sure, they would now be on the list, but Ho Hos and Fritos always took precedence.

Never one to waste time, I had the box of Ho Hos opened by the time my car had reversed out of the parking spot. I navigated out to the main road and proceeded to begin drowning my sorrows in the delectable goodness of chocolate cake and cream. Yeah, this was the life. It was so much better than going to the speed-dating event. I was waiting at the four-way stop, chowing down with reckless abandon, savoring the creamy deliciousness, when suddenly my car was rammed from behind. This initial impact pushed my car far enough into the intersection to run into the car to my left, which was making a left. I felt the two collisions, followed by a loud popping noise right next to my head. For a minute, I thought someone had fired a gun. But no, I could not be that lucky. It was only my airbag deploying. It wailed my chest and face, and the air was filled with smoke and dust. The Ho Ho that I had been bringing to my mouth became one with my face as my hand propelled upwards. I tried to breathe and inhaled dust and a bit of chocolate cake, which immediately had me choking and coughing. I reached down impatiently to unhook my seat belt, which had locked up. As I finally got it off, my door opened up from the outside. Without looking, I jumped out, happy to be free of my death trap, and promptly fell into the guy who opened my door.

Yup, there I was, covered in dust and Ho Ho debris, coughing and choking, spitting out powder and cake. My red curls now resembled a rat's nest, and my dress was riding dangerously high on my thighs. I was standing barefoot in the street with no way to get home. I was so ready to meet the man of my dreams.

"Are you okay?"

"Yeah, I'm ..." I was interrupted from replying 'fine' as I tried to look up at the face that belonged to the set of arms holding me up. The pain in my neck was immediate and intense. Shit, this was so not what I needed right now; par for the course for me, but not what I needed. Tears welled up in my eyes before I could stop them. I dropped my chin down and rested my head against the chest of the person supporting me. It didn't hurt that it belonged to a tall man. But at that point, I would have sunk my head into the soft bosom of just about anyone. "I think I hurt my neck."

His arms were holding me by the elbows. He had a firm grip. My mind was racing a million miles a minute. I was still pretty much trying to process what had just happened. It occurred to me that my car was probably totaled. Actually, I knew it was, since the airbag had deployed. I wanted to turn and look to see how bad it really was, but I was afraid to move my head. So, I simply stood there, held up by some strange man, head buried into his chest. I still wasn't able to see what he looked like, but his strength and support seemed like a good thing at the time. Okay, maybe this night wouldn't be a total loss. I reached up with my left hand to touch my

3

neck, and immediately felt pain in the front of my chest. I let out an involuntary whimper and wince.

Crap. I didn't want to seem like one of those weak, whiny girls. I didn't cry. I was the strong one. I always had to be.

"The ambulance will be here any minute. We'll get you checked out. Are you okay until then?"

I sniffed in, trying not to get snot all over his shirt. "Maybe. I think."

"Well, as long as you're positive."

I started to chuckle, but it hurt too much. I sniffled loudly. I was dangerously close to losing control of the mucus in my nose. I could endure a lot of embarrassment, but snotting on a stranger was just too much, even for me. "My neck really hurts. So does my chest."

"You probably have some pretty good whiplash and a contusion from the seat belt. Do you think you can take a few steps to get out of the intersection?"

"Um, sure. I, um," I faltered. This was going to sound totally whiny. Please don't let me sound like a complete baby. "I can't really lift my head. I'm afraid it's going to hurt too much."

"Squeeze your shoulder blades together, gently."

I did as the magic voice commanded.

"Now, see if you can lift your head a little."

I tried, and although it hurt, it was not as bad as I expected. I had my eyes squeezed shut in anticipation of the pain. I was slowly lifting my head when a high-pitched woman's shriek accosted my eardrums from my right. Even through all the cacophony of the traffic and distant wail of sirens, I knew that voice. There was no one else in the world who would say, "Avert your eyes!" to me. Reflexively, I turned to look. The pain shot down my neck and then everything went black for a moment.

"Stay with me here. I've got you."

I pushed down through my collapsing legs, tried to ground myself in reality and stand up again. "I'm trying to. I just thought ..." I trailed off. Had I heard what I

4

thought I had heard? It couldn't be. I had to be a little wonky from the accident. Yeah, that was it. Certainly I hadn't just heard my dead sister's voice.

CHAPTER TWO

Four hours later, I was still sitting on a plinth in the hallway of the Riverside Hospital, waiting to be seen. My neck hurt. So did my chest and shoulders. I was almost certain that I would have a might pretty bruise from the seat belt. I couldn't actually look, because my neck was in a brace. I still had no shoes, and my dress kept riding up. I wrapped the stiff white sheet around my lower body a little tighter hoping to keep the perverted looking bum across from me from getting a show. Not that I wasn't wearing good underwear because I was. At least this was one occasion where my mother had been right—always wear clean underwear in case of an accident.

I was leaning with my back against the wall, sitting upright. The fatigue of the day settled in and I ached everywhere. Fairly confident that I did not have a spinal cord injury, I wiggled my fingers and toes to give myself some reassurance. This was so not how this day was supposed to go. I gingerly lifted my left arm until I could peek at my watch without moving my head. It was around eleven p.m. I needed to go home and go to bed. Letting my arm sink downward until it flopped at my side, I took in a deep breath. Slowly exhaling, I mentally inventoried all the body parts that hurt. I quickly got discouraged and decided to take the shorter approach of inventorying the parts that did not hurt (earlobes and ends of my hair).

Seeing as how my ears were one of the few parts that did not appear to be injured, could I really believe what I thought they heard? It couldn't have been Aster. No way. She had been gone for more than seven years now. I tried not to think of her very often. Of course, that

6

was akin to telling myself not to breathe. God, I missed her. I wished she was here with me, holding my hand. Like the time when we were ten and I got dragged across a gravel road by our dog. I was terrified that the stupid animal would get away so I refused to let go of his leash. There were little tiny pebbles embedded into the skin on my knees. It took my mother hours to dig them all out, and it hurt like the dickens. Aster sat with me the whole time. She alternated between reading to me and singing to me to distract me from the pain. Closing my eyes, I could still see the hideous striped shirt she was wearing that day, and I could hear her voice reciting the words of Laura Ingalls Wilder. I thought she was so great entertaining me that day.

I thought of that day often. But tonight, in pain once again, I remembered, moments before Cinda took off, seeing Aster across the road with the neighbor's dog. The one that Cinda hated. Aster knew it. We weren't supposed to play with that dog. It had a mean streak. I never knew why Aster was with that dog that day. In all the excitement (and pain), I forgot to ask her. Looking back, it was easy to guess that she stayed with me while I was being patched up out of guilt. I guess I would never know.

Deep in this memory, I jumped when I heard a voice saying my last name.

"Ms. Cox? How are you doing?"

I opened my eyes. It was that nice guy who had pulled me out of my car at the scene of the accident. Here he was in the hospital. How had he found me? Wait, why was he here in the hospital? Was he some kind of deranged psycho who stalks car accident victims?

"Before you think I'm some kind of creepy stalker dude—"

"Too late," I managed to interject quickly. Then I smiled. Well, sort of smiled, since my cheek muscles hurt.

Deranged-stalker guy smiled back. He had straight white teeth, so he must have had good dental and orthodontic care. Okay, I could start referring to him as "good-dental-hygiene-deranged-stalker-guy." Good dental hygiene is important. So many deranged stalkers have poor dental care, and it pretty much gives them away right from the start.

"How are you feeling?"

"Pretty crappy. I kind of feel like I got hit by a truck."

Good-dental-hygiene, oh crap, you know who I mean, replied, "Well, you kind of did. The vehicle you were pushed into was a Ram."

"As in battering?"

"As in Dodge."

"Well, then that explains it, although the battering ram would have made sense too." I smiled a little more now. He laughed. I wished I could laugh with him, but God, everything really hurt. Maybe I was getting a little delirious from the pain, but this guy seemed kind of cute. No, not kind of cute, but really cute. "But, unless you want me to refer to you as 'Deranged-stalker-man' I might need to know your name. If that's okay."

"O.K."

I waited. "Okay?"

"O.K."

"Okay, normally I have a good sense of humor, but I've had kind of a shitty day. Everything hurts. My car is totaled. I have no money for a new one. To make matters worse, I lost my Ho Hos and Fritos in the car, which I totally needed today to comfort me because I was too chicken-shit to go to a speed dating thingy that my friend pressured me into. Then, I've been waiting here for hours. I appreciate you coming to see me, and for your help earlier, but can you just cut me some slack and tell me your name?"

"My name is O.K."

"Seriously?"

"Seriously."

"Wow that sucks. I thought my parents were bad, but I think yours take the cake."

O.K. laughed. "No, they did not saddle me with the name. It's my nickname, but it's what everyone calls me. I'm not sure I'd answer to my given name anymore."

"So what is your given name then?"

"Top secret information."

"Oh, come on. Give me a break. Can you not tell that I've had the most crap-tastic day?"

"Oh, I guess, and only because you've had a crap-tastic day. But you have to promise to keep it a secret. Deal?"

"Deal. Wait, let me guess?"

"You'll never get it."

"Now that sounds like a challenge." He looked skeptical. I decided to try looking desperate. "Oh come on, please? I've been here for over four hours, and I'm bored out of my gourd. Please?"

"I guess we can play, but only because you just rhymed 'bored' and 'gourd.' You get points for rhyming while in pain."

"How many points do I get for guessing your name correctly?"

"I don't even have to determine it because you will not get it. But if it makes you feel better, then guess away."

"Oscar?"

He shook his head and smiled.

"Oliver? Owen? Otto?"

"You're so cold, you're about to die of hypothermia."

"Otis? Ogden? Ozzy?"

"Getting even colder."

"Orenthal?"

"Orenthal?

"Yeah, like O.J. Simpson."

O.K. laughed. "I know. I'm just surprised that you knew his real name."

"I wouldn't have before the trial, but who doesn't now? So, not even close?"

"Nope, not even close." He sat down in a chair next

to my gurney and comfortably crossed his right ankle over his left knee. He clasped his fingers behind his head and relaxed back against the wall.

"Okay, then, I'm going to need a hint."

"Well, I don't know about a hint."

"Oh, come on already. Please?" I hated that I was begging. I hated that he was making me beg. I hated that I enjoyed begging him.

"Oh, I guess. The hint is that my first name does not begin with the letter 'O.'" He was very coy, and if I wasn't mistaken, he winked at me.

From the tone of his voice, it was obvious that he's played this game before. Shit, this was his standard line. No doubt about it. No way in hell am I going to be one of those girls who falls for a stupid line. Un uh, not me, not this time. Not gonna do it.

"Look, O.K., whatever your name is. I don't mean to sound like a bitch, but I'm not in the mood for your line right now."

"My line?"

"Yeah, your pick-up line."

O.K. smiled. He was not only smiling, he was laughing. Really belly laughing. What was he laughing at? Oh, shit. He was not only laughing, he was laughing at me.

"Are you laughing at me?"

"No," he choked out.

I tried to cock my head but the neck brace prevented me from moving. Neck brace. Accident. Airbags. Big hair. Oh God, what must I look like right now? My hand flew up to my hair and tried to smooth it down. "Oh, God, do I look that bad?"

He kept looking, and tried to stop laughing but couldn't. He was saved by an orderly who hastily entered from down the hall, "Ms. Cox, it is time to bring you to X-ray."

I was wheeled off in one direction while O.K. just sat there, still laughing at me. Good thing I'd never have to see him again.

CHAPTER THREE

"So there I was, accusing him of hitting on me. Little did I know that I was still covered in cornstarch from the airbag, my dress was stained and torn, and my hair was the size of a Jackson Five-era Afro. And to make matters worse, I had a bruise and road rash on my chest."

"Oh gosh, Es, that's awful."

I took a small sip of my green tea, staring down at the liquid. "That's not the worst part."

"How can it not be the worst part? It sounds like a dreadful day. And then, to have some creep following you around and trying to pick you up. You poor dear." Jillian cooed at me. Her appearance was in such contrast to her soft, motherly demeanor. With her blunt cut black hair and dark glasses, she bore a startling resemblance to Edith Head. She could dress up as Edna Mode from *The Incredibles* for Halloween simply by donning a black dress. But beneath that hard exterior was a soft-hearted cream puff.

"Yeah, no, it was even worse. I was eating a Ho Ho when I got hit. It smashed into my face. I went through the whole encounter with this guy with chocolate and cream smeared all over my face like a three-year-old."

Jillian's hand flew to her mouth.

"Oh yeah. I had Ho Ho cream in my eyebrow."

"Oh, Es, that's even more terrible."

"But wait, there's more."

"How can there be any more? How could it be worse than that?"

"Oh, it can be worse than that because that's my luck right now. You know, I thought moving to a new city

11

would actually be a fresh start. But no, I'm doing even worse here than I had been. It's like I'm under a black cloud or something."

"Why do you say that?"

"Because O.K. was not some deranged stalker with good dental hygiene. Oh no, he was my doctor. Yeah, he was there because his shift started at eleven, and I was his first patient."

Jillian froze, mid-bite on her Boston Cream. I gestured for her to close her mouth before she ended up wearing her partially masticated doughnut.

"Yeah, he was there to examine me. The whole, 'how are you feeling?' was not a good Samaritan gesture. He was just doing his job."

"Oh, Es, that's so embarrassing!"

"Tell me about it. I've never had a day like that. I was like a walking disaster—like something out of a sitcom. That is so not me."

"Well, at least you never have to see him again. Right?"

I shrugged. "I guess. I mean, I'd never be able to rebound from the embarrassment of thinking he was hitting on me. Ho Ho cream in my eyebrow!"

"Wait—why were you eating Ho Hos to begin with? I thought Saturday was that speed-dating event?"

I again looked at my tea for answers. No words of wisdom in the leaves. I guess that happens when you use a tea bag. I shrugged again. Well, I tried to shrug. My neck and shoulders were still pretty tender, and moving them hurt. "Yeah, I chickened out. I told you it wasn't my type of thing."

"Es, you know you have to get out more. You'll never find anyone sitting home eating Ho Hos and Fritos."

"How did you know I bought Fritos too?"

"Because I know your M.O. That's what you eat when you get stressed. Or need comfort. Or are happy. Or are sad. Or on days that end in 'Y.'"

"Yeah, but only on those few rare occasions. Otherwise, I pride myself on my healthy eating."

"This is true. You do eat so very healthy. I don't get the Ho Ho and Frito obsession."

"That's what happens when you grow up on a commune with hippy-dippy parents. I've eaten so much tree bark and grass in my life that my body craves some bad stuff. I never got it as a kid."

"Someday I want to meet your parents."

"Cheryl and Dean? Yeah, I don't think so."

"Awww, come on. I need to see where you came from. I need to see the people who produced such a wonderful child."

I shook my head slightly. I hated talking about my family. I was getting angina simply thinking about them. Jillian never pushed, but I could tell she didn't understand either. "You don't understand. I don't have a relationship with my parents. I don't talk to them."

"At all? How can that be?"

I shrugged. "They're totally not normal. I mean, obviously. I call them by their first names. Always have. But they see me as the odd one. To them, I'm the black sheep. I don't fit in. I never have and I never will. And at this point, I'm persona non grata."

"Why do you say that?"

"Because I'm too analytical. I don't read Tarot cards or tea leaves. I believe in Western medicine. I don't think that smoking a little weed will cure what ails you. I'm materialistic and like modern technology. And I ..." I broke off.

"What?"

"I believe that my sister is dead."

"What do you mean that you believe it?"

"Well, the most important detail in this story is that she left a suicide note. She wasn't stable, although my parents never wanted to see it. She disappeared one night and was never heard from again. She had been very ill and was an addict." I paused for a minute before saying, "But they never found her body, so my parents have always held out hope." I felt robotic saying it like that, but it had been so long, and I had been over it so many times. It had drained so much out of my life that I had to make the conscious decision to move past it. That was the final nail in the coffin between my family and me. I told Jillian as much.

"How many kids are there in your family again? Ten, twelve?"

"No, only seven." I smiled. It was amazing how people were dumbfounded when they found out the size of my family. It wasn't that big. It's not like we were the Duggars or anything.

"Which sister was it?"

"Aster."

"Was she older or younger? Where was she in the line up?"

"She was older than me by twelve minutes. We were twins."

"Identical?"

"No, fraternal. Cheryl's womb was the only thing we ever had in common."

Jillian put down her doughnut and wiped her hands. "You mean to tell me that your mom named her twins Aster and Esther? And how did I not know you were a twin?"

"I don't talk about it much. And yes, Cheryl did name us Aster and Esther. I was always jealous that Aster got this cool, ethereal pretty flowery name and I had the name of an eighty-year-old Jewish woman. Which wouldn't have been bad if we were Jewish, but my parents were originally Catholic."

"Do you want to talk about it?" I could tell Jillian was dying to know more.

"Not right now. Someday, I'll tell you the whole story, but I'm not up for it right now. I need to have a lot more alcohol before I even attempt to tell some of my family stories. But you want know the weird thing?"

"What?"

"So, after the accident, Dr. O.K. had helped me out of the car and I was standing there. I was trying to lift my head. I heard a woman scream."

"Was it the other driver?"

"No, that's the thing. I don't know where the scream came from. It was somewhere across the intersection. I'm positive that it was Aster."

"Why do you think that it was Aster?"

"Because it was her voice. I know it was sure as I'm sittin' here. But it was also what she said."

"What did she say?"

"She said something from when we were kids. She said, 'Avert your eyes!' It was a private thing. No one else in the world would know about it."

"What does it mean?"

"We always had to share a room, which was fine, but as we got older, privacy became scarce. One night Violet was in our room and she thought a bug flew down her pants, so she took them off. Aster yelled, 'Avert your eyes' as Violet disrobed. I don't know why, but we found it hysterical. From then on, whenever one of us went to undress, the other yelled that."

"Oh my God. Do you think it was her?"

"I don't know what to think. I've felt for seven years that she was dead. I've done battle after battle with my family to give up their hope and to let go." I finished the dregs of my tea and stood up. "I know that I am right. I just can't explain what happened."

"Do you think she was there, you know, in spirit?"

"I don't think so. But at this point, I don't know what to believe anymore."

CHAPTER FOUR

I tossed and turned, trying to get comfortable. Nothing worked. Damn whiplash. I couldn't sit, but I couldn't lie down either. It still hurt to turn my head. I guess it was a good thing that I didn't have a car to be driving right now. I wouldn't be able to anyway. I got up, popped another couple of Advil like they were Tic Tacs and went over to my computer.

I sat there, staring at the dark screen, hesitant to even turn it on. I knew what I was thinking of doing, and I didn't want to do it. I mean, I did want to do it, but, oh crap I was so confused. I knew I wanted to start researching, trying to find out what was happening to me. But I was scared. I needed to talk to someone about the situation. Not Jillian. She was too soft-hearted and naive. Despite the cruel and hard realities of our jobs with Franklin County Children's Services, Jillian was still shocked each time someone did something bad to another human being. It was why she was good for the job—she had faith in the human race. I considered myself good for the job because I had grown up in a family of dysfunction, and I understand how messed up things could really get.

The alarm on my phone beeped. I looked at the calendar reminder. I had physical therapy in forty-five minutes. Without a car, I was left to walk to therapy, so I needed to get going. As much as I had hated my beat-up, rusted-out, piece-of-shit mobile, it sure beat hoofing it everywhere. When the weather was bad, I took the bus, but I think I hated that even more. At least it was a warm day, but not too hot, especially considering it was the end of August. Thank you, global cooling. I would probably only be a little sweaty by the time I reached the clinic, but I threw on an extra coat of deodorant before leaving nonetheless. I pulled my unruly red hair up into a knot (or as close as my hair would let me) on the top of my head. It was more like a big fuzz ball. I would need my hair off my neck for the session. Plus, I was always looking for containment of my hair, which refused to be contained or defined.

Thirty-five minutes later, I was huffing and puffing up the large hill that led to the medical arts building where the PT clinic was. I couldn't run or work out because my neck and back were significantly jacked up. Three weeks had passed since the accident. I was still waiting on a rental car from my insurance. It had seemed like a good idea at the time to switch to that company with the cool commercials, but in hindsight, paying a little more for a company that actually delivered might have been a good idea. No longer would I be fooled by talking animals promising better prices. I was due to go back to work on Monday, and I would need a car to visit my clients. I needed to get that red tape unraveled soon. That was another problem for another moment. At this moment, I needed to get into the PT clinic so Kevin could work wonders and hopefully fix me once and for all.

Of course, recovering from whiplash and then speed walking to my PT session was probably not the best idea. I was often full of not-so-bright ideas. By the time I got to the door, I could barely stand up, let alone pull the freakishly heavy door open. Seriously, this was a place for people with physical problems. Why did the door weigh fifty pounds? As I was struggling with the door (I'd be damned if I would use the handicapped button), an arm reached over my shoulder and I heard a voice say, "Allow me, Ms. Cox."

I knew the voice without turning around. Of course, I couldn't turn my head, even if I wanted to, but luckily I didn't need to. Why was this guy always showing up? Why did I always have to look like an ass when he did show up? I don't think that looking like an ass was my baseline, but this would be the third time with this guy, so maybe it was. Was it the karmic rule of the universe that I should always embarrass myself in front of the adorable doctor with the killer grin?

I stepped back and allowed him to pull the door open for me. It appeared effortless on his part, like the door weighed no more than a sheet of paper. Huh. He probably worked out. Rescuer, doctor, perfect teeth, gorgeous brown eyes. I didn't need to add a most-likely fit and trim body. He was too perfect. He needed nothing more in his favor.

"I'm here for PT," I said as I walked towards the PT clinic door. Duh. I was such a dolt. Why was I always saying and doing idiotic things around him? When he was merely some anonymous person who had pulled me out of my car, I could form a coherent thought and not sound like an imbecile. But once I realized that he was not only a kind person (because what other type of person would help a stranger out during a car accident?), but cute, I seemed to have lost brain cells.

"I got that," O.K. said smiling. He nodded towards the door. "How's it going?"

"Other than the fact that I can't turn my head, I'm in constant excruciating pain, I still have no car, and I have to go back to work in four days, things are just peachy." I didn't mention that I was beginning to doubt my sanity thinking that I heard my dead sister just after the accident. Actually, I wonder if O.K. heard the woman screaming too? Maybe I should ask him. If he heard it too, then maybe I wasn't going crazy. If he hadn't heard it, well, then, I think the answer is pretty obvious.

"Wait, you don't have a car yet? How did you get here? Did someone drop you off?"

I could be crazy (completely to be determined), but I could have sworn that he glanced at my left hand when he said the word 'someone.'

"Um, no. I walked."

"You walked? Do you live close by? This isn't a residential section." Crazy again, but I know a look of relief crossed his face when I said that I was here alone.

"I live over off North High in Clintonville, in an apartment complex by the Steak 'N Shake."

"That's at least a mile away!"

"It's about a mile and a half."

"And you walked it?" He almost seemed incredulous.

"Yeah. You know, I always hated my car, but at least I didn't have to worry about anyone breaking into it when I had to drive into bad neighborhoods. Now I miss it dreadfully. At least the walking is good exercise. I can't really do anything else right now. It kind of keeps me a little sane as well."

"Are you not doing so well since the accident?"

I wanted to be flippant and brazen and shrug it off, but I couldn't. "Yes. No, not really. I didn't expect things to be this hard. I thought I'd get better faster. And ..." I trailed off before I got to the coo-coo part.

"Did you say you were going back to work on Monday?"

"Yeah, hopefully, as long as Kevin gives me the okay."

He smiled when I said 'okay.' "Do you still want to know what my real name is?"

I could swear he was flirting with me. Should I flirt back? Could I flirt back? It had been so long since I'd even tried. Last time, I thought he was flirting with me, I ended up sounding like a gigantic jackass. No, I was going to take the straight and narrow approach.

"Um, actually, I have to get into my appointment with Kevin's magic hands, but, um, there is something I would like to talk to you about. Would you be available to grab a cup of coffee sometime?"

"Far be it from me to keep you from Kevin's magic hands, although I now wish I were Kevin. My office is down the hall. Why don't you come over after and I'll give you a lift home? You might have to wait a few minutes, but I'm just catching up on some paperwork. Will that work?"

"Oh, um, sure." Holy cow, that was definite flirting. "I hadn't really expected you to actually say yes." Dammit. Where was my internal filter and why wasn't it working?

O.K. smiled again. He had the most delightful lines around his eyes. It showed that he smiled a lot. I liked that. Of course, with teeth as perfect as his, I'd be smiling all the time as well. He seemed like a happy-go-lucky kind of guy. Maybe he was the kind of person I should consider pursuing. The question was, was I the kind of person that he would consider pursuing?

CHAPTER FIVE

I sat in the waiting room of Dr. O.K.'s office. The secretary kept stealing glances at me out of the corner of her eye. It was apparent that she wanted to check me out but didn't want to be caught doing so. It made me wonder if there were girls here to go out with Dr. O.K. all the time. However, she wasn't very sly, and I caught her every single time. I was sure that I was a sight to behold. Black yoga pants and gray sneakers. A lime green, slightly fitted v-neck t-shirt. And then there was the hair. Piled on top of my head, the ginger curls had escaped containment and now it looked like I was wearing an electrocuted animal.

My hair was my arch nemesis. I hated my hair. It was red. But not really red; that was just the category I fell into. Honestly, it was orange. I never said that aloud because then came the inevitable comment ... carrot top. And it was curly. The only thing I had going for me is that it was not super thick, just moderately thick. When it was humid, it sucked moisture out of the air and grew to epic proportions. My whole life, all people ever commented on with regard to my appearance was my hair. No one ever saw past the domineering life force to my face, which I thought was remotely pretty. No one saw my eyes, which were the coolest color, half way between dark blue and dark green. No one saw that my skin was porcelain and flawless and that I looked younger than my age. Nope, they only saw the hair.

I hated my hair.

Aster was blessed with silky straight hair that was the color of sun-kissed caramels. I used to love to brush

21

and braid her hair when we were little. As I ran my fingers through it, I used to fantasize that it was my hair. I used to pray that I would wake up in the morning and our hair would have switched bodies. Aster did not like to do her own hair, let alone mine. Getting a brush through my hair could be akin to torture, so I never wanted anyone to touch it anyway (which, of course, propagated the cycle of tangles and torture). She was happy that I would take the time and effort to make her look nice so she didn't have to.

As I got a little older, I discovered that there were hair products specifically for people like me. My mother, in her hippy, live-off-the-land lifestyle, didn't really believe in them. She made her own soap out of left over fat from cooking (which became even more interesting when she went through her vegan phase). This did not lend itself to being able to make my hair look attractive. By the time I was in high school, I was sneaking off to the drug store and using my lunch money to buy conditioner and frizz tamer. Aster sympathized with my plight and helped me keep my contraband toiletries hidden from Cheryl. Sometimes, she would show up with a different product for me to try. The ones she got were always far superior to anything I would purchase. After a while, I figured out that Aster was shoplifting them for me. She was terrible at managing her money and there was no other way she would be able to afford them. I think she also liked the thrill of committing that act. It was the first of many red flags about Aster. But like everyone else in my family, I stuck my head in the sand and ignored it for much longer than I should have.

Anyway, I was there, relaxing in the doctor's office, knowing what horrendous thoughts the secretary must be having about my hair. I was pretty relaxed from the combination of Kevin's magic hands and the electrical stimulation machine. I may have dozed off, my head resting back against the wall. Next thing I know, Dr. O.K. is standing over me, clearing his throat gently. As my eyes flew open, my mouth snapped shut. Great. There I had been, sleeping, with my mouth hanging open like I was catching flies. Please, God, please let me NOT have been drooling or snoring.

"You look like you could really use a cup of coffee right about now."

"Do I look that bad?"

"No, you look tired, and you just fell asleep sitting up. That's a rare talent."

"That's me, rarely talented. Or better yet, barely talented."

"I highly doubt that. I bet you are full of hidden talents and wonders." Why did his words give me flutters in the pit of my stomach?

"Not so much these days." I stood up, smoothing my shirt down. Reflexively, my hands brushed my hair back up towards the wayward top knot and tucked the loose tendrils behind my ears.

He seemed to be staring at my hair. I was wondering if there was something caught in it. I covered the top of my hair with my hands, praying that there was not a bug caught in it. I finally had to ask him. "Is there something in my hair?" continuing to pat it, searching for an inconsistency in the texture.

He smiled. "No, not that I can see. Why do you ask?"

"You seemed to be staring at it. It's, um, rather thick, and sometimes things get caught in it. Once, I went on a date with a guy who picked me up on his Harley. When we got to where we were going, my hair had apparently acted as flypaper for all sorts of critters."

O.K.'s mouth dropped open.

"Yeah, and my date was so unobservant that I went the whole night like that. I'm sure that the waitress and every woman I walked by saw them and laughed."

"So I take it that date was your last with that guy?" O.K. held the door for me as we walked out. His legs were a bit longer than mine, and he walked with a hurried purpose. Probably trying to get rid of me as quickly as possible. In my half-asleep, still relaxed zone, I trailed

23

behind him. Try as I might, I just could not get my legs to speed up.

I laughed. "Oh, no. I married him."

O.K. seemed to take that in stride. "Oh, so you're married?"

I chuckled, trying to mask my huffing and puffing. "Not anymore. As if the bug thing wasn't warning enough, his name itself should have been a deal breaker."

"What's his name?"

"Dickie Cox."

O.K. stopped mid-stride, causing me to run right into him. Too late, I put my hands out to brace myself, but they ended up getting wrapped around his midsection and were dangerously close to grabbing his package.

His hands closed over mine and secured them at a more appropriate level. There was a split second when we stood there, me glued to his posterior, arms around his waist and him holding me in place. I wanted to exhale, you know like Whitney Houston, but that seemed creepy, even for me. Before I knew it, the moment was done, and he had turned to face me.

"You married a man named Dickie Cox?"

I tried not to notice that he was still holding onto my hand. I hoped I didn't have creepy-girl palm sweat, but was pretty sure I did. My mouth was dry for a moment and I couldn't seem to swallow. I nodded.

"Why did you marry him?"

"I asked myself that every day of our marriage. Probably because I was looking for love and acceptance. And you know how the song goes ..."

"What song?"

"The one that says I was looking for love in all the wrong places."

That made him grin again. God, he was so adorable when he grinned. "How long were you married?"

"About one year, which was about nine months too long." I swallowed again. This was my chance. "So, now you see why I'm so picky about knowing people's names.

I know you shouldn't judge a book by its cover—for Christ sake, my name is Esther Comely-Cox, but I'm never getting burned like that again."

"I know. I saw it in your chart. Never in a million years would I have pegged you for an Esther." He dropped my hand. The name did it every time. Just saying it aloud was repellent. It was a terrible name, and I swear I'm coming back in my next life with the most beautiful, melodious name I can come up with.

"Yeah, Cheryl, my mom, insisted that I hyphenate. I've been stuck with the name now about six times longer than the marriage was. But now, when I use my first initial on things, it ends up being 'E. Comely-Cox,' which sounds like one of those spam porn e-mails that you get."

We were walking again, reaching his car quickly. It was a Nissan Maxima, fully loaded. A nice ride with a lot of pep, but not the pretentious car you'd expect a physician to be driving.

Once we were settled in the car, he said, "Kingston."

Kingston? What did he mean by that? I wracked my brain for a possible clue. "Kingston? As in the first capital of New York state?"

"As in my mother's maiden name. She was the last one in the lineage to have the name, so she gave it to me."

"Okay, that makes sense, but I'm still not seeing where the O.K. comes in."

"That would be because my last name is Cole. So, my name is Kingston Cole."

I blankly looked at him. He glanced over at me and then put his eyes back on the road, his hands in a responsible ten-and-two position.

"Kingston Cole ... King Cole ... Old King Cole."

"O.K."

"Yep. I've been stuck with O.K. since I was four."

"Wow. Maybe my family doesn't seem as out there anymore." I paused for a minute. "You know, I think you should change your last name to 'Corral.'"

He smiled in response. "Not the first time I've heard that one. That was my nickname in college. It's strange to have a nickname based on a nickname." He put the car in park. I hadn't even noticed that he had pulled up to a coffee shop in the local strip mall. I was confused for a moment. I must have had a quizzical look on my face because he replied, "You wanted to grab a cup of coffee?"

"Oh, I didn't know you actually were taking me up on that."

"Of course. It's my treat on one condition ..."

I immediately became skeptical. I didn't like conditions. I had dealt with too many of them in my life. Warily I said, "What's the one condition?"

"You tell me how your family's names could possibly be worse than mine."

Ugh. The last thing I wanted to do was talk about my messed up family. I let the conversation drop as we entered the swanky coffee bar and got our respective drinks. O.K. was a gentleman and paid for mine, even though I told him he didn't have to.

"You cannot hold this against me," I said as I fiddled with my cup, again filled with green tea. People laughed when I told them about my family. I laughed too. It was ridiculous. Completely and utterly ridiculous. Saying it made me sound ridiculous too. And for once, I wanted to be taken seriously. I was still new in town. I had only been here since March, and really only knew Jillian well. I desperately needed company and someone to talk to, hence the reason for my aborted speed-dating attempt that led me to meeting O.K. in the first place. But mostly, I wanted this man to take me seriously.

I took in a deep breath, trying to tell my story without sounding like a complete and total flake. Never mind that I had no car, couldn't move my head all that well, and was dressed in yoga pants at this upscale, yuppie coffee bar. I knew that this story could put my ridiculousness over the edge. I swallowed and finally gained the courage to begin.

26

Before I could get the first syllable out, I heard a husky voice say, "O.K., there you are. I've been texting you for twenty minutes to let you know I was in the back room."

That husky voice belonged to a buxom blond. She had to be close to six feet tall and stood even taller in her fashionable heels. I didn't know designers by name, but I could certainly spot a quality pair of expensive shoes. She was impeccably dressed in a fitted-yet-classy navy blue sheath dress. She was even wearing pearls. O.K. stood up to greet her, suddenly embarrassed. Of course he was embarrassed. He was with me. Sweaty, messy, dressed in yoga pants in public, carrot-top Afro, no car, down-and-out divorced me. Oh yeah, with a spam porn name. Thank goodness I hadn't told him the family story. It spared me a small, albeit tiny, but still-tangible piece of humiliation.

"Oh, Melissa, I forgot we were meeting here. This is—" he gestured quickly towards me, "a friend of mine who needed a ride home."

"If she needed a ride, then why are you drinking coffee and tea?" She looked down at my cup and said the word "tea" as if it left a bad taste in her mouth.

"Esther has had a bit of bad luck recently, and I was—"

Before he could even explain, Melissa (who I was now referring to as Demon Melissa in my head) cut him off. "Well, we'd better get going. Our dinner reservation is in ten minutes. We need to get in so that we can get to the hospital for our shift. I can't believe you cut it so close." Demon Melissa then focused her attention on me for a nanosecond. "I'm a doctor as well. What exactly is it that you do?"

Although being a social worker is nothing to be ashamed of, I knew no answer would ever be good enough for the likes of Demon Melissa. So I gave her something to chew on.

"I run an internet porn site. We're always looking for older models for those fetish freaks. You should visit me at www.e-comely-cox.net."

Her mouth fell open in horror and disgust before she turned sharply on one of her nude patent leather heels. She marched proudly towards the door. It was only a fleeting glance over her shoulder when she reached the door that made O.K. go running after her.

He looked back over his shoulder and gave me a quick, "Sorry."

I sat there in shock. Did he really just run out on me? Was he really with that beast? It was only a few minutes after he'd gone that I realized three things. One: I don't want a guy who is whipped. As far as I was concerned, I never wanted to see O.K. again. Two: Here I was, even further from home, with no ride. And three: the keys to my apartment were sitting on the center console of O.K.'s Maxima.

Shit.

CHAPTER SIX

Going for a bus ride in five o'clock rush hour traffic was not what I had in mind, especially after Dr. O.K. had gotten my hopes all up for a more pleasant mode of transportation. I can't believe he ditched me. I can't believe I almost told him about the names in my family. Believe it or not, my family story was even more embarrassing than my hyphenated porn-star name. I thought it over as I rode the falsely fluorescently bright bus over to the hospital. I figured I'd wait there until Dr. O.K. came on duty. I hoped his shift started at seven rather than eleven. If it started at eleven, it would be a mighty long night. Waiting the two hours until seven would be long enough.

Even to me, who had lived through it, the story of my family sounded far-fetched. Once upon a time, my mother, Cheryl, may have been relatively normal. I'd like to believe so at least. She met my dad, Dean, at a church retreat for incoming college freshman. They were both eighteen. Cheryl was studying to be a librarian. Dean, a civil engineer. They lived in Upstate New York and it was 1967. My mom got a hold of a relatively new book by Roald Dahl that discussed the materialism and lack of moral guidance in society. My dad got a hold of some LSD. After hearing him speak at Rensselaer Polytechnic Institute, where he was in school, Dean religiously followed the Timothy Leary movement, and my mom followed Dean. One night, after some particularly potent stuff and a pretty trippy trip, my mom became obsessed with Charlie and the Chocolate Factory. As a result, my siblings (in order) are Charlie Bucket Comely (who is a girl), Violet Beauregard Comely, Augustus Gloop Comely, and Veruca Salt Comely. Baby Mike Teavee Comely was the last of that bunch, until Aster and I gave Cheryl and Dean quite the shock five years later. It was a good thing for Aster and me that there were no more names of the ill-fated children with the golden tickets.

Aster's full name was Aster Rain Comely. See what I mean? Even with the crappy last name of Comely, it sounded beautiful. It was melodious and earthy and rolled off the tongue. Her name conjured images of flowers, bathed in a light spring rain. Her spirit was infectious and could not be contained. Everything about Aster was buoyant and full of life. Her soul was as radiant as her beauty. She was my soul and the air I breathed. It seemed almost sacrilegious to be thinking of her and her beauty while sitting on this dingy city bus. I clutched at the physical pain that gripped my heart. I had not let myself think of Aster like this in years. I couldn't. It was simply too agonizing.

Her story was not so uncommon. Always dramatic as a child, Aster's behavioral outbursts had often been attributed to being from such a large family. My parents were often immersed in their causes and often not immersed in the lives of their children. At least not by the time Aster and I rolled around. We were often left in the care of our oldest sister, Charlie, who was twelve when we were born. But I knew Aster's behavior was not simply a result of our flaky parents. I mean, I had pretty much the same childhood that Aster did. Sure, we were fraternal twins, not identical. But we shared the same room, sat through the same home schooling lessons until we begged Cheryl to attend the public school, did the same chores, lived through the same chaos.

About sophomore year in high school, Aster developed this ever-so-annoying habit of waking me up in the middle of the night to talk. After a while, I realized that she wasn't really sleeping. She would pace around the room, and sometimes even sneak out just to go for walks in the dark. When she returned, she would wake me up and tell me about all these wonderful ideas and plans she had. Sometimes, she would tell me about how she had figured out that God was real and that she truly believed.

And then as quickly as that phase started, it would stop. Aster would be so very depressed, barely able to get out of bed. She went through phases of self-injury. But Aster was clever, and hid it well from others. I could see it though. I could see the pain and emptiness behind her eyes that fell on her like a curtain when she was in one of her "funks." I saw the wildness and sparkle, the reckless abandon in her eyes when she was in an upswing. A manic phase. Because that's what it was. No matter what wonderful euphemisms we came up with, we could not hide the darkness that lived with us. Precious Aster was bipolar.

Cheryl and Dean refused to accept it. They never sought advice, each feeling that their combined counsel was sufficient. They never told anyone the whole story. The high highs and the crushingly low lows. They never shared any of the gory details. Oh no, all they ever told was how wonderful Aster was. How creative Aster was. She was an actress. She was a producer. She was a dancer. She was a singer. She was a painter. She fronted a band. She worked with children. She worked with the elderly. She did it all. She was their all.

They never saw that her flitting from one thing to another was truly a sign of her uncontrolled mental illness. Sure, the creativity that it afforded her was spectacular. For those of us left in her wake, it was devastating. She was unreliable, to say the least. She abused drugs, probably as a way to self-medicate. She destroyed her body by starving it and mutilating it. She was not a sister or a friend anymore. Being with her was nerve wracking. It was walking on egg shells, never knowing who was going to show up. Never knowing that moment when it would all change and she would begin to cycle down. Needless to say, dealing with her was stressful. I would ask her what she was doing or why she was doing something. Her standard response was, "You wouldn't understand." And she was right. I didn't understand. Not for a long time.

It was not until I had taken many psychology courses and done some field work with mentally ill patients that I began to understand. Even when I had the name for what afflicted my twin, I was not allowed to use it. Cheryl and Dean had moved on to transcendentalism and believed that Aster's purity had been corrupted by society. I never knew what the hell they were talking about when they started transcendental-izing at me.

I tried talking to Aster about it but never found a willing recipient. I guess most people don't want to hear that they are mentally ill. Crazy. If I talked to her when she was in a manic phase, she blew me off, because there was nothing in the world she could not conquer. If I tried talking to her in a depressive phase, she shut me down with the "You wouldn't understand" canned answer. She honestly thought that she was the only person out there whose brain worked this way. How she could not see it was a mystery to me.

But the greatest mystery of my life would always and forever be how Aster could come home from band practice one night, eat a bowl of cereal, and then disappear forever two hours later. She had been functional at that point. She and the band had been working on new material and by reports had a great session. She was living at home at the time. She got home around midnight, and had her usual midnight snack of a bowl of cereal. She talked with my mom briefly. There was no fight, no conflict. Just the standard, "What did you do today?" We all knew never to ask *how* the day was, unless we were truly prepared for that response. Most of the time, we really didn't want to know. My mom went to bed and heard Aster go up shortly afterwards.

In the morning, there was no sign of Aster. Her keys and phone were still there, as was her wallet. She had left a note telling us all that she loved us and that she was sorry she could not have been a better person. The police were convinced that she had jumped off the bridge near my parents' house. That was the last time anyone ever heard from her.

We were twenty-four.

CHAPTER SEVEN

We kept waiting for her body to bob up. For some poor fisherman to find her. Spring went by and turned into summer. The "Missing" posters faded out and fell down. No one put new ones up. No one held out any hope. Except Cheryl and Dean. They hounded the police. Cheryl began contacting mediums and psychics and people who made her look on the straight and narrow by comparison.

I was lost without my twin. We were Yin and Yang. I was the anchor to her free spirit. But without her spirit lifting me up, I just felt weighed down by life. I was not the creative one, but I started writing. I wrote a letter, a plea to my sister to come home. But I didn't know what to do with it. There was nowhere I could send it that Aster would be able to read it. Because Aster was dead. Still, I could remember every single word of my plea to my sister to come home. It went:

> *Aster, if you're out there, please come home.*
> *Aster, if you're out there, please call someone*
> *just to let them know that you're okay.*
> *Aster, if you're out there, don't be afraid to*
> *come back.*
> *Aster, if you're out there, know that your*
> *family and friends are worried sick.*
> *Aster, if you're out there, don't do anything*
> *that cannot be undone.*
> *Aster, if you're out there, know that life is*
> *worth living.*
> *Aster, if you're out there, realize that you have*

talents and gifts that the world needs.
Aster, if you're out there, you have so many
people who care about you, and just want to
help.
Aster, if you're out there, know that there is
nothing so bad that you cannot get over it or
move on.
Aster, if you're out there, know that your
family, friends, acquaintances and total
strangers are praying for you.
Aster, if you're out there, realize that we all
feel helpless right now.
Aster, if you're out there, we're all afraid
you're already gone.
Aster, if you're out there, please come home.

I used to lie in bed and say those words over and over, like a mantra. Like a prayer. I prayed to Aster in the sky because no God ever answered my prayers. I knew my words were useless. They would help Aster come home about as much as I had been able to help her when she was alive.

It didn't take much psychoanalysis to realize that I became a social worker because of my experiences with Aster. I knew how mental illness could destroy a family. I knew that we, as a family, had desperately needed someone to swoop in and help us, but no one ever came. It probably would have helped if someone in the family had actually admitted that there was a problem and asked for help. Probably.

Feeling as desolate and alone as I had that first day without Aster seven years ago, I walked on autopilot from the bus stop, tears still streaming down my face. It had been so long since I had really thought about Aster like that. Oh, I thought about her almost every day. Usually something reminded me of her, or I saw something funny that I thought she would appreciate. I would think about something from our childhoods, which were so inextricably linked together. We used to say that people considered us one person. Like we came together and were not two separate people. While I may have, on occasion, pulled at those reigns that bound me to Aster, I never expected to be running totally free of her.

It sucked.

It sucked that I had seven more birthdays and seven more Christmases. I had seven more Halloweens, which was always our favorite holiday. I had seven years of anger and resentment and longing and bargaining. In short, I had seven years.

Aster was forever twenty-four. Forever that young, wild girl, not quite ready to grow up. Here I was, now thirty-one. I was pragmatic and responsible. I had a respectable job. I did have a failed marriage to Dickie Cox who, by the way, was a wannabe televangelical preacher, but I can't really be held responsible for that one—the marriage failing, that is. I mean, he was a wannabe televangelical preacher, after all.

A giggle bubbled up through my tears. I tried to choke it back and it came out sounding like a strangled cry. I had tears running down my cheeks. With my fair complexion, I was undoubtedly red and splotchy. Oh, and did I mention that I'm an ugly crier? This was me, pushing my way through the revolving doors into the lobby of the hospital. Crying and giggling and gurgling. It was no wonder that a passing nurse asked me if I needed help. I looked that awesome.

I ducked into a bathroom and was happy to discover that the bathroom was a private one. Once I had locked the outside door, I didn't have to worry about anyone walking in on me. I stared at myself in the mirror for a moment. I was shocked at how quickly the grief had overcome me and how completely it had overwhelmed me. I had put up walls around my feelings about Aster for so long that it surprised me how raw everything felt. Despite the fact that seven years had passed, those wounds still felt acute and fresh. I needed to stuff all that feeling back in the box and pull myself together. I splashed cold water on my face and smoothed it into my hair to try and calm the chaos up there.

I needed to blow my nose, which was red and full. I went over to the toilet paper dispenser and pulled. Approximately two squares of nearly transparent toilet tissue came off the jumbo-size industrial roll. I repeated this process about twelve hundred times to get enough tissue to blow my nose without covering myself in mucus. I cleared my nasal passages with a loud "honk" that echoed off the ceramic tile walls. I quickly washed my hands and opened the door.

Demon Melissa was standing outside the door when I walked out.

"Was that honking *you*?" she said with a perverse sense of delight. "That was disgusting."

"No, it was the goose I keep in my back pocket. He needed to use the facilities."

"What are you doing here? You don't look sick to me." She stepped back, giving me the up and down look. "I take that back. You look terrible."

"Gee, thanks. I need to find O.K."

"He's working," she said in a snotty, almost valley-girl voice. "He doesn't have time for you." The bitch literally looked down her nose at me when she said that.

"I need to speak with him, but that's really between him and me. I don't need your help, thank you very much." With that dramatic statement, I turned on my heel and walked away.

Rather, I attempted to walk, but instead with my right foot, I stepped on the toes of my left foot and face planted on the hospital floor. Right in front of Demon Melissa.

Fan-freakin'-tastic.

CHAPTER EIGHT

I've done a lot of embarrassing things in my life. Making a jackass out of myself was nothing new for me. There was the time that I peed my pants in front of the third grade class. There was the time I ate a rotten onion from the garden because I believed my older brother when he told me it was an apple. There was the time I ate liverwurst because my sister told me it tasted like candy. There was the time I tried, unsuccessfully, to dye my hair black (but that's a whole other story in and of itself). Then, of course, there was the whole Ho Ho cream in the eyebrows incident. All of those paled in comparison to how I felt meeting the floor in front of Demon Melissa.

And at that moment when you think something cannot get any worse, I looked up to see a pair of scuffed brown Clarks that just happened to be covering the feet of one Dr. O.K. Cole. To repeat myself, fan-freakin'-tastic.

"Oh my God, Esther, are you alright?"

I struggled to get up, shrugging off his arm as he tried to help me. I tried not to wince, but the fall had jarred my already fragile back and neck. I gritted my teeth and found resolve that I didn't know I even possessed as I stood up and lifted my head proudly. Demon Melissa was not even bothering to hide the fact that she was laughing at me. Outright.

Okay, this is where I have to question a person's judgment. Granted, I didn't know O.K. that well. He had helped me out a few times, and seemed relatively nice. I had known Demon Melissa for all of eight seconds when I gave her that moniker. If she had never opened her mouth, I would have said she was beautiful. However, the moment she opened her mouth, she became so unattractive. While I liked to look nice, I truly did believe that beauty came from within. Demon Melissa had nothing inside but pettiness and a mean-girl spirit. I had no need to be around a person like her. I could not wait to get my keys, get out of this hospital and never have to see these people again.

"Esther, are you okay?"

"I'm fine. Just clumsy."

"Oh, you sure are. Did you see that O.K.? She tripped over her own feet. I've never seen anyone *that* clumsy before, have you?" There was such a patronizing tone to Demon Melissa's voice that it was all I could do not to punch her.

Surprisingly, O.K. spoke up. "Really, Melissa? Did you take your bitch pill today or something?"

I was kind of taken aback. The way he had followed her out of the restaurant, I would have thought him totally spineless and whipped. Apparently, there was trouble in paradise. The internal me did a happy victory dance. The professional me (who I decided to channel instead) humbly looked down at my shoes, letting the tension zip back and forth between the two of them. If I was the catalyst for Demon Melissa showing her true colors, then so be it.

D.M. (as I was now referring to her in my head, you know, after I finished my imaginary victory dance) turned on her heel in a huff and stormed down the hallway. I would hate to be one of her patients tonight. I felt bad for the poor sap who came in needing a proctology exam.

Once her satanic presence was gone, the air seemed lighter. O.K. just shook his head. "I don't even know how to begin to apologize for that one."

"I wish I could say it is okay, but it's not."

"I know that."

"But I can say that it is not your fault. You cannot control what another person does or says. You can only control what you do and say."

"Wow, deep. Normally I'd pay my shrink two-hundred bucks for advice like that."

"I'm not sure if I'm more disturbed by the fact that you need a shrink, or that you pay them two-hundred bucks an hour."

"Someday I'll tell you the whole sordid story. That is, after you tell me your story about family names that you claim is worse than mine, but cannot possibly be."

Oh no, I was not going to get sucked back in again. No, sir, no way. Nope. I was not going down this path— "Sure, O.K. Some night when you get me good and snookered, we can trade war stories. I will have to have you sign a confidentiality clause though."

Mental head smack. Did I really say that?

O.K. smiled. Wow, those teeth really were perfect. They made his smile dazzling, like he belonged in a toothpaste commercial or something. I was mesmerized, staring at their sparkling whiteness. I *may* have crossed the line into creepy stare, because I suddenly became aware that O.K. was looking at me kind of funny.

"Sorry, I was staring at your teeth. They're brilliantly white. Kind of mesmerizing, really."

He closed his mouth and in a self-conscious kind of way and covered it for a moment with his hand. I had really crossed the line this time.

"I had horrible teeth as a kid. I only got them fixed in the last few years. I spent so long being self-conscious of my smile. It still throws me when people compliment me, but thank you nonetheless."

That was not the answer I had been expecting. He was much more candid than I was used to. It was refreshing but unsettling all at the same time. Unsure of where to go from here, I did what all suave, confident, self-assured people do—I changed the subject.

"Um, I left my apartment keys in your car. I need them."

"Oh my God, why didn't you say something at the coffee shop? How did you get here? I can't believe I left you! I'm such an imbecile. No, a jerk. A big huge one."

I smiled. I had not expected him to berate himself like that. It was endearing.

"Leaving me stranded for Demon Melissa was kind of a dick move."

"What?"

Uh oh, maybe I shouldn't have said 'dick move.' I kind of had a mouth like a truck driver, although I'd been making a concerted effort to reign it in. Then it dawned on me. The E-Z Pass brain. You know, when a thought comes into my head and immediately speeds through and out of my mouth without slowing down. I had actually said 'Demon Melissa' out loud.

This time, it was my hand that flew to my mouth. There was that moment that hung awkwardly in the air. And then, O.K. let out a laugh. A big, deep, belly laugh.

"Oh, that's rich," he managed to get out through his chortles. "She can be quite demonic, right?"

I didn't answer, afraid my big fat mouth would get me into more trouble. Again. As per usual.

"Esther Comely-Cox, I like you. I really like you. I wish I could bring you home, but my shift is just about to start."

Did he mean bring me home as in give me a ride or as in take me home and ravage me? I vote B. I looked at my feet sheepishly, not sure of how to handle the flattery and attention, and afraid that my face would (again) betray my more naughty thoughts. "Oh, that's alright. I can just take the bus. I need my keys though."

"Tell you what, come with me. My buddy is just getting off his shift, and I'll have him bring you home."

"I couldn't have you ask him. It's totally not necessary."

"Yes, yes it is. Come with me. But I have to warn you, he's slick. Be prepared to fight off any advances."

He took off down the hall and walked with his head up and with confidence. I tried to mimic his posture so that no one would question whether or not I belonged here. His badge was attached to his belt by some sort of retractable cord and he would zip it out to open the massive steel doors that sectioned off one corridor from another. He walked fast, but I was able to keep up. I guess being without a car for the last three weeks had at least one benefit (oh, and my butt was definitely firmer, just in case you were wondering).

We had taken enough twists and turns to thoroughly rob me of any geographical bearing when O.K. announced, "Here we are."

We were in a staff lounge. There was a large table in the center with an assortment of goodies covering the surface. For people in the health care profession, there was certainly a lot of unhealthy food. I would bet none of it was even organic. Cheryl would have had a field day with this one. This would be yet another arrow in her quiver against the evils of Western medicine. I could almost hear her saying, "And *these* are the people who you receive your health direction from? Look at them, filling their bodies with chemicals and refined sugars and poisons."

On the other hand, it had been hours since I'd eaten, and I was famished. My eyes grew wide surveying the bounty spread out before me. My stomach produced a large growl, which I'm sure could be heard three states away. I covered my stomach with my hands, but it was too late. Any eyes that were not already on me quickly swiveled in my direction.

I mean, what are the odds that my stomach would not only grumble, but also that it would sound *exactly* like it was saying the word "fuzzy?" In my case, pretty darn good.

A tall blond guy stood up from a worn, corn-flower blue couch in the back corner.

"Jesus, O—get that girl some food. What are you trying to do, starve her to death?"

O.K. turned and looked at me. "When *was* the last time you ate?"

I shrugged. "I dunno, around noon, maybe?"

Seeing as how it was now seven p.m., I guess the whole stomach growling thing made sense. I also knew I actually hadn't eaten at noon. I had eaten a yogurt and granola around ten this morning, and that was the only thing I'd had to eat today. I wasn't working and the cash flow was tight. I couldn't be spending lots of money on luxury items like food.

"You didn't eat at the coffee shop?"

I looked down at my feet, like a child being scolded. Before I could respond, the large blond made his way up to the front of the lounge where we were standing. Now that he was right before me, I recognized him as a pediatrician I had recently interviewed on a child abuse case.

I smiled when I realized this. He had seemed like such a caring and compassionate man during the tedious and uncomfortable interview. "Oh, Dr. Olsson. Don't worry about me. I got a date with some ramen noodles as soon as I get home."

"Oh, hey, Esther. How's it going? I mean other than this oaf starving you." Before I could even answer, Dr. Olsson kept right on going. "And what do you mean ramen noodles? Does anyone still even eat those? I haven't had to eat those since my intern days."

"Don't forget," I smiled in answer to him, "I'm a county-funded social worker. Every day of my career will be like your intern days."

O.K. seemed a little perturbed that Dr. Olsson was talking to me. Or that he seemed to know me. Or that he was being criticized for his treatment of a woman. Whatever the reason, O.K. was now clearly annoyed, his brow knitted. "Rob, how do you know Esther?"

"We've worked together recently on a case," he said shortly. "How do you know Esther?"

"Esther is standing right here, and Esther can hear you both. Esther is just tired and obviously hungry, and wants to go home."

They both looked at me. Dr. Olsson's face broke into a wide grin. I smiled right back. It was hard not to. I felt immediately at ease with Dr. Olsson, most likely due to the rapport we'd established during the emotionally draining case that had introduced us.

O.K. cleared his throat, drawing our attention. "Rob, I was going to ask if you'd bring Esther home. I had promised her a ride earlier, but got, um, sidetracked with Melissa. She—" he nodded towards me, "left her keys in my car and has been stranded since. I've got to get out to the floor, but you're off now right?"

Dr. Olsson smiled a wicked grin at me. "Oh, I'd be happy to give Miss Esther here a ride anytime." Now the words in and of themselves were innocuous, but he'd clearly layered on the innuendo. I guess this was what O.K. had meant about his friend being slick. I don't know why it didn't bother me, but it didn't. I guess there was a tiny (okay, HUGE) part of me that wanted to be flattered, especially after O.K. deserted me to take Demon Melissa out to dinner.

O.K. fished his hand in his pants pocket and pulled out the keys to his Maxima. He handed them to Dr. Olsson, who had a puzzled look on his face.

"What do I want the keys to your piece of shit for?"

I felt the need to defend O.K., since he had been trying to help me out, after all. "Hey, his car is not a piece of shit. I know—I was the proud owner of a rusted-out 1992 Mercury Topaz, which was a classic piece of shit until it became intimately and violently acquainted with the front ends of a Town and Country and Dodge Ram. Please don't insult my piece of shit, may she rest in peace, by calling his," I nodded towards O.K., "brand new, V-6, fully loaded turbo Nissan Maxima a piece of shit."

"Wow, this girl's got moxie. I like her." Dr. Olsson smiled at me.

"I don't know if it's really moxie, or really 'I just want to go the hell home right now.'"

Both doctors smiled at me. Rob said, "Okay, I'll run down and get your keys out, and then come back up and escort you home. Why don't you have a little something to eat while you wait." It was not a question; it was a statement.

I was pretty hungry (not to mention poor), so I meandered over to the table. The lounge had started to clear out as some of the staff went out to start their shift. I looked over the goods on the table. There was a pan of curry chicken and rice from a local Caribbean restaurant. There was one of those fancy fruit arrangements where the fruit is all cut up and skewered to look like flowers. I took a pineapple star and some chocolate dipped strawberries from there, as well as a small scoop of the curry chicken and rice.

I sat down with my plate and looked up. O.K. was hovering near the door. "I've got to run. Will you be alright?"

I smiled. "I think so, unless I get food poisoning, which would totally be my luck."

"I'm sorry to leave you in the lurch."

"It's no big deal. You've helped me enough."

"I guess I should be saying that I'm sorry to leave you with Lurch."

"Aww, he's not that tall." I smiled again.

"Can I call you sometime?"

At this point, I had shoveled a forkful of chicken into my mouth, so I covered my mouth and said, "Sure."

And with that, Dr. O.K. was gone. Again.

CHAPTER NINE

"Did you get enough to eat?"

I leaned back into the luscious leather seats of Dr. Olsson—Rob as he instructed me to call him—'s BMW. Of course he drove a BMW. The seat warmer radiating a comforting heat on my sore back, combined with my full belly, made me feel drowsy.

"Mmmm, plenty," I said, the sleepiness coming through in my voice.

"What did you have?"

"I had the curry chicken and rice, some fruit, a little coffee cake. And a cookie. Or three."

"Those cookies are the best, aren't they?

"Yeah, who makes them?"

"I do." That woke me up.

"Shut up, you do not."

"I do too. I like to bake when I get off work. I'm usually a little keyed up, and it helps me relax." He paused for a moment, and I was trying to think of something that would not sound totally insulting. He continued. "You can say it—it's pretty girly of me. Nothing I haven't heard before. My parents owned a bakery in North Dakota, so it's in my blood."

"I may or may not have been questioning your masculinity, but now I'll say you can bake for me anytime. Those cookies were unbelievable. I'd ask for the recipe, but I don't bake."

He clutched at his heart. "You don't bake? What kind of woman doesn't bake?"

"What kind of man does? Turn left at this light."

"Touché," he said, as he easily glided the car on the road. "So, if not baking, what do you do to relieve your stress? I imagine it must be great with your line of work."

"I drink heavily."

"Oh, well, that's a good coping strategy."

"No, I try to laugh and not take myself too seriously. And I tap dance. It's hard to be in a bad mood when you're tapping."

"I would think so. But a better question would be is it hard to tap dance when you've been drinking heavily?"

I laughed. "I've honestly never tried it, but next time I do, I'll let you know how it turns out. I imagine it will not go well. I have a hard enough time staying upright while sober. Sometimes I resemble Bambi the first time he goes out on ice."

"Bambi was a boy?"

"Yeah, pretty sure. They did refer to him as the 'Prince of the Forrest.' It's the next right, first building on the right."

As I was chauffeured for the second time today by a handsome, funny doctor, I had to chuckle at my situation. I had moved to this city six months ago. In that time, I had had exactly zero dates with anyone. I hadn't even been hit on, let alone asked out. Pretty much the only males I dealt with were through work. So, that meant they were police officers or the people that I was investigating for child abuse or endangerment. My office was all females, except for our boss, Tom, who was about nine hundred years old and married to the scariest woman I'd ever seen. At one time, I had harbored a fantasy about a police officer, but most of the ones who showed up on a case had hit the doughnut shop about five hundred times too many.

Anyway, now it seemed like attractive doctors were coming out of the woodwork. I guess I didn't need that speed dating that I chickened out of after all. On the other hand, if I hadn't chickened out, I wouldn't have been at the market where I was hit by two cars.

"Earth to Esther. Come in Esther."

I snapped back to attention. "Sorry, got lost on my own little thought train there for a minute."

"Thinking about anything good?"

"Nah, just life."

He laughed. "Oh, is that all?"

"Yeah, nothing big." I turned to face him. He had put the car in park and was angled towards me. "Dr. Olsson, I—"

He cut me off. "For the love of God Esther, call me Rob."

"Alright already. No need to get snippy. *Rob*, I was trying to thank you for helping me out today. I do really appreciate it."

"But now you owe me."

I was a bit taken aback by his statement. "Um, yeah, I guess I do."

"And I will accept your repayment when you accompany me to dinner tomorrow."

"How is making you drive out here again repayment?"

"Because you will be gracing me with your presence, your wit, your charm, and that unbelievably sexy red hair."

You know, I had actually forgotten for a few minutes that I was cursed with this mop. Reflexively, my hand went to my hair and tried to smooth it down. Maybe it wasn't so bad after all.

"Okay, with words like that, how can a girl refuse?"

"That was my plan," Rob said with a wink. My heart fluttered a little. He was attractive. No, scratch that, he was hot, like some sort of 6'4" Norse (or Swedish? I don't know, I'm bad at these things) god.

But when he did something like smile and wink, he was absolutely adorable.

"Deets?"

"Deets? What are deets?"

"The details. What are the details for tomorrow night?"

"Ahhh, the details. Why didn't you say so in the first place? Way to make a guy feel old and out dated. How old are you anyway?"

"I'm a year away from my thirtieth birthday."

He smiled again. "Oh clever little Esther. You want me to believe that you are twenty-nine. I would completely believe it, except for the fact that I've seen you work. By the time you would have gotten your Masters' degree, which all social workers need, you would have been twenty-five. You are not in an entry-level position, which makes me think you have experience. And the way you handled yourself on that case, I believe you have more than four years experience. So how much experience do you have?"

It was my turn to put the innuendo on. "I have enough experience. Enough to be very good at what I do." Then I smiled and winked.

Gosh, it was fun just to flirt again.

That certainly caught him off guard. Tomorrow night was going to be fun.

CHAPTER TEN

The pants, skinny and black. The shirt, hunter green and sequined. The hair, well, holy shit, the hair was awesome. Just the right amount of curl and volume. No appreciable frizz. Damn I was looking good. Just in time for my date with Rob. For once, it seemed like the heavens were smiling down on me.

I had woken up this morning in significantly less pain than I had been feeling since the accident. The insurance company finally came through with a rental. Can you believe that the guy in the Dodge Ram who T-boned me claimed the accident was my fault since I "ran" the stop sign? That was what the holdup had been all along. Anyway, the powers that be had finally done their job, and I had a rental (at no cost to me) and a check coming my way for my car. Or what was left of it.

I was in a great mood as I got ready for my date with Rob. We were going to a bar to see a band play but would grab a bite to eat there first. The band was due to come on at nine, so Rob was picking me up at eight. I pulled on my knee-high, high-heeled boots over my pants and put a slouchy black blazer on over the sequined tank top. Big sparkly chandelier earrings and a chunky bracelet completed the look. I put the essentials—money, license, lip gloss, breath mints—in a silver wristlet and I was good to go.

Just then my phone rang. I fished it out of my pocket and looked. It was my sister, Veruca. I hadn't talked to her since right after I moved to Columbus in March.

"Hey, Veru. What's up?"

"Oh, not much. Did I catch you at a bad time?"

I looked at the clock on the microwave. "I've got a few minutes. I've got a date picking me up in about ten."

"Ooohh. A date! Tell me all about him. No, what are you wearing? Where are you going? More importantly, how's the hair? Oh, I bet it's going to be so much fun."

Veruca was in her late thirties. She had four kids and a good-for-nothing husband. She never got to do anything, let alone anything fun.

"The hair is actually kicking ass for once. We're going to see a band at a bar. We're going to eat there."

"Oooh, pub food." She lowered her voice to a whisper. "Are you going to get a big, fat juicy burger?"

There was a long while when we were growing up when Cheryl and Dean were vegetarians, which meant all us kids were too. All we wanted were chicken nuggets (we didn't even hope for that big yellow arch kind, because we knew it was way too corporate). Still, all these years later, we all kind of harbored a little guilt when we ate meat, but it didn't stop us.

"I'm not sure what I'm going to get. I'll have to see what's on the menu."

"So, who's the guy?"

"His name is Rob. He's a pediatrician. I met him through work a while back, but ran into him at the hospital last night and he gave me a ride home."

"Hospital? Why were you in the hospital again? Are you alright?"

"Yeah, it's a long story, but I left my apartment keys in the car of another doctor. I went over to the hospital to get them back. He had to work so Rob offered to drive me home."

"Wow, two doctors?"

"Yeah, I know. I don't know that anything will happen with either one, but hey, a girl can have fun, can't she?"

"That sounds like something Aster would say. She was always dating several guys at once."

After the crying jag on my way to the hospital last

night, I didn't want to get started thinking about Aster again. My makeup looked pretty good, and I didn't want to have to re-do it. I quickly changed the subject. I told her about the accident and the troubles I'd been having with the insurance company. "And today, I finally got a rental car and they are sending a check for the Topaz."

"That's good. Are you getting a lot for it?"

"No, of course not. It was a twenty-one-year-old piece of shit. Maybe I'll be able to afford another piece of shit."

"You know you could always ask Cheryl and Dean. They would probably help you out."

I bristled. "Yeah, I'll figure something out."

"Esther, this is getting old. When are you going to stop being so stubborn?"

"Stubborn? I'm not being stubborn. I just refuse to let them live in their crazy denial."

"Can't you see they need to hold out hope?"

I so did not want to be having this discussion right before I went out for the evening. I again changed subjects. "I only have a few minutes. How are the kids doing?"

That set Veruca off in another direction altogether, and I listened to her rant and rave while I put the finishing touches on my makeup and hair. She was still going when my buzzer rang, and as I walked down the stairs. Rob was standing at the bottom of the stairs, and I signaled to him that I'd be off in a second. He looked positively delicious in his pale blue v-neck sweater and dark jeans. I was so distracted by his good looks that it took me a moment to realize my sister was still droning on and on. I was finally able to interrupt Veruca long enough to tell her I had to run and that I'd call her soon.

"Sorry about that. Once my sister gets going about the kids, she doesn't even stop to breathe," I said as I got into his Beemer again. He held the door for me. Holy crap.

After he walked around and got in his side, he picked the conversation right up without missing a beat. "How many does she have?"

"Four—ages nine, seven, four and two."

"Oh, wow, she's got her hands full."

"Yeah, and when she gets going it's hard to get a word in edgewise. I think she's so starved for adult conversation that she forgets that it should be a give and take."

"Does she work outside the house?"

"Oh, you're good."

"Yes I am, but we'll get to that later." Oh my God, swoon. "But how did you mean in regard to this conversation?"

I couldn't help but smile. Unbelievably hot and sexy, but adorable as well. There had to be a big flaw in there somewhere. "The fact that all mothers are working mothers. Some also have an outside job that pays as well."

"I'm a pediatrician, remember? Those moms are my bread and butter."

"And I'm sure you know how to butter them up, don't you?"

He laughed. "I've been accused of flirting with a harried, frazzled woman once or twice."

"Why?"

He shrugged. "I guess because my nurse and front office staff think the things I say border on inappropriate."

"No," I laughed. "Not why do they think you are flirting, but why are you flirting with these women?"

"Because if I don't, who will? They show up in my office, exhausted. Spent. Worried. Doing the best they can. Doubting their abilities and instincts. I look at these woman who have sacrificed everything to raise their kids. Making them remember that they are special and beautiful is the least that I can do for them. If they feel good, that will be reflected in how they are able to parent their kids."

"That's brilliant. I wish our pediatrician had thought of that."

"How many kids do you have?"

I was confused for a moment. "Me? Oh, no, I don't have any kids. I meant when I was a kid. My mom had a bad experience with the pediatrician who saw Charlie, and that was it. She never took us to a pediatrician again. I'm guessing if the pediatrician had complimented her, instead of criticizing her for a cat scratch, I think things may have been a lot different."

"A cat scratch?"

"Yeah, Charlie pulled the cat's tail and the cat scratched back, as cats are known to do, and rightfully so. The pediatrician basically told my mother she was careless, and that Charlie would probably be scarred for the rest of her life."

"From a cat scratch?"

"Yeah, I know, no big deal, right? Well this guy was super old school and went on a tirade about cat scratch fever and my mom ended up walking out of the office with a toddler in one arm and a newborn in the other, and never returned."

Rob laughed. "I bet he had a really successful practice."

"I wonder what that guy would make of the cases that you and I see nowadays. I guess maybe he did see horrible stuff back then too. I guess people have been abusing their children for centuries now."

"What a pleasant and uplifting thought."

I smiled. His sleek car slid into a parking spot at the bar. A bright neon light flashed a picture of a martini. "I'll try to keep it less depressing from now on."

"But the short version of that story was that you do not have any kids."

"None that I'm aware of. I have an ex-husband, but the only thing that remains of him is his crappy last name, which brilliant me decided to hyphenate. I haven't felt like shelling out the dough to change my name back. What about you ... any kids?"

"None that I'm aware of." Smart aleck.

"Any ex-wives?"

"Plural? You must have a lot of confidence in me."

"I have eyes. You didn't answer the question."

"I have an ex-fiancée who still pops up from time to time." We got out of the car and headed toward the door. I stopped before going inside.

"Not that it's any of my business, but how often is time to time?" I couldn't help but wonder if this was going to be an issue. Was she the type to lie in wait and put a horse head in his bed?

"Whenever our hospital shifts overlap. She's a doctor also."

Oh no. Even worse. I knew where this was going already. "Let me guess, Melissa?" I was proud of myself for leaving off the 'Demon' part.

He cocked his head incredulously. "Yeah, how did you know? Have you met her?"

CHAPTER ELEVEN

My burger arrived, juicy and greasy, and so large I was worried I'd dislocate my jaw trying to eat it. I couldn't wait. I knew that this being a first date and all, I should cut the burger in half and eat it daintily. But no, I picked that sucker up with both hands and took a big 'ole bite. Damn it was good. The bacon and the cheese and the special barbeque sauce, in combination with the pretzel bun (the man who invented the pretzel bun is a genius, by the way), brought happiness to my mouth. I had been grocery shopping on such a limited budget, and hardly ever ate out, that this burger (and steak fries, and beer) seemed like a luxurious gourmet dinner to me.

"I take it it's good?"

Rob was politely eating his Reuben, looking civilized. I'm pretty sure I looked like a caveman eating. "It is so very good. I haven't had a burger this good in a while."

"You looked a little, um, satisfied over there. I was getting jealous. I was hoping to bring that kind of look to your face."

"You're bad!" I threw my balled napkin at him. I had gone through several napkins already. Did I mention that I was a messy eater? I loved chicken wings but refused to eat them in front of anyone I wasn't already in a serious committed relationship with. Because if the guy was on the fence at all about me, after seeing me devour wings, he was sure to be out of here. "It's been a while since I've had a good burger. I don't eat out much anymore."

"Why not?"

"No fun eating alone. I only moved here about six months ago and I haven't met many people outside of work."

"Work ... let me guess ... middle-aged, burnt-out women, overweight cops and pedophiles."

"Yeah, pretty much. Kind of slim pickins. Jillian Reznik at work actually talked me into going to a speed-dating thing, but I chickened out. I went to the store, bought Ho Hos and Fritos instead, and wound up getting my car totaled. It was a kickass night."

"But that's when you met O.K., right?"

I was surprised that he knew this. Did that mean O.K. had been talking about me? What was he saying? Was it good stuff? Why was I thinking about O.K. when I was on a date with this super-hot guy. "Yeah, he was at the accident scene. Then, after waiting in the E.R. for over four hours, he showed up. I thought he was some creepy stalker guy and accused him of hitting on me. I didn't know he was a doctor there to see me. And the best part ... I was covered in the powder from my airbag deployment, as well as the remains of the Ho Ho that I was shoveling in my face when I was rear-ended and then T-boned."

"I bet you looked totally hot."

"Totally." I smiled. He smiled intensely back at me. I needed to deflect the attention off of me for a minute. "Tell me a little bit about yourself."

"That is way too open ended for me to be able to answer."

"Okay, I told you an embarrassing story about me. You tell me one about you."

"Okay, I will keep it in the food-related mishap genre. So, while I was in college, I was dating this girl. She was from California, and was, um, rather focused on her appearance."

"That's being nice and tactful."

"Well, she had a killer figure. She was gorgeous and had aspirations of being an actress. I had met her while I was doing some modeling on the side to help pay the bills."

Looking at him, it was not hard to believe at all that he had been a model. "Where did you go to school?"

"This was when I was at NYU for undergrad. So we were in the city, and went to this little hole in the wall Italian restaurant. The food was out of this world. We ate our dinner, and things were really going well. I was on my game and fairly confident that after dinner, um, well, you know."

"Third date?"

He laughed. "Yeah, pretty cliché, I know, but I was twenty-two and thought I was all that. So we ordered dessert. I was really impressed that this girl would order dessert. A lot of girls won't eat in front of a guy, especially the models. I hadn't really paid attention to the fact that she had gone to the bathroom at least three times during dinner."

"Oh no."

"Oh yes. Now, I would realize that a female who is 5'9", weighs one-hundred and fifteen pounds and eats more than I do probably has some serious issues. She had eaten about half of her tiramisu, and then pushed the plate away and went to the bathroom. I figured she was done, so while she was in the bathroom, I ate the rest of it. When she came back, she freaked out on me."

"Because you had eaten her dessert?"

"Yeah. She started ranting and raving about 'did I know what she had to go through to be able to maintain her figure?' and stuff like that. She basically told me that she had purged to make room to finish her tiramisu."

"Oh, that's gross."

"That's not the worst part."

"How can it be worse than that?"

"Because she then picked up her fork and stabbed me with it."

"She did not!"

"She did so! I have the scar to prove it." He held up his hand, and in the dim light of the bar I could faintly make out four tiny dots on the back of his hand.

"Okay, that may just beat Ho Ho cream in my eyebrows."

"You didn't say that you had the Ho Ho cream in your eyebrows. Oh, no, you definitely win."

Conversation with Rob was easy and it was fun. There were a lot of innuendos and flirting. It was pretty obvious what Rob had in mind for later, but it didn't seem to bother me that much. Maybe because he exuded sexual confidence. Maybe because I was lonely and was in a dry spell. Maybe because he was working hard on getting me drunk. Either way, it was all good with me. Too soon the band started its warm up, and then it became harder and harder to hear each other. We stood up and walked over to the back of the dance floor, directly in front of the band. Somehow, I always had a beer in my hand. No sooner had I finished one, when another magically appeared. I glanced sideways at Rob. He'd had a beer at dinner but now was drinking soda.

I leaned over and motioned for him to lean down so I could yell over the band into his ear. "Why do I feel like you're trying to get me drunk?"

"Is it working?" He turned slightly and yelled back at me.

"Perhaps. Maybe my next one should be a water."

"Buzz kill."

I playfully elbowed him and tried to ignore the sparks that touching him ignited. Shit, it was going to be hard to be well behaved later.

The band was awesome. They played a lot of '70s and '80s music, but threw in some early '90s alternative here and there. The male lead singer had a great vocal range, and several of the band members played different instruments to vary their sound. The lead singer looked to be in his early or mid-thirties, while the rest of the band seemed closer to forty.

As a result of attending all of Aster's shows when she was in bands (plus the fact that my parents were anti-television, so we only had a radio in the house growing up), I knew pretty much all of the songs the band played. They were playing a lot of classic rock. Stuff the older people in the bar seemed to enjoy, but older than my demographic. It didn't bother me—I knew all the songs. And, when I drink, I sing. So, before I knew it, I was singing along pretty loudly with the band. By this time, Rob and I had moved up a little closer and I was standing directly in front of him. The singer noticed that I was regularly singing along and called me up there.

"You in the front, Red! You've sung along to every song so far. Time for you to get up here!"

I laughed and shook my head. I was not the one who got up in front of people and sang. That was Aster. My voice wasn't terrible, but I lacked the confidence that Aster had possessed in spades. The singer called for me again, and led the crowd in a chant of, "Red! Red! Red!" Even Rob joined in. Since I had been drinking rather steadily for a while, it suddenly seemed like a great idea. I drained the rest of my beer, and shrugged out of my blazer, handing both the bottle and the blazer to Rob before I marched up to the band.

The singer asked me if I knew the song that they wanted to play, which, of course I did. The classic rock duet, a hit in the late 1970s had been popular in our house. My brother, Augustus, hated it. Every time it came on the radio, Aster and I would call him in, telling him his favorite song was on the radio. I still smiled every time I heard it, thinking of how gullible he was every single time.

I knew every word of the song and was ready to go. The lead singer gave me a few instructions and helpful tips, and then the band started to play. There was barely time for my nerves to kick in. As soon as I started singing, I felt awesome. Okay, perhaps that was my liquid courage. Either way, I felt comfortable up there with the lights blazing in my face and all eyes on me. The lead singer and I had an instant chemistry that was almost magical. The words came easily, I think I was in tune, and I was even able to dance a little without looking like I was having a seizure. I think. I hope.

I was surprised at how I could really see the faces in the crowd. Rob was smiling and laughing. He looked like he was proud of me. He had a devilish twinkle in his eyes. The lead singer was engaging, and it was fun playing off him, singing the duet about the couple promising forever to each other just so they could have sex in the back seat of the car. I felt like such a natural up there. Too soon, I was hitting the last note of "Paradise by the Dashboard Lights," pulling the mike away as I faded out. The crowd erupted in applause. They were chanting, "Red!" over and over.

"How 'bout one more? Got it in you?"

I couldn't resist. I was hooked. It was fantastic being up here. I could see why Aster liked it so much. The second song, a Jim Croce classic, hard to believe, was even more fun to sing. I sort of didn't want to be done after the second song. The crowd was again chanting "Red!" I threw my arms up in the air and took a big bow. As I returned to the upright position, I saw the woman standing at the very back of the bar, right by the door. She was staring at me. I stared right back. Her hair was shorter than it had been, but there was no denying it.

It was Aster.

CHAPTER TWELVE

I tried to get through the crowd as quickly as I could. I kept pushing, but people were in my way. I kept my eyes on the back of the bar, trying to find her again. People kept stepping in front of me, stopping to tell me what a great job I had done. Normally, I would take the time to relish the compliments. I didn't have the time for that right now.

Aster.

I was certain it was her. Sure, her hair was shorter than she used to wear it, and she was a bit heavier than she had been when she ... died? Disappeared?

I faltered for a moment. What if I had been wrong all this time? What if I had not been looking for her all this time when she was out there? What if I had given up hope when I should have held out hope?

I couldn't think about that now. I had to know. I had to find her. I finally reached the door and threw my weight against it to push it open. The air had turned chilly and it assaulted me. I was hot and sweaty from being on stage and I crossed my bare arms over each other. I looked right and left. There was no one out there. There were no cars that were pulling out of the parking lot either. Where could she have gone?

I sank down on the curb, all that adrenaline draining instantaneously. Elbows resting on my knees, face in my hands, I questioned everything.

"Hey—you okay? You ran out so fast."

I looked up to see Rob standing over me. From way down on the curb, he seemed so tall. He must have sensed the height discrepancy was too much for me to handle and sat down next to me. He asked again, "Are you okay?"

I shook my head. "I don't know."

"Did you freak out about being up on stage? You seemed so confident up there until you bolted. I would never have guessed that you were nervous."

"I ... wasn't. I mean, I was a little nervous getting up there but it was fun. That's not why I ran out."

"Oh, why?"

"I ... thought ... I. Shit this is crazy. I don't know." I wagged my head back and forth in disbelief. What was happening to me?

"Esther, I don't know you all that well, but I know enough to know that something just happened. Did you have too much to drink?"

"No, I don't think so. Maybe. I honestly don't know what to tell you." I wanted to tell him what happened. I really did. Before I could even get the words out, the lead singer of the band came up.

"Red! You were awesome up there. Why'd you split like that?"

Rob looked at me expectantly. I looked from Rob to the lead singer and stood up. Rob stood up with me.

"Sorry, I guess I needed some air," I mumbled. It was lame, I know, but it was all I could manage at that moment.

"Red, you ever sing in a band before? You got some serious chops."

"Nah. I have done some mean sessions of karaoke when I've been totally lit though. I never got your name, by the way," I said, easily deflecting the course of the conversation.

"Name's Albert."

I looked at him. He was probably around my age. Short, buzzed brown hair did nothing to hide the male pattern baldness creeping in. Large silver earrings in each ear and a full sleeve of tattoos. Nope, definitely not an Albert to me.

"You gotta name, or you gonna stick with Red?"

"Esther."

"Never in a million years would I have pegged you for an Esther."

"Well, I wouldn't have pegged you for an Albert, so I guess we're even then."

I looked up at Rob and smiled gently. I could not let him know what had happened. He would think I was bat-shit crazy. Maybe I was, but I didn't want anyone else to know it. I tried to summon up some bravado.

Rob smiled down at me and held me steady, his hands gripping onto my arms. I smiled back, drawn into his presence. I couldn't help but lick my lips, staring at his.

Albert cleared his throat. "Hey guys, remember me? Still standing here. I can tell you are ready to get out of here, but I need to get Esther's info."

I tore my gaze away from Rob and looked at Albert. "Why do you need my info?"

"That's why I came out here. Well, I wanted to make sure you were alright, but I also wanted to talk to you about doing some gigs with the band."

"Me?"

"Yeah, we've been talking about adding a female sound for a while. We've tried the same stunt that we pulled with you tonight a few times, but we just usually end up getting some really drunk chick who sounds like a dying cat. The guys thought we hit the jackpot with you. You interested?"

"I have no idea. I never really considered it before. My sister was in a band. It was always her thing, not mine." I paused for a moment. It had been fun up there. Maybe I should at least think about it. "You know, I'll think about it. Let me give you my info and give me a call. I think I should at least explore this."

"Hell yeah you should."

I swapped info with Albert and he went back inside. As I slid my phone into my back pocket, I turned to Rob. "You wanna get out of here?"

"What did you have in mind?"

Could he still be interested in me? I mean, this guy was Hot (with a capital 'H'), and we had really seemed to be hitting it off. He had appeared to like it when I was singing. He had looked almost proud that I was with him. Of course, then I go and act like a super-freak, tearing out of the bar like my pants were on fire. Chalk another one up for Esther the Awkward.

Once back at my apartment, I let him in and he made himself comfortable on my super comfy but otherwise impractical white couch. Rob refused the offer of a drink and sat patiently while I made myself a cup of chamomile tea. With my steaming mug in hand, I sat down on the opposite end of the couch, tucking one leg under me and faced him.

The sad thing was, in this moment, I really needed a friend. I wanted someone to talk to. I looked at Rob, lounging on my couch like a lion watching his prey. He was hot and he was sexy. I was lonely and really needed some comfort. I really didn't know this guy from Adam, but he was there and he was willing. I needed to figure out if I was.

I put my tea down on the coffee table and leaned back, fatigue washing over me. Even after seven years, Aster was still exhausting me, sapping my energy. Crap. Here I was with this super-hot guy who appeared to have one thing on his mind and all I could think about was my sister.

"Can we talk for a few minutes?"

"No, I'm done talking."

I straightened my spine and bristled at that response. "What's that supposed to mean?"

Before I could get another word in, he leaned forward and kissed me. Gentle at first, but it quickly deepened and grew hot and heavy.

Oh, that's what he meant.

Yeah, I was fine being done talking too.

CHAPTER THIRTEEN

I tossed and turned. Another night of no sleep. I was too hot, then too cold. My pajama pants kept creeping up and getting tangled on my legs. I had a headache. I got up, took some Advil and drank a glass of water. I munched on some pretzels, dipping them in the jar of peanut butter. Tired of eating, I laid back down, but wasn't even drowsy. I tried to read, but the words made no sense swimming across the page in front of me. Whether I wanted to admit it or not, sleep was not going to be a reality for me tonight. Too many thoughts were running through my mind with the force of a freight train. I tried to slow the train and analyze the thoughts. Aster ... singing in a band ... hallucinations ... was I going crazy? ... Rob ... mmm, kissing Rob ... Okay, that train had officially derailed.

I gave myself a few minutes to ponder the Rob situation. He was really very attractive. If I had to be honest, which it was hard not to be at three in the morning, he was too attractive for someone like me. Other than the hair that made me stand out (usually because it was standing up), I was pretty average looking. I was just on the shorter side of average. Other than my hair, I was non-descript. If I had been blessed with the straight mouse brown hair that Veruca, Violet and Mike had, I'm sure I would have always blended into the background. As it was, as a child, even the bright red curls often did not prevent me from being overshadowed by the life force that was Aster.

Why would someone like Rob be interested in someone like me? I had a job that was a lot of hard work that paid diddly squat. Overworked and underpaid was a spot-on description for any social worker anywhere. I moved every few years. I was on my fourth city since I got out of school. I had no roots and little contact with my family. I had a flaky, religious freak, ex-husband out there, and an even flakier family with whom I didn't get along.

I did have a fairly decent figure and kept relatively in shape. I had to work out to balance the stress of my job. That was a benefit of being alone. It didn't matter if I got up super early to run, or hit the gym at eight o'clock at night. I ate fairly well, except for tonight. Jeez, I can't believe I gorged on the burger like that. I probably looked like I was making love to it.

Despite all that, Rob had seemed interested in me, hadn't he? I mean, he initiated the kissing. Oh, and it was delicious, have no doubt. That man could certainly kiss. I have not had a make-out session like that in, oh, I don't even know how long. Frankly, I can't remember the last time I had even kissed a guy. And he hadn't been drinking, so it was not like it was a mutual drunken hook-up either. Even though it was great, I was glad I kicked him out before things got too hot and heavy. Sure, I was an adult and could do with my body what I wanted to, but I wasn't sure I wanted to. Oh, there was part of me that *definitely* wanted to, but you know what I mean. Ultimately, I knew I was looking for someone to spend my life with. I could wait for the good stuff for a little while longer, if he is the right one.

Plus, I had a lot of shit going on in my head right now.

I was really afraid I was going crazy. That thought made me get up and start pacing around my apartment. I wished it was bigger so I could pace more. Although I was generally familiar with mental illness, I pulled out an abnormal psych textbook from the bookshelf in my living room and curled up on the couch. I found the textbook to be a bit outdated and moved to a Google search at my computer desk.

I looked up hallucinations first. I went to the online encyclopedia, although I knew not all of the information could be trusted. I figured I had enough knowledge to weed out the crappy information. Auditory hallucinations, what I had experienced when I thought I heard Aster at the scene of the accident, were common in paranoid schizophrenia. Great. Just great. Luckily, there was a link to a support group for people who suffer from auditory hallucinations, but no other mental illnesses. Too bad that wasn't going to be me, since I had the visual hallucination as well. I book marked it, to be on the safe side.

The more I read on hallucinations, the more concerned I became. What if it wasn't mental illness? What if I had epilepsy or a brain tumor? There were a lot of medical reasons for hearing and seeing things that weren't there. That thought freaked me out even more. Could there be something going terribly wrong in my brain? How would I find out? Oh, crap. To find out, that would require extensive and invasive medical testing. Not to mention expensive.

I was still new to the job and had been out of work for the last three weeks. This last move had put a dent in my savings, meager as they were, and I needed a new car. I didn't have the extra financial resources to spend on medical bills, on top of the ones that I had already racked up in the accident.

The other possibility was the beginning of mental illness. Somehow, that didn't sit well with me. I mean, no one wants to have a mental illness which is why so many of those afflicted live in denial for years. Aster certainly did. My parents never admitted it either. They liked to refer to Aster as "free-spirited" or "sensitive." Sometimes they even went so far as to call her "temperamental." I think years of drug use had warped their brains. They honestly did not believe there was a problem. Often it takes a crisis or hitting rock bottom for a person to even realize they have a problem. I didn't want to be one of those people.

I Googled "bipolar disorder," which is what Aster had. I was relieved that this didn't really fit me. I didn't seem to have the periods of mania and depression. Certainly nothing that I considered manic behavior. Sometimes, I was sad, but nothing out of the ordinary. I could be lonely. I missed my family and missed my twin, even though having her in my life had brought nothing but heartache. I was a divorced woman, thirty-one years old, kind of a drifter and living in a town where I knew no one. I didn't think occasionally feeling a little down was abnormal.

Next, I searched "paranoid schizophrenia." I didn't think I fit the criteria for that either, but maybe I did? I didn't think I had disrupted thought processes or emotional disturbances. I was a tad scattered, maybe with a touch of attention deficit, but certainly not disrupted thoughts. Right? Maybe I couldn't see it in myself, just like Aster couldn't see it either. I would not live in denial while things spiraled out of control. I needed to get evaluated as soon as I could. If I was developing a mental illness, I would act proactively and responsibly. I would get into counseling and on medication if I needed it. I would face this and would treat my symptoms and do the best I could to remain as functional and productive as I could.

There were other mood disorders, but I was getting too bleary eyed to continue searching much longer.

I went into my bedroom and opened my bottom file cabinet drawer where I kept all my employment benefit information. There was an employee assistance program that I could avail myself of on Monday morning. Or as soon as I got settled back into work. Slightly relieved to have a plan of action, I tried to finally go to sleep.

But the sleep didn't come right away. Instead, I thought about the night I realized that something was really wrong with Aster. We were sixteen. She was in a cycle of not really sleeping. Part of the reason she couldn't sleep was that her mind would race. I used to sneak peeks at her journals. The shit she would scribble down during these times was unbelievable. It was closing in on five a.m. and she had been up all night. I had been tossing and turning, not unlike now, waiting for her to come back. She finally ran back into our room yelling, "There is a God! Es, you gotta believe me. I've got it all figured out and now I know, I believe—there is a God!" Her hair was wild. Her eyes were wild and detached. I knew, in that moment, that there was something terribly amiss with her. My heart shattered a bit in that moment because I knew our lives would never be the same, from that moment on.

Rolling over, I tried to block the memories from assaulting me, causing my mind to race like Aster's used to. Worn out from the stress, I finally drifted off.

It never even occurred to me that there was any other explanation for why I heard and saw Aster.

CHAPTER FOURTEEN

"Hey, Charlie! Do you have a minute?" I knew I was grasping at straws calling my oldest sister, but I was hoping she would provide me with some comfort. I had the best relationship with her out of anyone in my family. It was not great, but I knew that she wouldn't hang up on me.

"Sure, Es. Any time. I just dropped Tristan off at basketball, and now I'm sitting in the car until he's done."

"You just sit there the whole time?"

"It gives me sixty minutes all by myself. I usually bring some work and do it. I get to listen to satellite radio and jam out all by myself. Sometimes, I look forward to it. But don't tell Dave. I like to make him feel guilty about all the running I have to do."

"You know I'm not going to tell anyone in the family."

"So, what's up?"

"Not much."

"C'mon Es. I know you. You don't call unless something's up."

"I guess I don't call a lot, do I?"

"No, but it's understandable. We all handle grief in our own way. You were more affected than any of the rest of us."

"I don't see that I was any more affected. She was everyone's sister."

"But you guys were different. Always together. Then the thing with Cheryl and Dean. It is understandable that you pulled away. I wish you hadn't, but I know why you felt you had to."

"See that's the thing. I know that I said I never wanted to speak of it again, but I, um, I need to talk about it."

Charlie laughed, a deep throaty laugh. "I won't tell anyone that you needed to talk. It will be our little secret."

I laughed too, because there was no such thing as a secret in our family. Gossip spread through it like wild fire. Even the most guarded things came out eventually. I knew that Charlie wouldn't mean to tell anyone what I was about to tell her, but she would. She would tell Gus, who would tell Mike, who would tell Violet and Veruca. I didn't care that they would all find out eventually. I just needed to talk.

"Do you remember when Aster started having problems?"

"What do you mean?"

"You know, when she started showing signs of mental illness?"

"It's funny. Well, not funny really, but now that Tristan is fourteen, I've been thinking about that a lot. I've been worried for a long time that he would have it too. But now that he's a teenager, and doing all the typical teenager stuff, I realize how atypical Aster was for her whole life. It became glaringly obvious when she was about fifteen."

"Don't you think we all were a bit on the atypical side?"

"We were raised by unconventional parents in an unconventional household. But we were still normal kids. We did normal kid things. Aster did not do normal kid things."

"Sure she did." I didn't know why but, even after all this time, I still felt the need to defend her.

"Cutting yourself is not normal. Being a pathological liar is not normal. Sleeping with every guy who smiles at you is not normal. Doing drugs is not normal. Refusing to get out of bed for a month is not normal."

"But don't you think part of that was her looking for boundaries? For Cheryl and Dean to stop acting like our friends and start acting like our parents?"

"Yeah, if it was normal teenage stuff. Aster took it all to a whole other level. And that was before she added in the unpredictability and irrationality that drug use introduced."

"She really was pretty unstable, wasn't she?"

"Yes, she was. I don't know how none of us saw it. Well, none of us but you."

"And then I became the bad guy for calling her on it."

"Well, putting a name to it, at the very least."

"I never got why that made me the bad guy. To me, I was calling a spade a spade."

"You're not a parent yet—"

"Not that I know of, at least."

Charlie chuckled and carried on. "So it may be difficult for you to understand, but one of the hardest things about being a parent is accepting that your child is flawed. From the moment they take their first breath, you want to believe that he or she is perfect. And then, as they get older, you want to believe that you are doing the best job parenting them. We all know that Cheryl and Dean were not the best parents. They probably shouldn't have had kids, let alone seven of us. They were and are too interested in themselves and their relationship with each other to be there for us. For the six of us, we learned to lean on each other. We kind of parented ourselves. It's pretty surprising that the six of us turned out to be quasi-decent human beings. Aster highlighted all of their shortcomings. Even the best parents would have had trouble dealing with Aster. She out matched them from day one."

"So you don't see me as having the same type of issues that Aster had?"

"God no. You were always so analytical and practical. Pragmatic, but caring and compassionate. I have to say, you are totally in the right field."

"Um thanks, I guess."

"But the funny thing? If someone looked at a picture of you and Aster. A still, posed one, not a candid one because that would give everything away, but if you were just sitting there—only based on your appearances, I'm sure most people would assume that you were the wild, out-of-control child while Aster was the prim and proper rule follower."

"I know. It's always thrown people for a loop. They expected it of me, and I never acted out. They never expected it of her, and she consistently shocked the hell out of people. And while I never wanted to be her, sometimes I was so jealous of all the attention she got. Even if people seemed to like me or were interested in me, once they met Aster, they kind of forgot all about me."

"You were always in her shadow."

"Yeah, and most of the time I was fine with it, but sometimes I wished people could see the real her and the real me. But that's beside the point."

"So, then, what is the point? Why are you asking about Aster? What's up?"

"Okay, this is going to sound totally crazy, but wait and hear me out."

Charlie listened patiently as I explained the accident and then hearing Aster yell our phrase after. Then I told her about the band thing and seeing her there. I could not believe how out there it sounded. She was quiet for a few moments and I was almost afraid that we had been disconnected and that she hadn't heard anything.

"Charlie?"

"Yeah. I'm just thinking. I think the first time was the stress of the situation. I'm sure someone screamed. I think you heard Aster because your brain wanted it to. Haven't you ever been positive that a song lyric said one thing, and then been shocked to find out that the real lyric is not what you swore you heard?"

"Yeah. That makes sense. I was thinking about asking O.K., that doctor who helped me out at the scene, if he heard anything."

"I think that's a great idea. You should follow up on that."

"And seeing her in the bar?"

"I think you saw someone who favored or even resembled her, and she was so in your mind that you thought it was her."

"I guess that's plausible. It certainly seems like a better answer than a brain tumor or schizophrenia."

"Oh, Es, I don't think you are crazy, not at all. You are very stable and level headed. I don't see any of the things in you that I saw in Aster."

I sighed in relief. "That's what I needed to hear. With you being twelve years older than us, I figured you'd have the best perspective and memory on the situation."

"Don't forget, I practically raised the two of you."

"Yes, you did, and I still need you." I couldn't help my voice from breaking as the tears started to flow.

"I know, honey. You've not only lost your other half, but you lost the rest of your family as well. I can't even imagine how hard it must be for you."

"You know, sometimes, when I allow myself to think about it, which isn't often, I get so mad at Aster. Not only did she take her life, but she took mine as well. I'm still here trying to pick up the pieces."

CHAPTER FIFTEEN

"So, I hear you're quite the singer."

"Rumors of my talent have been greatly exaggerated. Besides, you shouldn't believe everything you hear."

O.K. laughed. "No, I guess not, but I think I need to judge this one for myself."

"Well, in two weeks, I'm making my official debut with the Rusty Buckets."

"The Rusty Buckets?"

"I know, it's a bad name, but they, I mean we, are working on it. We've been practicing already. It's pretty amazing. Albert, the other singer, and me really hit it off. We just mesh so well. It's kind of freaky. But I'm sure you didn't take time out of your busy working doctor schedule to hear about my bar band career. What's up?"

"Um, actually I did call to ask you about that. I thought it was really cool, and a bit on the surprising side, too."

"Why would it be surprising?"

"I don't know, maybe, I, um ..." he trailed off, at a loss for words.

"Maybe because I can barely walk without falling over myself, so getting up in front of a crowd would not seem like a smart thing to do?"

"No, yes, I just thought you, oh, I don't know."

"Are you actually tongue tied, O.K.?"

There was a silence on the other end of the phone. Perhaps I should not have taunted him. When would I learn to keep my big mouth shut?

"Um, I still owe you that cup of coffee that we started and never finished. Although, you ordered tea. Green tea, if I'm not mistaken."

"You mean the cup of coffee and the ride home that you promised, but left me high and dry because of Melissa." I could not help the word 'Melissa' from coming out of my mouth like something had left a bad taste in it.

"Yeah, and in addition to a cup of coffee and a ride, I owe you an apology."

"I don't know, O.K. There seems to be more here going on than I am privy to, and I don't want to be caught in the middle."

"What do you mean?"

"Weren't Rob and Melissa engaged?"

"They were. They broke up about a year ago."

"Right. And you desert me for Melissa and shuffle me off to Rob. I go out with him, and now you're asking me out? I mean, you are asking me out this time, right?"

"Yeah, I was. I mean, am. Rob said that you guys went out once."

"So he told you about our date?"

"A little. He told me about the singing, and that the band offered you a gig."

Hmmm ... interesting. Do men gossip like women do? Even as estranged from my family as I was, both Charlie and Veruca wanted the dirt from my date with Rob. I was surprised that they both called me after. In all honesty, I missed the close camaraderie that I once had with my sisters. With the five of us, there were alliances from time to time and divisions based on age. Charlie was twelve years older than Aster and I. Growing up, Charlie and Violet, who are only eleven months apart, were always together, just due to their close proximity. Veruca was sort of stuck in the middle, surrounded by the boys. She aligned herself with whomever had the best deal. Until Aster started acting out, and then disappeared. All the relationships shifted and became skewed, and I found myself on the outs with everyone.

"Esther? Are you still there?"

"Oh, sorry, I got distracted."

"What distracted you?"

"I saw a shiny object."

"Really?"

"No, I was actually wondering if men gossip the same way women do. Two of my sisters wanted the dirt after my date with Rob, and I was wondering if Rob was spreading any dirt about me that I should be aware of."

"What kind of dirt would there be for him to spread?" O.K. was clearly fishing.

I laughed, "Oh, no. I don't kiss and tell."

"So you admit that you kissed?"

"Stop fishing!"

"I'll stop fishing if you agree to go out with me. Just once, to talk."

"Okay."

"What?"

"What, what?"

"You said 'O.K.'"

"No, I was saying 'o-k-a-y,' not your name. I think I'm going to start calling you Kingston instead, just to avoid confusion."

"So you are agreeing to the date then?"

"Why don't you come over here and let me cook? I like to cook, and it gets boring to cook for myself." Wow, I sounded like a loser.

"Oh, my God! You cook too? Please tell me that you have some major flaw, other than going out with Rob?"

"I'm going to ignore that comment, although I do want a full explanation of what's going on. And, of course, other than the hair, I do have major flaws."

"The hair is not a flaw. The hair is, well, I don't even know how to describe it, but it is something. Doesn't count as a flaw. You need something else."

"Okay, how 'bout I may or not be going crazy?"

"I highly doubt it. And if you are, I have a good shrink, remember?"

"How could I forget? But I can't afford two hundred bucks an hour. Hell, I can't afford two hundred bucks period. I have to settle for the crappy free kind. I think I'm screwed."

"Well, tell me what's wrong, and I'll tell my shrink and then tell you what he says. I'll pass along his advice to you."

"Isn't he going to question it if you keep developing hysterical pregnancies?"

"Oh, is that what it is? We covered that last year. I can already help you with that one."

I laughed. I had to hand it to O.K. No matter how bad I might be feeling, he always said something to put me at ease and make me laugh. No doubt about it, Rob was hot, and he seemed like a decent guy. Of course, he really didn't want to talk or listen to me explain what had happened. I'm fairly confident he'd only wanted to get into my pants. And since I didn't let him, it wasn't too surprising that I hadn't heard from him in the two weeks since. It hurt a bit but wasn't surprising.

"You know, with our track record, this dinner is destined to go epically wrong."

"Maybe, but it's worth a shot. At least we'll get a good laugh out of it, right?"

Even I couldn't disagree with that logic.

CHAPTER SIXTEEN

"I can't believe it! Nothing catastrophic happened." We were relaxing on my couch after a tremendously successful and, might I add, delicious dinner.

"Ssshh ... don't say that out loud. The night is not over yet." O.K. leaned forward and put his finger on my lips to silence me. He held it there for just a moment too long, and the moment was now tense. But a good tense. Sexy tense.

Somehow, his touching my lips had made me want desperately to kiss him. Somehow, I had gone from gloating to thinking about kissing O.K. I sat back to break that moment. I couldn't think about kissing O.K. That would complicate things unnecessarily. I didn't need that. I wanted it. No, wanted the kissing not the complication. Shit. Why could I not stop feeling his warm touch on my lips?

"I know. I really need to learn to stop tempting fate."

"Yes, and not to tempt fate, but that dinner was awesome. You can cook for me any time." He smiled, showing those beautiful teeth again. And he had one dimple, and crinkles around his chocolate brown eyes. His hair was a bit disheveled, and he was in need of a haircut.

"You need a haircut," I blurted out. Damn that E-Z Pass brain.

He ran his hand through his hair, which tousled it even more. Hmm, perhaps I should not have been drinking that wine with dinner. But I'd opened the bottle to make the piccata, and it seemed like such a shame to let it go to waste.

"I know, I'm overdue. I usually go every four weeks, but I had to cancel my appointment with Michele last week. She can't fit me back in until next week. So I have to look like this until then."

By now, his hair was pretty much standing on end, and I couldn't stand it anymore. I leaned forward on my left hand and tried to smooth his hair down with the other. He reached, putting his hand over mine. I was so wrapped up in his tender touch that I did not realize my left hand was sliding off the front edge of the couch until I pretty much face planted in his lap.

Yup, my face to his crotch. 'Cause that's how I roll.

O.K. started laughing, and picked me up. "You know, I usually wait until the second date to ask for that."

I was sure my face was as red as my hair. I looked at O.K., who was laughing, and I lost it. I burst out laughing. We were both laughing so hard that it was getting hard to breathe. I had a tear or two rolling down my face and my cheeks hurt from laughing.

Finally, catching my breath I said, "I honestly cannot remember the last time I laughed that hard."

"Me neither!"

"Good God, I am a disaster of epic proportions."

"Not epic, just sort-of continental."

"Continental?"

"Yeah, bigger than a country, but not quite global."

"Yet."

"You've crashed your car, accused me of hitting on you, fell asleep in my waiting room, face planted twice, with one ending up in my lap. I'm not sure how much worse it could honestly get."

"Did you hear about my date with Rob? I may have had a slight break with reality."

"He didn't say anything about it. And I don't want to know. Really. I mean, other than the band thing, which, by the way, is totally cool."

"That part of the night was really cool. I never pictured myself up singing with a band. That was my sister's thing. I was always on the sidelines, watching. Which I was fine with, until I realized how kick ass it feels to be up there with a mike in your hand."

"Okay, that's all I want to hear about your date." He shifted uncomfortably.

"Does it bother you that I went out with him?"

He fiddled with the button on the back couch cushion for a moment. He appeared to be choosing his words carefully. "It's just that since Rob and Melissa broke up, well, Rob's been ..."

"Active? Friendly? Slutty?"

He smiled. "You could phrase it that way."

"I kind of had that suspicion. I mean, he was really nice and all, but not the kind of guy you take home to meet Mom and Dad. Not that I will ever bring anyone to meet them since we don't talk, but you know what I mean."

"You ever gonna tell me the family story? You've alluded to it a few times, and I've got to admit that my curiosity is piqued." I knew he was changing the subject and warily I let him. I had to know if he heard Aster too.

"Um, it's kind of heavy, and I don't know that I want to get into it right now. But that reminds me, I have wanted to ask you something." Make it sound light. Make is sound breezy. Don't make it sound coo-coo.

"Okay, shoot."

"The day of the accident? Right after you helped me out of the car, and were coaching me through trying to lift my head—do you remember?"

"Yeah, I was holding onto you and then you almost passed out. I was kicking myself for getting you out of the car without waiting for the paramedics to arrive."

"So, in between the holding me and the passing out, as I was lifting my head, I heard a scream. Did you hear that?"

He was pensive for a moment. "Yes, come to think of it, I did. A woman, right? That was when you jerked your head up, and then went down."

I swallowed hard. "Do you remember or could you make out what the woman screamed?"

He shook his head. "I don't know. I wasn't really paying attention. I was more worried about you."

"But you definitely heard a scream."

"Yes."

"And it was a woman."

"Yes. But why does all this matter?"

"Okay, this is where I go completely overboard and break with reality." I told him how I would swear it was Aster, who had been dead for seven years.

"So, she disappeared or committed suicide?"

"Well, she left a note, and then was never seen again. She didn't take her phone, purse or even wallet. Her bank account, meager as it was, was untouched. None of her stuff was gone."

"And you thought she killed herself."

"Even though Aster and I were fraternal twins, we were closer than regular sisters. We really were two halves of a whole. Literally, yin and yang. I used to feel her, and I have never felt her since she disappeared. It was like I was suddenly in the atmosphere without gravity pulling me back down. I know, with every aspect of my being, that Aster committed suicide. But I really, really hate talking about it."

O.K. was quiet for a minute. I sank back into the couch, weary from the emotional rollercoaster I had been riding the last few weeks. Unable to stay still, I got up and went into the small galley kitchen to wash the pans from dinner. We had cleaned up the rest previously, but I had left my pans to soak. I started scrubbing them, taking out my anger and frustration on them.

"Wow, remind me not to piss you off anymore."

I startled, surprised that O.K. had followed me into the kitchen. He was leaning against the counter, watching me. I gave him a tight smile. "I'm not angry with you. I'm angry with Aster, and there is nothing I can do about it."

"Why are you angry with Aster?"

"I'm angry that she pulled me into her tangled web. I'm angry that she was sick and did nothing to get better. I'm angry that she gave up and ended her life instead of fighting for it. And I'm mostly angry that she left me all alone."

And with that, a tear escaped down my cheek. Tears twice in the last hour. One from joy and one from sadness. Perhaps I had more bipolar tendencies than I wanted to admit.

My hands were still submerged in the sink full of bubbles, so I pulled them out to dry them. Slowly, I turned to face O.K., my hands still gripping the sink behind me.

"And now, to make matters worse, I think I'm going down the same road of mental illness that Aster was on and it scares the living shit out of me. What if I end up just like her?"

O.K. took two steps towards me and closed the gap between our bodies. He gently took my face in his hands and said, "Have you ever considered that there might be another reason for seeing and hearing your sister?"

"What else can it be other than I'm headed for a room in the Pecan Manor?"

"Pecan Manor?"

"Yeah, you know, the nut house."

"I wouldn't go reserving you a room there yet."

"Oh yeah, why not?" I stuck my chin out slightly in defiance."

O.K. leaned in and gave me a very light, very soft kiss on the lips. It completely disarmed me, which I think was his plan.

"Have you ever considered that Aster might still be alive?"

CHAPTER SEVENTEEN

"No."

"No? That's it? No, you haven't considered it, or no, she is not alive."

"NO," I said more emphatically. "No, there is no way Aster can be alive." I pushed off the sink and put my hands on his chest. With a slight force, I pushed him out of the way and stormed around him. "And I think you'd better go."

"No."

I whirled around to look at him. "What do you mean no? You can't refuse to leave my apartment." I stomped out to the living room and started picking things up and slamming down.

"Esther, calm down."

"No, I will not calm down. How could you say such a thing? There is no way in hell that Aster is still alive!"

"Why do you say that?"

"Because, I, well, if she was ... shit." I was standing in the middle of the floor. I wanted to sink to the floor and weep, but I would not let him see me like that.

O.K. stood about four feet away from me, just watching. I seemed paralyzed for a moment. Finally, I gestured for him to sit down. He sat on the couch. I sat across the room in the mission-style leather armchair. Thoughts raced through my head, and I tried to organize them before I opened my mouth. After a few moments, I laid my head back, closed my eyes and talked.

"I've been through this with my parents over and over. This is a battle I'm a veteran of, and I refuse to revisit it. They refuse to believe that Aster would end her life. They spent all of their time and energy, not to mention money, searching for her. I'm angry with them for not giving up on Aster, and they're equally as angry with me for giving up on her. Yes, I gave up on her. But she had given up on herself. I knew it. I could tell by her behavior that had escalated and escalated. The crushing depression that followed was even more agonizing. They were not with Aster the nights that she would wake up out of a sound sleep, in a panic because she felt like she was being engulfed in never-ending despair."

Gently, O.K. said, "That sounds terrible, and like such a burden to carry. How old were you?"

"Her behavior started becoming erratic when we were about fifteen or sixteen. You have to understand, we were inseparable. Even if there was an activity only one of us did, the other usually hung around. Then, Aster started taking off, disappearing. She became secretive and defensive. By the time we were seventeen, she was anorexic and was cutting."

"Jesus. What did your parents do?"

"Nothing. Cheryl and Dean are hippies who believe that children will flourish best in an environment of total love and acceptance, and all negativity should be avoided."

"What the hell does that mean?"

"It means they never told us no."

"Never?"

"Well, that was the thing. They're all crunchy and organic and believed that television and materialism are the roots of all evil, so we weren't allowed to watch TV, and we never had new stuff. The best you could hope for was some good, not super-old stuff from Goodwill."

"Wow."

"Yeah. But wait, there's more."

"Oh, I can barely wait to hear this."

"This really doesn't have to do with Aster, per se, but more to the dysfunction that is my family. My parents were pretty into drugs for a while in the '60s, especially the psychedelic ones. My mom, after a particularly potent trip, became obsessed with *Charlie and the Chocolate Factory*."

"Like Willy Wonka?"

"Yeah, but the book. This was before the movie. She became convinced that the story of the children was an allegorical message for all that was wrong with society. Gluttony, greed, sloth. And that the only way to pure goodness was abject poverty."

"Those sound like some of the seven deadly sins to me."

"Yeah, but by this time, my mom was pretty anti-organized religion, so she didn't see it that way. She saw that Roald Dahl was passing a message along personally to her. Of course, she totally missed the message that the parents were responsible for their children turning out so horrid. She could only see that the external forces corrupted the children. She only saw what she wanted to see. But, nonetheless, she was obsessed and my five older siblings are named after the children in the story."

"You can't be serious."

"As a heart attack." I opened my eyes, but still couldn't look at him. I dropped my head, and became focused on my hands which were clasped tightly in my lap. The really embarrassing part was coming next.

"You do not have a sister named Veruca Salt."

And there it was. "Actually, she's married now, so it's Veruca Salt Comely Jefferson. I have a sister, Charlie Buckets, as well as Violet Beauregard, and two brothers, Augustus Gloop and Mike Teavee."

"Holy shit. How many kids are there?"

"Aster and I made seven. I have absolutely no idea where our names came from. And as much as I hate my name, I guess on some level I should be happy that we were not named 'Oompa' and 'Loompa.'"

"Now, that would have been a tragedy."

I smiled weakly. I was now pretty focused on playing with the large brown tortoise-shell button on my green sweater. It was a comfy sweater, and it was my favorite. I wished it was a suit of armor to protect me from all the hurt that I had endured with my family. I knew I would need to make eye-contact with O.K. again at some point soon, but I wasn't ready yet. I could not believe that I had lost my shit like that. The anger at his suggestion that Aster might be alive simply had overtaken me. I knew it was from battling my family for so long. I knew it had nothing to do with him. I knew I needed to have better control over it.

"I'm sorry for lashing out at you like that. And for pushing you. I don't know why I did that."

"You don't have to apologize."

"Yes, I do. It is inexcusable. That was totally wacko of me."

"Moderately wacko, not totally. I only go for moderately wacko chicks anyway. I draw the line at totally wacko."

I sat up suddenly, and looked at him. "O.K., what is going on here?"

"What do you mean?"

"I mean, I keep spilling my guts to you. And then you make a comment about going for chicks like me. But, well, not to sound old fashioned, what are your intentions towards me?"

"Shouldn't your father be asking me that?"

"I don't speak with my father, remember?"

"Oh, right. So, you really have no contact with your family because of this thing with your sister?"

"Stop changing the subject."

"Esther, you're the one changing the subject. We were talking about your sister and your family."

Wow, the night had deteriorated fast. Here we were, sniping at each other. Practically yelling. This was not how I had seen the night progressing. Especially after that moment on the couch, and after he kissed me by the sink. This was me, totally blowing it. Figures.

"See, I don't even know how to ... shit. I fuck everything up."

"Esther, just calm down for a minute. I know I got you all riled up, and I'm sorry for that. I didn't know talking about your family would be this upsetting."

I smiled tersely. "That's why I'm better off not talking about them."

"I can see that. I won't bring it up again, unless you want to talk about it. Deal?"

My tense smile relaxed into a more natural one. "Deal. But you do need to tell me what is going on here."

"We're hanging out. And we were having a good time, until I brought up a subject you told me not to, but I was a stubborn, nosy ass and pushed the issue anyway. You had a tiny hissy fit, and now we're all better. We should probably kiss and make up."

"NO!"

O.K. looked hurt. "Well, that was a clear refusal. I guess I'd better get going then." He stood up and went to the wrought iron coat rack by the door. He was trying to get his barn jacket down without knocking off my four hundred jackets.

"No, O.K., that was not what I meant. I meant that I need to know what's going on before any more kissing can happen."

He turned and looked at me, in the process knocking over the whole coat rack. Luckily there were enough coats to cushion the landing. O.K. squatted down to try to pick up the coats that were all over the floor. I went over to help.

"Seriously, why does one person need so many coats?"

We righted the coat rack and I finished replacing all the coats. "I've moved around a lot and lived in a lot of different climates. Plus, in regard to the subject of family that we are not discussing, I have a lot of rebellious behaviors. I never had a lot growing up, so I overcompensate by hoarding now. But stop changing the subject, for the love of God!"

"I don't know what you want me to say Esther."

"Why don't you start with telling me what's going on with you and Melissa? Are you together or what? How does Rob factor in? Isn't he your friend? How could you do that to him? And then how do I factor in?"

"Melissa? Why would you think anything is going on with me and Melissa?"

"Because you obviously had a date with her the night you left me in the coffee shop."

O.K. laughed, closing the gap between us once again. "No, we had a presentation for Grand Rounds that we were finishing up for the next morning. I had to get it done. It was a work thing only. After everything that happened with Rob, I would not touch her with a ten foot pole."

"What did happen with Rob?"

"That's not for me to tell, but I could ask you that same question."

"We went out once. I thought we had a good time, but I haven't heard from him since. Not sure what happened."

"Are you interested in him?"

"Maybe. I don't know. Probably not."

"Are you interested in me?"

CHAPTER EIGHTEEN

"So what did you do when he asked you that?"

My head was down on my desk, buried in my folded arms. I was recounting for Jillian the disastrous details of my date with O.K. "I cannot believe I screwed things up so completely and so quickly."

"Awww, honey, you don't know that you messed things up that badly."

"Oh yes I did. I doubt if I'll ever hear from O.K. again."

"Well, what did you do?"

"I tackled him, pinned him against the wall and kissed him good and hard for a good long while. It was fantastic. Rubbed him up and down pretty good too. Then I felt guilty for accosting him and told him he needed to leave. I pretty much shoved him out the door."

"Oh, that's not good."

"No, it's not. Jillian, I had two dates with two handsome, funny, cool doctors in two weeks and neither one has called since. I totally freaked out in some manner, not on one, but on *both* dates."

"At least you're consistent."

"Consistently nuts that is."

"Have you considered calling ... who? Who do you want to keep dating?"

"I don't know. I think O.K. is a bit more in my league. Except for when I freak out, we always have a really good time together. Rob is like movie-star, Norse-god handsome. Seriously, I think he was a model while in college."

"Esther, I'm disappointed in you."

I lifted my head and looked at Jillian quizzically. "Why?"

"Judging that poor man based solely on his looks. I would have expected better of you than that."

"Oh, the whole, 'judging a book by its cover' thing? I guess I was doing that. I still don't know. I was kind of instantly attracted to O.K. Probably because he was acting like the knight shining armor to my damsel in distress. Over and over. And his sense of humor. We seem to really get each other. On the other hand, with Rob, it seemed to be more, um, just physical chemistry?"

"Sex?"

"Yeah, that's probably all it would be. But I bet it would be fantastic and hot."

"Really?"

"Yeah," I sighed. "I could tell when he kissed me. It would be like, throw everything on the floor and do it on the desk hot."

"I've never had one of those." It was Jillian's turn to sigh.

"Me neither, but I think Rob held that potential."

"And what about O.K.? What was kissing him like?"

"It was definitely passionate, but in a different way. I don't know how to explain it. Still good. Just different. Comfortable. Like coming home. Like a shoe that fits perfectly." The warning alarm on my phone sounded. "I guess we'd better head into our meeting."

Jillian and I headed into our department meeting. It would be a long, boring hour. I had clients to see and phone calls to make. I didn't need to sit here, wasting my time, listening to Tom, my out-of-touch boss drone on and on about the stuff I was doing already. Nonetheless, I tried to be diligent and listen. But, in spite of my best efforts, my mind wandered. I wrote up a list of songs that I would propose to The Rusty Buckets as additions or substitutions to the song list. And try as I might not to, I thought about O.K. and Rob. I was making a mental pro and con list of the two of them when the meeting finally wound up.

Not like it really mattered anyway, since neither one was calling. I told Jillian as much, after the meeting.

"That's bullshit."

"Jillian! Did you actually swear?" I pretended to be mortified, but secretly it amused me. It was so out of character with her personality. I was a good bad influence on her.

"Yes I did. Why are you waiting for either one to call you? Don't your fingers work? You can call them, you know."

Holy shit, why hadn't I thought of that? My head was so far up my own ass right now because of all the Aster stuff that I hadn't even considered the thought of calling Rob. Or O.K. Or both.

"Which one do I call?"

She looked at me and laughed. "Oh, to be young again and have such quandaries!"

I laughed right back. "Jillian, you're forty-two. You're not exactly over the hill, you know."

"Yeah, but Bruce and I have been married for nineteen years. I missed out on all this wild dating stuff. We've been together for over twenty years. Do you know I've never kissed two different guys in the same week?"

"Well, in my defense, it was the same month, not the same week. And I have to say, also in my defense, Rob kissed me, but I kissed O.K."

"Then I think there is your answer."

"What answer?"

She shook her head, with an amused look. "About which one you call. Rob had to kiss you, but you kissed O.K. You should call O.K. You went after him. You pursued him. I think it must be him that you are more interested in."

Her logic made sense. Why couldn't I see that? We were packing up our things, ready to get on the road for the day. We'd be off in different directions, and I wasn't sure when I'd catch up with her again. That was a difficult part of my job. There was a lot of solo time in the car, going from client to client. We were all overworked and excessively underpaid. I was in my car as much as I was in my office. It made for some lonely days sometimes. The clients and their situations were so dire and needy, that it really sapped your energy. Just having another person like Jillian to commiserate with made a huge difference. I was so lucky to have her to talk to and get her sage advice. I was still playing catch up from my three-week sabbatical, so I probably wouldn't get back into the office during normal business hours until the end of the week.

"I'll fill you in when I have news!" I shouted to her as we were both getting in our cars. She waved, and we were off.

CHAPTER NINETEEN

I dragged my tired little rear end up the stairs to my apartment. Some days, my job was draining and this was definitely one of them. I was still tired and sore from my neck injury, although it was certainly getting better. At the end of a long day, my fatigue reduced my tolerance for pain, so my neck bothered me more. Today had been one of those days that I hate. I had to remove a child from his home for neglect. The fact that the child had a terminal illness only made matters more dramatic. I hated that I had to remove the child, but I hated that his parents weren't taking care of him even more.

It was easy to see that I had a lot of baggage that I carried from my childhood into my job. Although I couldn't have verbalized it when I was younger, as an adult it was easy to see that we were, to some extent, neglected by Cheryl and Dean. They were all consumed with their relationship with each other and whatever set of beliefs they were touting at the moment. There were too many of us running around all the time for any real structure. We moved a lot, as well. It was probably why I was so transient now. I'd never had real roots. My family was more like a tumbleweed, drifting where the wind dictated.

I only wanted to draw myself a hot bath, pour a glass of wine, and think about anything but work or my family. The tub was running, and I was struggling to uncork a new bottle of Shiraz when my cell started ringing. I dashed across my apartment to find my large shoulder bag, where my phone was nestled deep inside. By the time I finally pulled the phone out, it had stopped ringing. I looked at the display. It was Charlie. I was touched that she was checking in on me. Even though my relationship with my parents was non-existent, and strained with my siblings, I wanted to believe that someone still cared about me, even just a little. I would call Charlie back after my tub, when I was relaxed and ensconced in my fuzzy fleece pajamas.

I put the phone down on the counter and then realized the tub was still running. I went and turned it off. The water was on the hot side, so I could afford to let it cool for a few minutes. I looked around the bathroom for my wine, but it was nowhere to be found. I walked back out to the kitchen and finished pouring my glass. My phone lit up again as Charlie's name marched across the screen. Huh. I had a few minutes before the bathwater would be cool enough, so I answered the phone.

"Hey, Charlie! What's up?" I picked up my wine glass and took a tiny sip. Because of my neck injury, I still couldn't hold the phone between my shoulder and ear, and I found it awkward to hold the phone with one hand and drink with the other.

"Oh, Esther, I ..." she broke off. Charlie was crying. She never cried. This was not good.

"Charlie, what's wrong?"

"Esther, it's Dean."

Her words hit me like a ton of bricks right in the gut.

She continued. "He's in the hospital. They think he had a heart attack."

"Oh my God. What ... how ... when ... what's the prognosis?"

"We don't know yet. He wasn't feeling right and Cheryl took him in about four o'clock this afternoon. Preliminary tests indicate a heart attack."

"What are they going to do?"

"There's talk about transferring him to Rochester— to Mayo—to do a catheterization and then possibly surgery, depending on what the outcome of the cath is."

"How's he feeling?"

"Pretty awful. They gave him something when he got to the ER to open up his blood vessels, and it has given him a really bad headache. He says that's worse than the chest pain. I'm on the next flight there."

A pang of hurt and sorrow gripped my heart. My last words to my father, to either of my parents for that matter, had been in anger. What if those were our last words to each other?

"Should I come?"

There was a deafening silence on the other end of the line. After what seemed like an eternity, she said quietly, "I don't know. You know how he feels."

I was glad that this was a phone conversation, so that no one could see the hurt on my face. Charlie hadn't said that to be hurtful; she was simply being honest. I knew the score, and had for a long time. She was just repeating it.

"Well, thank you for letting me know at least."

"Esther, you know that's not how I feel. I'm thinking that it'd upset Dean if you came."

"Of course it would. Because he wants to see Aster, not me, and I can't do that for him."

"It's not right."

"No, it's not. I know you only have Tristan, but can you imagine ..." I broke off, unable to continue that thought. I didn't need to continue though. Charlie knew where I was going with it.

"Esther, I know it doesn't mean that much because I'm your sister, not your mom or dad, but I love you. I always have and I always will. I wish there wasn't all this drama so that we could all be together. It's bad enough that we lost one sibling. We don't need to lose another."

"I'm not lost. I know right where I am. I can't accept their denial and the hypocrisy."

"And Cheryl and Dean can't accept your honesty and candor. They'd rather keep their heads in the sand."

"But you let them. You allow their foolishness to continue. You feed into it by supporting them."

Charlie was quiet. Shit, I hadn't meant to hurt her when she was taking the effort to reach out to me. "Yes, Esther, I enable their ridiculousness, but not for the reasons you may think."

"Why do you do it then?"

"I'm not strong like you are."

"What do you mean by that?"

"I need their approval. I know that it is silly, but I need them to love and approve of me. I'm not strong enough for it not to matter, even though I know how wrong they are most of the time. I know I should walk away, just like you did, but I'm not strong enough to."

"I always thought I was weak because I ran away with my tail between my legs."

"Oh no, Es, you are the strongest of the lot. You always have been."

I mulled this over for a moment. Quietly I said, "I always had to be. Being with Aster took a lot of strength."

"Yes, I guess it must have. I don't know how you handled her all the time, but you did. From the time you were toddlers, you could get her to cooperate when no one else could. You were like the Aster whisperer."

"But that never mattered to Dean. He only ever saw Aster. He only used me to get to Aster. I know everyone used to joke that as twins we were a two-for-the-price-of-one deal, but I think Cheryl and Dean would have been more content if they'd only had one. I know they only ever wanted Aster, and when she was gone, they couldn't deal. And they certainly could not shoulder any of the burden of having a mentally ill child, so I became the scapegoat. I have been disconnected from the family since Aster started getting sick, which has been half my life. I had to learn to be strong, not because I wanted to, but because there was never anyone there to support me."

"I know. We failed you terribly. I don't know that I will ever forgive myself for that."

"Charlie, you're my sister, not my mother. You've been more of a mother to me than Cheryl ever was or will be, but you still shouldn't have had to provide for me what Cheryl should have. I know you love me, and you know I love you. That's enough."

"Aww, Es, there you go again. You're my baby sister. I'm supposed to be guiding you, not the other way around."

"I look at it that you and I are the bookends and it is our collective job to keep everyone in between upright. I just couldn't keep Aster on the shelf any longer."

"You did the best you could. You did better than the rest of us. And yes, we're the bookends, but shouldn't that have been our parents' role?"

CHAPTER TWENTY

After the phone call with my sister, even a long, hot bath and a glass (or three) of wine did nothing to relax me. I hated the way things were with my family. I hated that I had no communication with my parents. I hated that my father could be dying. I hated the fact that, even on his possible deathbed, he wouldn't want to see me. Seriously, how messed up is that? I knew Charlie was right, that my presence would probably only upset him more. It was good of her to call and let me know. I took a miniscule amount of comfort in the fact that Charlie still considered me part of the family, even if no one else did.

I picked up my phone and called O.K. If for nothing else, I needed to apologize again for acting like such a freak. I was usually very even keeled but this whole Aster thing had set me on edge.

"Hello?"

"Hey, O.K. It's Esther."

"Hey Esther! What's going on?"

"Not much. Just thought I'd check in and see how you're doing." Wow, with stellar, engaging conversational skills like that, it was a wonder I didn't have guys crawling all over me.

"Are you okay? You sound a bit down."

"I know you must hate this, but can I ask some medical advice?"

He chucked a bit. "Don't worry, I get it all the time. My favorite is when someone wants to show me a lump while I'm in the middle of grocery shopping. I've actually had to stop people from dropping trow in the middle of Kroger."

"You say people, as in more than one?"

"You have no idea. So whatever you have to ask me, it cannot be that bad. But if you need something that requires you to pull your pants down, I'd be happy to come right over and look."

In spite of myself, I smiled. "No, it's nothing like that."

"Dammit. Maybe next time."

I paused, trying to pull myself together before I asked. "What do you know about heart attacks?"

His voice immediately shifted to professional mode. "That's a pretty big topic. Are you having chest pain?"

"No, no, not me. I guess my dad had a heart attack."

"Oh, Esther, I'm so sorry."

"I guess they took him in and gave him some medicine to open up his blood vessels, but it gave him a wicked headache, and he said he'd rather have the chest pain than that headache."

"Nitro. That was the nitroglycerine. It is a vasodilator and opens up all the blood vessels, including the ones in the brain. It causes a massive head rush, so to speak. But it sounds like he's somewhat stable, if he's able to complain about his head?"

"I guess they're transferring him to a larger hospital so they can do a catheterization and then they'll decide on what happens next from there."

"Where do your parents live?"

"They're in the southeast corner of Minnesota, Winona County. I guess they're transferring my dad to a hospital in Rochester."

"Mayo?"

"Yeah, I think."

"When are you leaving?"

"Leaving?"

"Yeah, are you flying or driving up there? How long of a drive is it?"

"Um, I honestly have no idea from here. I haven't been out there since I moved here. And I'm not going. I was told my presence would only upset Dean more."

There was silence on the other end of the line. Finally, O.K. said, "I don't know what to say to that."

"Yeah, I know. Pretty messed up. Charlie's keeping me updated, which is good of her. I feel like she's caught in the middle, which is really hard on her, but at least someone is keeping me in the loop."

"Do you really think it's the best decision not to go?"

The tears that I'd been holding back since I talked to Charlie started to flow. At least we were on the phone and O.K. couldn't see what an ugly crier I was. I tried to not sniffle so maybe he wouldn't even guess I was crying. Again. "No, I want to go. I want to see my dad. I want to have a family again, but ..." I faltered. How do you tell someone that your family doesn't want you? I was rejected from the tribe and asked to leave the island. There was no going back. "I'm trying to respect Dean's wishes."

"His wishes?"

"Yeah, the last time I saw my parents, my father told me that I was no longer part of the family." I had not admitted that to anyone. I usually told people that I didn't get along with them. I never told anyone that I had been shunned.

"That's bullshit."

"Excuse me?" I was taken aback by his reaction. He seemed angry.

"That's bullshit. You don't kick people out of the family. That's why it's family. Even Jeffrey Dahmer's family still loved him. There is nothing that you could have done to warrant being expelled from your own family."

I think at that moment, I fell in love with O.K.

Through my tears, I smiled. I wish he could see that he was able to put a smile on my face. "Thank you for saying that. It was what I needed to hear, even if you did just compare me to a serial killer."

I'M STILL HERE

He chuckled. "You know what I mean. You don't have to get into it, if you don't want, but what could you have possibly done that your family thought they were better off without you?"

"No, this can of worms is already open. I insisted Aster was dead."

"That's it?"

"That's it. For three years after she 'disappeared,' my parents held out every hope. There were fliers and searches. They literally spent hundreds of thousands of dollars. Cheryl and Dean were paralyzed. They could barely go to work. Cheryl became obsessed with psychics and mediums, trying to find her. They set a place for her at every meal. They talked about her as if she was going to walk through the door at any minute. Every Christmas, there was a pile of gifts for her. It drove me mad. They would not even entertain the idea that Aster was dead."

"Wow, that sounds rough. What did you do?"

"Believe it or not, I tried to bite my tongue. I tried to subtly suggest that they consider the idea that Aster had committed suicide. It all fell on deaf ears. I grew bitter and resentful, and visited them less and less. I was working by this time, and had moved to St. Paul, so it seemed natural that I drifted away. But the final straw came the last time I went out to see them." I stopped for a minute and took a deep breath.

"You don't have to go on." O.K. was being so patient, so kind.

"Yes, I have to. I need to say this out loud. So, I make the two-plus-hour trek from St. Paul to East Podunk, where they live, for Sunday dinner. But it's not just Sunday dinner you see, it's also my birthday. I didn't think there'd be any kind of celebration, knowing it would be too hard on them because of Aster. I gave up celebrating my birthday after Aster died."

"You stopped celebrating your birthday? Why?"

"How do I make them celebrate me when my twin isn't here to celebrate? Plus, I didn't want to. Our birthday was always something we did together. I hate that I've had seven without her. So, anyway, I walk in, and the place is decorated all in pinks and purples, with balloons and crepe paper streamers everywhere. The entire family is there. I'm all pleased. I couldn't believe all the fuss was for me, finally coming to visit, and they were finally going to acknowledge me. Then I see it on the sideboard—the birthday cake." The words were tumbling out of my mouth. I had to get them out fast, otherwise I would choke on them. "Pink and purple had never been my favorite colors. They were Aster's colors. I'm a redhead, so I could never wear pink. I always preferred aquas and greens. But, even though Cheryl had gotten the colors wrong, I was still happy that she did this for me. So, I take a peek at the cake, all pink and purple. And on the cake, it says, "Happy Birthday Aster! We love you!"

"Wait—it was a cake for Aster, not you?"

"Yup. I had been invited to a birthday party for Aster."

"Aster was your twin though? I'm ... I ... I don't understand."

"Yeah, at that moment my patience snapped. They were having a party for Aster, hoping that if it was decorated perfect enough, got the right kind of cake, she would come home. I totally lost it. Cheryl could not see why I was upset. You wanna know what she said?"

"I'm not sure I do, but shoot."

"She said, 'You don't even celebrate your birthday anymore!' So, she didn't think she had to
acknowledge my birthday, but needed to acknowledge Aster's."

"That is so messed up."

"I know. And I had stopped celebrating my birthday because it was too hard to celebrate it without Aster. How could I ask my family to celebrate me when Aster was dead? I said as much, and that sent my dad off the deep end. He started yelling, 'How dare you say such a thing?' and 'There is no proof that my precious Aster is dead!' Of course, I run my smart-ass mouth off and tell him that there is more proof that she is dead than alive and that they needed to accept that. I mean, she left a freakin' suicide note, for Christ's sake. He said he will never accept it. I told him that he needed to, or I couldn't be around them anymore."

"I don't think I even want to know what he said."

"He said that he would never give up on Aster. And that since I had given up on her, I had given up on the family, and that I was no longer a part of the family. And that was it. That was the last time I saw or talked to my parents."

"I don't even know what to say."

"I bet you're sorry you took my call. You'd better start screening."

"Oh, I'm sorry all right. I'm sorry that your family is a bunch of asses. I'm sorry that you've had to go through all of this. I'm sorry that you're hurt and alone. But I will never be sorry that I took your call or that I met you."

Yup, that did it. I was in love.

CHAPTER TWENTY-ONE

Dean was going to need a quadruple bypass. I guess the years of smoking weed cancelled out the years of vegan eating after all. He was doing all right, anxious for the surgery. My parents had never been big believers of Western medicine, and I bet it was getting Cheryl's gall that she couldn't fix this with acupuncture, incense and essential oils. Charlie was keeping me updated, but was also keeping it from the rest of the family that she was in touch with me. They would not be pleased to know that I knew.

That was the irony of the family. I talked to Charlie the most, probably about once or twice a month. I talked to Veruca several times a year. I did not talk to Violet, as she was aligned with my parents on the Aster issue. Gus and Mike were men, so they weren't really big on the phone anyway. I got occasional e-mails or texts from them. But all of them kept it secret from each other and from my parents that they spoke to me. I was the black sheep. The pariah. The red-headed, well, you know.

I wanted to tell Charlie to tell Dean that I was asking for him. I could not send my love, because I was not sure that I loved my parents any longer. Love should be reserved for people who respect you and care about you. My parents offered me neither caring nor respect. Jillian, whom I'd only known for six months, offered me more caring and respect than my parents did. Plus, I didn't want to put Charlie in the middle, so I said nothing. I didn't want her subject to the ostracizing that I had faced. And despite all my parents had put me through, I really wanted to be there. I wanted to be able to hold my mom's hand while she waited and to hug my dad one last time. I wanted to be a part of my family again. Maybe I was crazy.

Damn Aster. This was all her fault. She may have thought through her suicide, but maybe she didn't. What she certainly did not consider is how it would impact the rest of us. She single handedly tore our family apart. She took away my best friend and other half and then took my family with it. I was seething and stewing in my own anger when my thoughts were interrupted by my cell phone. It was a good thing. I needed the distraction before I broke something or hurt myself trying (because let's face it, that was probably what would happen). Plus, I was sitting in my new piece-of-shit car (because, even with the insurance payment, I couldn't afford anything better), and I didn't want to break it already. As it was, the passenger's side rearview mirror was held on with duct tape. Luckily, the Ford Escort was black, and the previous owner had used black duck tape, so it was not that obvious.

"I think you need to go," said O.K. excitedly. "You need to go to your family."

"I want to, but I can't. They don't want me there. I would only cause more problems."

"You don't know that. What if they're being as stubborn as you are? What if your dad wants to see you to make amends, but is saying he can't because you wouldn't come even if he asked?"

"I never thought of that."

"I thought maybe that was the case. You can thank me later. I came up with a plan that will knock your socks off. And then I have an even better idea for a way you can thank me."

"Okay, O.K. Lay it on me. Well, the first plan, I mean. Not that I don't want to talk about the other thing, 'cause ... shit, I'm a moron. What's your plan?"

He laughed at my stuttering and stumbling. I really did love his laugh. His voice was soothing to me and I felt good talking to him. "Would you drive up there? How long of a trip is it?"

"I would have to drive. I can't afford a plane ticket and a rental car. I honestly have no idea how long it would take. Hang on ... let me put it the GPS." I pulled my GPS out of my work bag, plugged it into the car and put in the addresses. "It says here a little over ten hours."

"Perfect. When is the surgery?"

"Tomorrow morning. I guess he's stable and being monitored, but they still want to get this taken care of as soon as possible."

"Naturally. Do you trust me?"

"I did until you asked me if I trusted you. Usually when people as you that, it's because they're going to do something that is not deserving of trust."

"Good point. I need you to take a leap of faith and trust me on this."

I don't know why, but O.K. had this ability to soothe and put me at ease, even in the most difficult of situations. His words were like an elixir for my soul, and I did trust him. And that was difficult for me to do and even harder for me to admit.

"What do you want me to do?"

"You need to drive up there. He'll be in surgery for a good four to six hours, at minimum. Pack your bags, make arrangements to take time off and whatever else you need to take care of, and then go right to bed. Set your alarm for two a.m. If you get some sleep now, and get on the road then, you should be there about the time he's getting out of surgery."

The plan sounded valid. I had run scenarios through my head before and had come up with something similar. I hadn't thought about driving in the middle of the night, but O.K.'s plan made sense. I wasn't sure if I should admit that to O.K. or not. I was taking a leap of faith in trusting him, so I could take the leap in admitting that he had come up with a good plan.

"Okay."

"What?"

I sighed. How many more times would I do that? "No, okay as in I'll do your plan. It sounds like a good idea." I looked at my watch. It was four in the afternoon. I could be home and in bed by six. I would take a melatonin to help me go to sleep. I hadn't been sleeping well, so being tired was not a problem. My ass was dragging already. Going to bed in two hours sounded wonderful.

"O.K., thanks for caring. I really needed a friend, and you've been that. You've been more than a friend. I can't thank you enough. I'll call you from the road and let you know I got there."

Even though the plan called for early sleep, I did not think it would come so easily. Perhaps it was the fact that I had some kind of plan, some kind of direction. Perhaps it was because I hadn't slept well in weeks. Perhaps it was the melatonin. Whatever the reason, sleep came fast and deep. In fact, it was a little too deep, and I was still fast asleep when there was a pounding on my door.

Still groggy, I opened my eyes and tried to figure out what that banging was. My alarm was playing music, but it had failed to awaken me. I stumbled out of bed, nearly falling because I was tangled up in the sheets. I looked at my clock as I hastily tried to silence the music. It read two-ten a.m.; I had overslept by twenty-five minutes. Thank goodness that banging woke me up.

Wait, why was someone banging on my door at two in the morning? This could not be good. The only people who banged on doors in the middle of the night like this were the police, and only when they had bad news for you. I moved even faster trying to get to the door, this time stubbing my toe on the wooden threshold in my bedroom doorway. I hopped the rest of the way to the door, yelling, "Coming!" so whoever it was would stop the banging. I unlatched the deadbolt and was surprised to see O.K. standing on the other side of my door when I opened it up.

"You were supposed to be up by now."

"I may or may not have slept through my alarm. What are you doing here?" I asked, rubbing my eyes and then letting out a large yawn. You know, the fly-catching kind that is oh-so attractive.

"I came to make sure you got up and got on the road."

"That's very sweet of you. Come on in while I get myself together." He stepped inside and looked at me with a Cheshire Cat grin.

"What?" I said with a frown. I thought he might be laughing at me, and especially at two in the morning, I had little sense of humor about such things.

"You may or may not have a *minor* case of bed head—" my hands immediately flew to my mop, trying to tame it "—and a pillow crease down the side of your face."

Please shoot me now.

I hustled to the bathroom to take care of my needs, as well as brush my teeth. I pulled my hair back into a low ponytail and splashed some water on my face. I had packed all my make-up already. I figured I didn't need to look pretty for my solo drive.

I found O.K. in my kitchen with two large travel mugs of coffee poured. "I know you usually drink tea, but this is your Keurig, so I figured you must drink coffee sometime. How do you take it?"

"Black."

That answer gave him pause. "Nice."

"When your parents make you be vegan for a while, you develop a taste for things without dairy. Guess that was one of the few things that kind of stuck with me."

"Are you still vegan?"

"Good God, no. Frankly, we all cheated behind our parents' backs every chance we got. We all hated it. I think we did that from the time I was about eight until sixteen maybe?"

"You were drinking coffee then?"

"If it was organic and fair trade. My parents didn't let a little thing like caffeine stunting a child's growth deter them from what diet they thought was best. From what I hear, they are now on a paleo diet."

"Isn't that pretty much the antithesis of a vegan diet?"

"Cheryl and Dean are very consistent about their inconsistence. I still feel guilty when I eat meat though. But I crave it something fierce. Didn't Rob tell you about our date?"

"No, not really, other than the singing part. I really didn't want to hear anything." Did I detect a hint of jealousy in his voice?

"So, he left out how I pretty much made love to my bacon cheeseburger at the table then?"

"Yeah, somehow he omitted those details. I'd love to hear a play-by-play. Or better yet, see it." He winked at me. It made my stomach flutter.

"Well, that will have to wait until I get back. I need to get on the road." I had to focus.

I picked up my bags, which were right by the door. I had thrown in the last-minute stuff—the chargers, my books, my iPod—while O.K. and I were talking, and I needed to head out.

"Yeah, that's the thing. Thinking about it, I don't think you should be driving ten hours in the middle of the night alone. And I'm not sure your car would make it anyway."

"What are you talking about? This was your idea in the first place! You got me all psyched to go. I can't not go now." I huffed out of my door and waited for O.K. to leave so I could lock the door behind me. I continued to huff down the stairs and to my car. When I got to my car, I noticed a duffle bag on the ground behind my car.

"What's this?"

"Oh, that's mine," said O.K. "I can't let you drive all by yourself, so I'm coming with you."

CHAPTER TWENTY-TWO

O.K.'s mind was set, and there was no dissuading him. Frankly, although part of me was a little perturbed that he sprang this on me, there was a larger part of me that was going, "Squeee!" with joy that he wanted to do this for and with me. I was incredulous that he would dump everything to drive me up. Why would he do this for me? I would have to ask him. I was still trying to wake up. Those deeper thoughts would have to be processed a bit more at a later time. Since O.K. seemed totally wide awake, and I was still waiting for the coffee to kick in, I let him take the first shift with driving. He had insisted on taking his car after all.

The hours passed and we made good time. Except for the large tractor trailers, there wasn't a whole lot of traffic for the first several hours of our trip. We stopped when we needed to, but otherwise it was the open road and us. Congestion picked up as we moved through central Illinois approaching Chicago around the morning rush hour, but we stayed on the outer belt and didn't lose too much time.

O.K. told me more of his life story. I felt like we were always talking about my messed up family and me, and I wanted to know where O.K. came from. It turned out that O.K.'s life story could not have been more different from mine. He was an only child, and he had grown up in a small city about thirty miles east of Columbus. He had gone to Ohio State, so he'd lived his whole life in Ohio. His mom had passed away from breast cancer when O.K. was in high school and his dad quickly remarried. His stepmother, who he called "Mom," had two kids from her first marriage, so O.K. finally got the siblings he'd always wanted.

"So, you call your stepmother "Mom?"

"Yeah. Why? Is that weird?"

"No, I think it's funny. I don't call my mom "Mom." My parents have always insisted that we call them by their first names."

"I noticed that you referred to them that way. I just thought it was because you were estranged."

"No, it's because they're strange. From the time we were little, that is what we called them. So when most parents are mimicking babbling for their kids to say 'Ma-ma' and 'Da-da,' my parents were trying to get us to say 'Cheryl' and 'Dean.'"

"Somehow, it doesn't quite have the same ring, does it?"

I laughed. "No, not at all. And it totally negates the whole normal childhood speech development thing. But things like that never mattered to Cheryl and Dean. They lived, and still live, in their own world where they think the normal rules don't apply."

"So, they live in Minnesota now? But that's not where you grew up, right?"

"No, I didn't grow up in Minnesota. We didn't move there until I was eleven."

"Where were you before that?"

"We lived in upstate New York, but we moved around there a few times. Then we went to Colorado for about six months before we landed in Minnesota."

"See, I'm kind of jealous of that. I still live within a half hour of where I grew up. I went to college for a semester at Miami, which is a little north of Dayton. I didn't like it, so I transferred to Ohio State. And I stayed there for med school."

"But to me that sounds wonderful. You have roots. You have a home. I feel like a transient vagabond. And with each move, I lost a sibling or two. Charlie, the oldest, is twelve years older than us, I mean than I am. Once we started moving, it was time for the older kids to

113

go to college. Or they were working and didn't want to leave. With each move, the family was smaller and smaller. By the time we landed in Minnesota, it was only Mike, Aster and me left."

"I bet that was hard."

"Yeah, the family kept splintering. Now, Charlie lives outside Albany, New York. Violet lives in New York City. Gus lives in Boulder. Veruca lives in St. Paul—she moved to Minnesota because of her husband's job with 3M, not because of my parents. And Mike is in Oregon."

"Wow, you are all really spread out, aren't you?"

"Yeah, and I keep moving myself. Looking for a place to call home, I guess."

"Where have you lived?"

"Since leaving Minnesota, I've lived in Vegas, Boston, Florida and now Ohio. But always big cities. I've had enough of the country living."

"Did your parents always live in the middle of nowhere?"

"Yeah, pretty much. On the outskirts of civilization. Maybe a small town. Easier to maintain their hippy lifestyle when you're not on a cul-de-sac."

The conversation was easy, but so was the quiet. It was not an uneasy silence. We were okay being in each other's space without the need to fill the void with useless words. It was easy to get lost in my thoughts. I was nervous. About seeing my family. That Dean wouldn't make it. That he would and he would be angry with me for coming.

We had decided that we would be stopping at the next rest area for fuel, food and facilities. We were approaching Wisconsin and were really making good time. We'd found a radio station that played pretty much anything from the '70s through current day. We'd gotten a good thirty minutes with that station, singing along to the eclectic mix of music. The static started creeping in, and rather than search for a new station, I turned the radio off.

"I feel that I need to warn you. My family, it's ... it's not like yours."

"No one's family is like mine. And no one is like yours. We're all different."

I shook my head. "No, that's not what I mean. I mean, my family. Well, we're related by blood, but that's it. We just happen to be people who share DNA. It is not the loving, caring, supportive environment that it should be. You need to know that before you walk in."

"I'm just your chauffeur." He looked over and smiled at me. "I'd say it doesn't matter to me what they say, but it does. I don't want you to be hurt again. I think they've hurt you enough."

I returned his smile.

"So who all will be in Minnesota?"

"Everyone."

"They're all there?"

"Yeah, Cheryl wanted everyone to come in to be together. They purposely scheduled Dean's surgery out a day so that he would have a chance to see all of his children before he went in."

"But ..."

"He no longer considers me his child. I'm surprised he consented to the surgery without having seen Aster first."

"But that's crazy."

"I know," I shrugged. "It is what it is though. It hurts. He yearns for a daughter who chose not to live and ignores the daughter that does. I wish I could change it, but I can't."

We were stopped by this point at the gas pump. The morning sun was bright and the fall air was crisp. I got out of the car and started stretching. When I stood up, O.K. was standing there in front of me. He looked directly into my eyes. I could see the sadness that his eyes held and I knew it was for me. He took me in his arms and hugged me. I put my head on his shoulder and held on to him.

Standing there, in his arms, he said to me quietly, "You are deserving of love and respect. You have done nothing wrong." I closed my eyes as he said this, the tears slipping slowly down my cheeks. "I cannot imagine what special powers Aster must have held that have prevented your family from seeing what a remarkable and wonderful woman you are. It is their loss." With my body pressed up against his, it didn't matter how bad my family was. All was right in the world.

"Thank you for saying that. I try to tell myself that, but I don't always listen to me." I lifted my head and looked at him, giving a weak smile, which was the best I could do.

"If you don't listen to you, who else will?"

I put my head back down on his shoulder and let him hold me for a minute. I could have stayed there forever, but a rather impatient (or you could say nasty) woman in a minivan started yelling, "Pump or get a room. Either way, MOVE! Jesus Christ!"

O.K. broke the hold, but not before giving me a quick kiss on the top of my head. "Why don't you go in and order me a breakfast sandwich and coffee while I pump. I'll meet you inside."

We ate quickly, took care of our other needs, and got back on the road with a full tank of gas, full bellies and empty bladders. Two more states and I would be with my family for the first time in four years. How would they react? I wanted to think that they would be happy to see me. I wanted Dean to treat me like the prodigal daughter returned, but I was more confident that I would still be treated like Judas the traitor.

I was driving now, and O.K., despite the coffee in his hand, appeared to be dozing off. I reached over, removed the coffee and put it in the cup holder. He wasn't dozing off; he was in a dead sleep. I guess doctors were used to grabbing sleep where they could. Thinking about my family was exhausting. I knew nothing I did would change their minds. My parents would always see Aster as their golden child, the light in their world.

I kept stealing glances at O.K. who was zonked out. He was really adorable. I had thought he was attractive when I first fell out of my car and into his arms, but his support and friendship had made him downright irresistible to me. I focused on this for a while. I needed to think about something other than my messed up family. So I thought about O.K. while I drove. There was a small part of me that wanted to pull off of I-90 and into a hotel so I could have my way with him. I wondered what he would think of that. He was so sweet and thoughtful towards me, but I didn't know if he saw me as a friend, a charity case, or something more. I would not be one of those psycho girls who read too much into everything and misinterpreted every little nuance. I would play it cool and calm and let him take the initiative.

"What's going on between us?" I blurted out, waking him up.

"Huh? What? Did you say something?" O.K. was obviously a little groggy. He must have been in a deep sleep. Oops.

"Oh, I, ahh, I, um was just singing along with the radio." I turned up the volume a little and prayed it was a song I knew. "Sorry to wake you up. Go back to sleep."

He shifted around and was quickly back out. I did start singing along but tried to keep my voice low. Singing helped me pass the time, and before I knew it, we were in Minnesota. Literally, in the home stretch.

CHAPTER TWENTY-THREE

"I guess if you're going to need an operation, being a patient at the Mayo Clinic is probably the best you can hope for." O.K. was looking around as we walked in the main doors of St. Mary's Hospital. One of the two hospitals of the Mayo Clinic that put Rochester, Minnesota, on the map, St. Mary's housed the experts in heart surgeries, including cutting-edge use of robotics and transplantation. I'm not going to lie, it was reassuring that Dean's doctor in Winona had pulled some strings to get Dean transferred here. Especially considering that Dean was such a critic of Western medicine. I had much more confidence that Dean would make it through the surgery and have a good outcome, having been a patient at the world-renowned Mayo Clinic.

Like most large hospitals, there was construction all over the place, which made it difficult to get from point A to point B. I could tell O.K. was itching to pull out the "doctor" card and geek out with the great minds that were here, but he was trying to stay cool and aloof. Perhaps he was trying to impress me with his cool? Dammit, there I was, overanalyzing and over interpreting his every move. Again. I gave myself a mental slap on the forehead and continued to get lost as I tried to find the cardiac surgical waiting room. The patient representative at the front information desk had indicated that Dean was still in surgery.

Following directions from the third person I asked, I finally found myself in the correct wing. But try as I might, I could not force my feet to take one more step closer. I didn't want to cause a scene, and I knew my presence would do nothing but. I looked at O.K. and whispered apologetically, "I don't think I can do it. I can't go in there."

He took my hand and said, "That's okay. You don't have to for now. Why don't you text your sister and ask her to come out here. Then you can at least find out what is going on."

I simply stood there, holding his hand and looking at him. I think I was trying to draw strength from him. I don't know what I would have done without him in that moment. I had been on my own for so long. Even as a teenager, everyone supported Aster, including me. I don't think it ever occurred to my family that I needed support as well. I nodded and gave O.K. another tight smile. "Okay, I'm going to text her. I can do this." My words were as much for me as they were for him.

I was still preparing myself to text Charlie when a nurse in scrubs exited the waiting room. She looked at us standing there, obviously nervous. Obviously afraid to go inside. "May I help you?"

O.K. nudged me slightly. Drawing in a deep breath, I said, "Um, my father's in surgery. He's having a quadruple bypass done."

"Have you received any information on him yet?"

"Um, no. I, we, just got here. The rest of my family I'm sure is in the waiting room. I was working up the courage to go inside."

The nice nurse smiled, almost a bit patronizingly. "There's coffee and refreshments inside. It's much more comfortable in there than standing out here in this hallway."

"Oh, it's not that I'm afraid to go in the waiting room per se, it's more, well, I'm estranged from my family. They don't know that I'm coming. I don't want to cause a ruckus going in there, but I'm anxious to know how he's doing. Is there any way that you could get me an update on my father? His name is Dean Comely."

"No, I'm afraid I can only give information to the people that he's indicated."

"I understand. We'll go inside in a minute."

The nurse hustled off and I had to start prepping myself again. There were people all over the place, but I was still surprised to be tapped on the shoulder. "Yes?" I said, addressing a male nurse in pale green scrubs.

"I didn't mean to be eavesdropping. My name is Carson, and I was your father's nurse for the last few days. You're his daughter?"

"Yes, I am and this is my friend, Dr. Kingston Cole. I haven't seen or spoken to my father in a number of years. I've been a bit out of touch with the family. But I, well, I couldn't stay away when I heard he was sick. I just don't want to upset everyone by walking in there."

"Praise Jesus!" exclaimed Carson. "Your father's prayers have been answered!" Carson was a bit on the flamboyant side. He had dyed canary yellow hair that looked even brighter against his cocoa skin.

"'My father's prayers? I think we may be talking about different people. The Dean Comely I know is not at all religious. He is the definition of a lapsed Catholic."

"Oh, don't I know it, Sugar. But that man, well, I've been prayin' for his heart to open up. He told me the only thing that could make it happen is for his daughter to show up, and well, here you are. He said he did wrong by you and he needed to make amends and tell you he was wrong before his work here was done. He's gonna be so happy to see you. He said he messed up so badly, and he was afraid he'd never get to fix it. But here you are. Tell you what, I'm gonna go get an update for you. I can't wait 'til that cranky ole man wakes up. I'm gonna tell him that Jesus came through for him big time."

I smiled at O.K. Things were going to work out. Dean was ready to apologize. He wanted me back in his life. He knew what he had done wrong. He knew how he had hurt me. He didn't want to die before he made amends. I leaned against the wall, needing something to keep me upright after the relief flooded through me.

Slowly, I sank down so I was sitting, back against the wall and knees to my chest. O.K. sat down on the floor next to me.

I started talking. "I know that I should be strong, but you don't know what it means to me that he knows he was wrong. I mean, my parents have hurt me in indescribable ways."

"Oh, you described them pretty well."

"The sad thing is, they're not bad people. I don't think they willingly set out to hurt me. I don't have kids, so I can't say, but even though I know you're not supposed to have favorites, they probably couldn't help it that Aster was theirs. And when she got sick and got out of control, they couldn't handle it."

"Couldn't or didn't?"

I shrugged. "I don't know. Part of me thinks that their brains were so warped from drugs and lifestyle brainwashing that they literally did not have the ability to handle it. I don't think they ever set out to hurt me. I became the scapegoat, because I was there too. They lashed out at me because I was a reminder of everything they lost with Aster. I can rationalize why they did it."

"But it doesn't make it acceptable."

"No, it will never be acceptable. But I'll do my very best to let the hurt go and move on. This is such a huge step. The least I can do is meet him halfway."

O.K. put his arm around my shoulders and I snuggled into him. "And I will never be able to thank you enough for, well, for everything you've done. I wouldn't be here right now if you hadn't made me, and then to put everything on hold to drive up here with me ..."

O.K. interrupted my rambling with a kiss. It was slow and gentle at first, but the intensity started to build. I was needy, hungrily devouring his mouth.

"Lawd, you two ought to get a room!" Carson was back.

O.K. broke away with a huge grin on his face. His eyes never left mine. "If I had a nickel for every time I've heard that ..."

"You'd have ten cents," I finished. I turned my attention toward Carson and, wiping my mouth, said, "Were you able to get an update?" I stood up and brushed off my bottom. I was still in the yoga pants and fleece that I had slept in last night in preparation for a long day in the car. I didn't even want to think about what the hair was doing.

"They're closing him up now. He came through great. There were four arteries that needed to be bypassed and another that they put a stent in. He'll be in recovery for a few hours and will go to the CICU for the night. He is stable and should have a good recovery."

"Oh, thank God."

"Praise God is right. I can't wait to tell him his prayers were answered."

"Thank you Carson for all you've done. You will never know how much it means to me."

"No problem. I wish I could be there to see his face when he sees that his long-lost daughter came back for him. I tole him and I tole him, 'Keep the faith and she will come back.' And here you are Miz Aster, here you are."

I froze, my blood cold. "What did you call me?"

"Oh, I was just trying to be polite by adding the 'Miss.' I guess with a name like Aster, adding the 'Miss' makes it sound a little too close to disaster."

"You called me 'Aster?'"

"Well, that's your name, ain't it? How many long-lost daughters can Dean have? There's a whole mess of kids in the waiting room as it is."

I stood up ram-rod straight. "I'm his *other* daughter, Esther."

CHAPTER TWENTY-FOUR

"I don't know how to say this without it sounding awful."

I looked at O.K. Was he really going to kick me when I was this down? We were sitting on a bench outside of St. Mary's. After the wonderfully enlightening interaction with Carson, I high tailed it out of the hospital, leaving O.K. in my wake. He caught up with me, standing in front of the main doors. I'm pretty sure I had a bewildered look on my face. I didn't know where to go or what to do next. I wanted to just go, get the car and drive home. So what that I had been on the road for almost eleven hours already today? I could drive twenty-two hours out of twenty-four. I had enough anger to fuel me.

I continued to stare at him blankly. He sat down next to me. "I know I'm going to muck this up saying it, but hear me out."

I nodded, still unable to form words.

"In my experience, sometimes, women—or people," he quickly corrected, "sometimes can over exaggerate situations to make things a little more dramatic than perhaps they actually are. While I certainly believed what you had told me about your family, there was part of me that wondered if you were being dramatic or had a narrow perspective about the situation."

"You thought I was making it up?" I was furious. I was going to rip his head off.

"No, no, no!" he jumped in quickly. "I did not think you were making it up at all. I thought that maybe your point of view was somewhat skewed, being colored by your own personal experiences."

"Where are you going with this?"

"I'm sorry that I thought you may have even had a tiny bit of a skewed perspective, because you don't. Not at all."

"Yeah, what's your point?"

"Your family is really fucked up."

I looked at him and then burst out laughing. I'd never heard O.K. use that kind of language before. It seemed funny that now, of all times, he drops an F-bomb, and it's about my family.

"Yes, yes they are."

"When you talk about how unreasonable they are, it doesn't seem real. It does not seem like reasonable, rational people could act in such a blind way."

"Well, that's where you've got it backwards. They are not reasonable or rational. Part of me wonders if Cheryl and Dean are delusional. Lord knows they've done enough drugs to have a little scrambled eggs up there. Knowing that Aster was bipolar, perhaps there's a touch of mental illness in them as well. There is such a strong genetic component."

"Could be."

We sat in silence for a few minutes, watching people race in and out of the hospital. I wondered how many other people were going in to visit family members who did not acknowledge their existence. Probably none.

"What do you want to do now?"

"I want to get into the car and drive home."

"Really?" He looked at me. I stared back.

"Really."

"You don't want to see your dad at all?"

"And say what? Hi Dean. Drove over ten hours to see you. Sorry that I'm alive but Aster isn't. Wish I could make it the other way around for you."

"Don't say that!"

"That's what he thinks. And what do I say to my mom? Hi, Cheryl. Remember me? I'm your youngest daughter. You know, the one whose birthday you forget, but you remember my dead twin's?"

"You're not even going to go in and talk to your mom?"

"Nope."

He huffed.

"What was that huff for?"

"I just don't get it."

"Get what?"

"You guys lost a family member. It should make you appreciate each other all the more. Instead, it has done nothing but drive you apart. Do you know what I would give for one more chance to see my mom?"

"I know. I know I should seize this opportunity to see her and make amends, but I'm not strong enough or big enough. I can't take one single more instance of them shitting all over me and cursing me for being the one to still be here. I can't go through it again."

He was quiet for a moment. "You're right. You shouldn't have to. I want to go up there and shake some sense into those people. I just don't understand how they cannot even acknowledge you. Can't they see what a brilliant, wonderful, beautiful person you are?"

"But I'm not Aster, and that is all they'll ever be able to see."

He reached over and took my hand. It seemed like O.K. was always holding my hand or holding me up these days. I didn't want to become reliant on anyone, but I found myself wanting to lean on him, both literally and figuratively. I couldn't let myself though. Hadn't my family shown me that love and dependence only cause hurt?

I pulled my hand out from his and sat up. I would depend on me. I didn't need anyone else. "I'm fine now. Let's go."

"Are you sure?"

"Yes. They don't need me, and I don't need them. I don't need anyone." I stuck my chin out stubbornly. I tried to pretend I didn't see the hurt in O.K.'s eyes. I stuck my chin out a little bit further. My arms were crossed over my chest. I would take ownership of that look later, but now I was too busy wallowing in my own self-pity. The only other thing I could do to make my point would be to flop on the ground and kick my legs.

"Esther!"

I looked up dully.

"Esther! Is that you?"

Charlie was running out of the hospital toward me. Breathless when she reached me, she panted, "Esther! You're here! You came!" She grabbed me and hugged me tightly. Limply, I hugged back.

"Esther, why didn't you come inside? Why are you out here?"

"I'm leaving."

"No, you have to come in!"

I shook my head. "I can't. I just ... I can't go through it all again. I tried, but I can't put myself through it. Not again."

"What do you mean?"

"I was in there. We—" I gestured to O.K. "—were inside, outside the waiting room. We talked to one of Dean's nurses, Carson."

"Oh, yeah. Isn't he a trip?"

"Yeah, I thought so too. He was going on and on about how Dean was praying for his daughter to come see him. How he had done her wrong. How he had messed up and needed to fix it. It made me so happy. I couldn't believe that he had finally realized that. And then he called me Aster."

"Oh, no!" Charlie clutched her heart.

"Oh, yes. Once again, Dean is holding out hope that Aster comes back, but doesn't give a shit that he has another daughter out there. I mean nothing to him. I mean less than nothing. He doesn't even tell people that I exist. I can't—"

"I'm sure he wouldn't act that way if he saw you. I'm sure he's hurt that you've left him too. You need to go in and see him. Tell him you're sorry for staying away so long."

"Tell him that ... I'm sorry?"

"Yeah. He may give you the chance to apologize."

"I'm not the one who did something wrong. He told me to get out and never come back."

"Well, you know how upset he is about Aster."

"You're defending him?"

"No, I'm not defending him. I just, well, I think he shuts you out as a defense mechanism. It was so hard on him, losing Aster, who we all know was his favorite. I don't think he can bear the thought of losing another daughter. So he shuts you out and pretends you don't exist as a defense mechanism, so that he's not hurt by you not being around."

"That's the stupidest thing I've ever heard."

"No, and if you apologized for always picking fights, then he would probably let you stay."

"*Let* me stay?"

"Esther, be reasonable. He's not so bad. He's so upset that Aster isn't here. He's been through so much, losing her. Just listen to him, to what he has to say."

I couldn't believe that Charlie, who was the most reasonable out of the whole clan, was defending him and putting the blame back on me. "I'm done listening. C'mon—" I turned to O.K., "—I'm ready to go now."

Charlie's walls were up and I could tell she was now on the defensive. She looked over my shoulder to O.K. "I assume you're *one* of the guys she's dating." There was spite and malice in her tone. I could tell she hoped that O.K. didn't know about Rob so that she would get me in trouble.

O.K. didn't take the bait. I wanted to kiss him. He cordially extended his hand. "I'm Esther's friend, Kingston Cole."

Charlie was annoyed that he hadn't taken the bait. "Are you gonna make her come in or what?"

"First, Esther is a grown woman, and I consider it disrespectful to talk about her when—" he leaned closer

to Charlie and continued in an exaggerated whisper, "—
she's *right here!*" He held one hand up to block that the
other hand was pointing at me. "Second, Esther and I
don't make each other do anything. If Esther wants to go
in, which, with the way you all treat her, I can't imagine
she does, she will. Third, I think you need to pull your
head out of your ass for a minute and consider Esther's
feelings."

Charlie's mouth hung open, unable to form words.

I really needed to kiss him now.

I couldn't remember the last time anyone had
defended me. Actually I could, and it had been Aster.

CHAPTER TWENTY-FIVE

We ran out of steam after only three hours on the road. I, personally, was physically and mentally exhausted from the day. We decided to get a hotel room at the Cambria Suites as we passed through Madison, Wisconsin. It would be the last large city until we reached Chicago, and that seemed like too far to drive.

I thought it would be awkward getting a hotel room with O.K., but somehow it wasn't. He didn't put up a fuss when I told him that I was paying. I suspect he knew that I was not up for fighting about it. I was happy that the room was under $100 for the night and was pleasantly surprised at the cool decor and amenities for such a discounted rate.

We dropped our bags and I flopped on the bed.

"I can't remember ever being this tired."

"I can. It was called residency."

"Do you still work those kind of hours?"

"Good God, no."

I rolled over and looked at O.K., who had sat down on the bench at the end of the king-size bed. "But you are still at the hospital and have a private practice?"

"Yeah, I'm in the office two and a half days a week. I do surgery two days a week. I work one to two evening shifts at the hospital and then take call every fourth weekend."

"So you had been on call the night of my accident?"

"Yeah, I got called in to come and see you."

"But then the night that we had coffee ..."

"I had my shift then. That was a long day, since I was in the office all day first."

"So you work a lot."

O.K. was bent over, taking off his shoes. I liked the fact that he wore his scuffed brown oxfords with his jeans. As opposed to me who traveled in glorified pajamas, O.K. was wearing halfway decent clothes. Although, since it was now around five in the afternoon, he too was starting to look a little rumpled.

"I guess I do. I don't have a lot else going in my life. I took on the extra hospital shifts after my last relationship ended. I'd rather be busy working than home by myself or out bar-hopping, trying to prove how young and virile I am."

"So if you were in a relationship, you wouldn't work quite so much?" Damn, that sounded like I was fishing. Not to mention desperate and needy as well. I pushed myself off the bed. "I'm going to go take a shower." I needed some space before anything more flew out of my mouth.

The hot water felt good beating down on me after such a long and stressful day. At least I didn't have to worry about running out of hot water. As the water pelted my back, I wished that I could shut my mind down and stop thinking. About Aster. About Cheryl and Dean. About Charlie. About O.K. Mmm ... O.K. Oh God, O.K. was on the other side of the door. What was going to happen tonight? He had been nothing but a perfect gentleman. Would he make a move on me? Would I make a move on him? Was I ready to enter into a relationship at this point? Did he want a relationship? I knew I didn't want a casual fling. Those were too draining. If I was going to put effort in, it would be for a real relationship. After all, I was thirty-one. I already had a failed marriage. I had no family. I wanted to find a life partner, not just someone to roll in the hay with.

Lost in my seemingly endless train of thoughts, O.K. scared the bejeezus out of me when he started banging on the door. "You okay in there?"

I stuck my head out of the shower. "Yeah, fine. Just finishing up." I turned off the water and looked at my pruney hands. I guess I had been in there a while. The bathroom was like a steam room. With my luck, I would probably set off a smoke alarm when I opened the door. I turned the fan on, dried off, and liberally lotioned up my body, which was now dried out from the shower. I brushed my teeth, as I feel compelled to do after every shower.

I hadn't planned on spending the night with O.K. when I packed. Hell, at that point, I hadn't even realized he was planning on coming with me. As a result, I had packed the pajamas of a lonely single woman. Penguins adorned the bubble-gum pink fleece bottoms. The long-sleeve, fitted gray t-shirt likewise had a penguin on it. At least the bottoms were low rise and fitted through the hips. While I certainly wouldn't consider them sexy, at least they weren't frumpy. I decided to put my bra back on though, because the t-shirt was a bit on the flimsy side. Plus, at my age, the girls could always use a little support.

I quick finger combed through my hair, applied some anti-frizz product, and I was finally ready to face O.K. again. I had no makeup on. My hair was wet. I was wearing ridiculous pajamas. It never occurred to me that O.K. might be hungry and want to go out to dinner or get something to eat.

"I guess you're planning on staying in tonight then?"

I looked down at my outfit. He was sitting on the bed, watching the news on television. "You know, I didn't even think about it. What time is it?"

"It's almost six."

I laughed. "My clock is all off. I feel like it's midnight."

"Understandable. It's been a long day."

I sat down on the bed next to him. Well, it was a king-size bed, so we could have fit about four other people in between us. "You can say that again."

"It's been a long day."

131

I smiled and playfully whacked him. "I can get changed again, so we can get something to eat."

"No, you look comfortable. Why don't we order in and eat here?"

"Sounds perfect. Are you sure you don't mind?"

"No, not at all."

We poured over the menu. I ordered a steak while O.K. ordered a burger. We got a bottle of wine, since we both agreed that a bottle of beer each probably wouldn't be enough on a night like tonight. O.K. hopped in the shower while waiting for the food to arrive. He was done in about a nanosecond. He came out in gray sweats and an Ohio State t-shirt. His hair, which he'd gotten cut since our disastrous date, was still wet, and he had shaved. The aroma of nice aftershave drifted off him. I took a deep breath, enjoying the smell of him.

I looked down at my pajamas again. I felt like an idiot. "If I had known you were accompanying me on this trip, I would have packed better pajamas."

"They're, um, interesting. Penguins?"

"I like penguins. Penguins are cute. They're birds that persevere even though they can't fly. I used to want one for a pet."

He laughed. "Really?"

"Yeah, I'd have dreams that I would find a stray penguin in a sketchy pet store and bring it home. There was always part of me that was disappointed to find out it was a dream."

He looked at me like I had four heads.

"Oh, come on. Tell me that you don't have weird dreams from time to time."

"Honestly, I don't really remember them most of the time. I think I sleep pretty deeply."

"I wish I didn't remember them most of the time. I can't tell you how many times I've woken up pissed off at someone because they were an asshole in my dream. It was really interesting the time I dreamt that I got into a fistfight with my sister-in-law. We had a family gathering the next day and it was all I could do not to punch her."

"Remind me never to be in your dreams."

"Well, they're not always violent you know."

"Oh really? Tell me more ..."

Shit. Why was I always such an asshole? When would I ever learn to think before I spoke? I was saved by the room service delivery. Although there was a small table and chairs in the corner, we decided to sit on the floor and eat. I leaned back and let the bed support my back.

"I hope you don't mind sitting on the floor," O.K. said, in between large bites of his burger. He devoured it in such a way that I knew I did not have to be self-conscious about eating. He managed to balance his plate on his lap successfully but also managed to drip ketchup down the front of his shirt.

"Um, you have a little something ..." I handed O.K. a napkin.

He laughed, wiping his shirt. Somehow, using a napkin only managed to smear the ketchup more. "I Berted."

"You what?"

"I Berted. I had a roommate in college, Bert Sandstrom. I'd come home, and Bert would be lying on the couch with like a double-decker sandwich on his chest. He never used a plate. He'd have food all over himself. And every time he ate, he spilled food down the front of himself. Of course, he pretty much always wore white too. There was always mustard on his shirt. So anytime anyone spilled, it became known as Berting."

"I wish I'd known that years before. I've been Berting for a very long time. I'm very good at it." I took another sip of wine. "Especially when I've had a lot of this." I held up my glass in toast.

O.K. toasted me back. "To Bert."

"What a day," I sighed after I had drained my glass. "I just can't, I just, I, I'm speechless."

O.K. leaned over, closing the gap between our shoulders and kissed me. When he finally broke away, he said, "You don't need to say anything."

"Just tell me one thing, and then I'll shut up. Is this more than a random hook-up?"

"I don't normally take several days off work, drive all day only to turn around and drive back for my random hook-ups."

"You don't?"

"Esther, I know this might be hard for you to believe, but I like you. A lot. More than a lot. I have for a while. Every time we went out or tried to go out, things got interrupted. I knew you needed a friend for this. I wanted to be that friend. I want to be more than that."

"Why? I'm such a mess. Even my own family doesn't like me."

"That's their loss. You are remarkable. And spunky. And strong. And charismatic. And beautiful. Did I mention beautiful?"

"You know, I don't think you ever did. But I need to tell you something before you say anything else."

"That doesn't sound good."

"It's not. I can't stand that stain on your shirt. It's driving me nuts."

"Wha—my shirt?" He looked down with a confused look on his face.

"Yes, your shirt. I can't stand it. I can't handle your Bert. You need to take it off. RIGHT NOW." I grinned at him.

With a matching grin, he took his shirt off.

I grabbed his face in both of my hands as I rose up on my knees to straddle his lap, all without breaking the kiss. I must have Berted as well, because before I knew it, my shirt was off too.

Oh my.

CHAPTER TWENTY-SIX

I couldn't stop smiling. Yes, it was that good. Both times. We slept in and ate a leisurely continental breakfast. By late morning, we were back in the car, headed south on I-90 again. Despite the catastrophic events in Minnesota, the mood in the car was light. I guess a good romp will do that for you. We chatted, quizzing each other about various things in our pasts. Favorite songs and movies were covered, as well as food and books.

"Biggest regret?" I asked.

"Biggest regret or mistake?"

"Are they two different things?"

He paused, mulling it over for a moment or two. "I was engaged a few years ago."

"Do you regret not getting married?"

"No, not at all. Cathy and I had dated since college. She stuck with me all through med school. I was dragging my feet about committing to her. I pushed out getting engaged, and then insisted on a long engagement. I used the excuse that I was trying to finish medical school. And then I was beginning residency. Money was tight. I didn't want to spend the money on a big wedding."

"How long were you together?"

"In total, eight years."

"Ouch."

"I know. I knew for a long time that Cathy was not the right person for me, but it was easy and comfortable. She was there; she got along with my family. I loved her, but knew I wasn't in love with her."

"Did she know that?"

"I want to believe on some level she did, but I don't think so. If she knew, then it would excuse how I acted, but in all honesty, nothing can excuse what I did."

"What did you do?" I hoped it was not something that was a deal breaker for me. I liked him, and I did not want this thing to end before it really started.

"I cheated on Cathy. I knew it was wrong, but I justified it by, well, I lied to myself to make me feel better. That way, when she found out, she called it off and it wasn't my fault. I could blame her."

"You blamed her for your cheating?"

"No, I could blame her for calling off the wedding and breaking up with me. I wish that I had been adult enough to end things without having to resort to cheating. I knew that she would not be able to live with it, so I think that's why I did it."

"Wow."

"I will forever feel badly that I did that. I should have just been honest with Cathy and myself and ended things."

"Yeah, you should have."

"Thanks for the support. What about you? Biggest mistake and regret."

"For me, they are two different things. Biggest mistake was marrying Dickie. It was right after Aster disappeared. Things were awful. Simply awful. I think I thought Dickie would rescue me from the chaos in my life and take me away from it all and I could be part of a family."

"Was he not a knight in shining armor?"

"Um, no. He was a whack-job. A religious zealot who actually believed the malarkey that spewed from his mouth. He told me that Aster had been sick because the devil was in her heart. And that she was being punished for my parents' sins."

"He did not say that."

"Yes he did. I have never been a violent person, and I found myself wanting to punch him. All the time."

"Why did you marry him?"

I shrugged. "It was impulsive. It was stupid. I was looking to escape. I wanted someone to take care of me."

"But that's not your biggest regret?"

"No," I said quietly.

There was silence as I tried to gather the strength to say what I had to say.

"When Aster went missing, and there was the note and everything, and even the police said that she was gone, I was relieved. I will always regret that the first thing that crossed my mind was relief. I was relieved for me and my family that we wouldn't have to ride the Aster roller coaster anymore. I was relieved for Aster that she was no longer tormented. But mostly, I was relieved that I would no longer have to deal with all the shit she put me through. What kind of person is relieved that her sister, her twin, has killed herself? I regret that I am that kind of person."

"You can't regret that you felt relief. I'm sure dealing with Aster on a daily basis was draining and taxing."

"You have no idea. It was my life. Every day was spent putting out the fires that she started, or just keeping her going. I never knew who she was going to be when she walked through the door, and it was exhausting. Sometimes I marvel that I was able to finish school. I never knew what each day would bring."

"Where did you go?"

I could tell he was changing the subject to help me feel better. I let him lead me. "I did my undergrad at Winona State. I stayed at home when I was there. By the time I was done, I needed to get away, so I went to Minnesota for grad school. It was the first time I was away from Aster."

"What was she doing?"

"Who knows? Drugs. Singing in a band. Working in a gas station. It was terrible, but I had to get away. I think if I hadn't I never would have gotten out. I think she would have sucked me down with her."

"I think the only thing you should regret is that you didn't leave her sooner."

"Why would you say that?"

"She was the sick one, not you. Her illness overtook your life. You are lucky that you were able to persevere through all of it to get your education."

"I don't see it that way. If my sister had had cancer, I would not have wanted to run away. I would have stayed by her side, donating whatever body parts she needed, taking her to treatments. I would have fought with her, not against her."

"It's not the same thing."

"How can you say that? You're a doctor. How can you not see that people with mental illness are just as sick as someone with cancer?"

"I don't disagree at all. But it's not the same thing because if Aster had had cancer, everyone would have admitted it and faced it. Aster would have sought treatment, and the family would have pulled together to collaborate and do everything to help Aster beat it, right?"

"I guess," I shrugged.

"I would guess, especially seeing your family assembled at the hospital for your dad, that if Aster had a traditional illness, no one would have denied that it was there. One of the most frustrating things about treating mental illness is that it is such an uphill battle for people to even admit that it is present."

"You're right."

"Of course I am." I looked at him to see if he was really being that smug. He was laughing.

"I think if you want this relationship to work, then you need to admit that I'm usually right." Oh shit, I just said we were in a relationship. What if that totally freaked him out and scared him off?

"Yes, dear."

So did that mean we were in a relationship? I would think so. Right? I playfully slapped him on the arm and sank back into my seat. After a minute I said, "You know, sometimes I hated her. I mean, I loved her more than anything, but I hated who she turned into after she got sick. I just wanted the old Aster to come through the door. What kind of person hates her sister for being sick?"

"You want to know what my over-priced shrink would say?" Without waiting for an answer he continued. "You didn't hate Aster. You loved her. You still do. You hated the disease. You hated that she was sick. But there was nothing anyone could do about her getting sick. You couldn't control it. So, you got mad at Aster."

"Why did she have to get so sick? Why did she have to leave me? I would have helped her through it. I was too selfish, only thinking about me and my needs. If I had known that she was going to kill herself—well, I would have stayed. School could've waited. She couldn't."

With those words hanging in the air, I fiddled with the radio until a halfway decent station came in. I sang along with the song, almost not realizing I was doing it. I was so used to being in the car by myself. Singing along was a stress reducer for me, especially when I was working. Most of the time, I wasn't even aware that I was singing.

After a song or two, O.K. asked, "So when do you make your official debut with the band?"

"Saturday night." I paused. "Oh crap, what day is it?"

"It's Thursday."

"Oh, God, is that it? This seems like it's been the longest week."

"I guess it probably has been for you."

"I feel like the days have been about forty-two hours long each. I should call Albert and touch base. I think we're supposed to rehearse tomorrow night."

"Are you nervous?"

"No. Maybe. A little."

"I would think it'd be natural to be a little nervous."

"I'm partly nervous about the performing, but I think I'm more nervous because of what happened last time."

"Rob said you killed it."

"Oh, I did. I was awesome. Obviously, it got me the gig."

"I see that humility is a strength as well."

"Shut it. You know I'm kidding. Didn't Rob tell you what happened after?"

"No, he didn't indicate that anything had gone wrong."

"Not wrong, per se, but, well, I don't know how to say this without sounding crazy so bear with me. When I finished the second song, I looked up, and I swore I saw Aster standing at the back of the bar. I tore out of there, trying to catch up with her, but she was gone. I didn't tell Rob what I saw, but it was hard to cover up tearing out of there like my pants were on fire."

"Holy shit."

"Yeah, I know. That's what convinced me that I was starting to lose it."

"I don't think you are. You know that."

"How else can you explain it?"

"Do you believe in spiritual connections?"

"Ghosts?"

CHAPTER TWENTY-SEVEN

"Yeah, no. I don't believe in ghosts. I'd like to believe that there is an afterlife, but I don't think people hang out in between planes of existence to complete unfinished business or communicate with loved ones." I could not hide the disgust in my voice. Just thinking about the thousands of dollars Cheryl had spent trying to get a message from the great beyond angered me.

"Just throwing it out there. I didn't mean to offend."

"No. We've been down that road. Again and again. Let's put it this way—none of the mediums, psychics or quacks that Cheryl paid was able to communicate with Aster. I can't tell you how many ridiculous Tarot card readings I've been to. I had to draw the line when Cheryl wanted to start doing online Tarot card readings."

"Gotcha. I won't bring it up again. Maybe in times of high stress, you connect to her. Obviously, you were thinking about her when you were singing, right? She was definitely in your conscious mind. Then, combined with the adrenaline rush from singing, you thought you saw her."

"That's the most plausible, reasonable explanation I've heard so far. Okay, you can stay." I smiled at him. I really did like him. He was on my side. It was nice.

He returned the smile. "That's good, because you're in my car, and we're still not even to Dayton yet. We have about two hours left. I hope you can put up with me that long."

"I'm surprised you still want to be with me after all the drama. I swear my life is usually pretty quiet. I usually keep all the drama at work. I see enough of it there."

"Yeah, I can imagine."

"I couldn't even imagine some of the horrors that I would encounter before I got into the field. I just wanted to help families like mine who so needed help."

We talked about work and how boring our lives really were for the rest of the trip. The time sped by, and before I knew it we were parking in front of my apartment. O.K. carried my bag up to my apartment as I fumbled with the keys to unlock the door. Even though it had only been a little over a day, I felt like we had been together for weeks. We just fit together right.

The apartment looked the same as it had when I left. But I was different. For the first time in a very long time, I did not feel alone. O.K. had given me the feeling of belonging that I had sought since Aster had vanished from my life. I turned to him and gave him a hug. He let me stand there, holding onto him. But even more, he was holding me back.

"Do you want to stay?"

He leaned in and gave me a kiss. It started soft and tender, but quickly grew more passionate. Finally, he broke away. We were both panting a bit.

"I would love to stay, but ..."

Just when I was getting comfortable, he drops this on me? What the heck? Did I totally misinterpret the whole relationship thing? Crap, I was that psycho girl. Time to back peddle. "You don't need to come up with an excuse. If you don't want to stay, you don't have to. What I don't need is an excuse or a lie. Please be honest, and we'll be fine. Obviously, it won't be the worst thing I've ever heard."

"I want to stay, but I think I should go home. I have a feeling we're going to be spending most of our nights together. I'm going to take this one last night to get my shit together."

I tried not to let my disappointment show. I asked him to be honest, and he had been.

"And by getting my shit together, I mean I need to clean my house so that you can come over and not be afraid to use the toilet."

"Oh, so your literal shit."

"Yes, pretty much. And I need to catch up on laundry, since I have a large collection of clothes with Berts on them. I now know how much that bothers you."

"If you recall, it bothered me when it was on the shirt your were wearing. I felt the need to remove the shirt. I *think* that worked out very well. At least it did from my standpoint."

"Now that you mention it, I think I should *not* do my laundry, if that's going to be your reaction."

"Oh, look at that—" I took a step back and pointed at his shirt. "I think you may have Berted again."

He looked down at his impeccably clean shirt. "No, I'm fine. But you, my dear, are a terrible mess. I think we need to remedy that right now."

"What did you have in mind?"

O.K. was playing with the bottom of my shirt, running his fingers along the bottom hem. "Look at this. You're all wrinkled."

I held my arms tight at my side. This was fun. I knew I had a shit-eating grin on my face. "I think my shirt looks completely fine."

"No, it is really wrinkled. And perhaps a little dirty. I think this needs to go in your laundry, stat." His hands were busy underneath my shirt, running up and down my back. He leaned in, kissing my neck. In between kisses, he said, "Yeah, I think you really need to get out of these clothes."

I tried to resist but his kisses and hands and body pressed up against mine were making me weak in the knees. "I think I'm okay for now."

O.K. pulled back. "Quick, pretend your choking!"

"What?"

"You know," he said, and motioned, putting his arms up above his head.

"Only because you're cute." I lifted my arms above my head and before I knew it, my shirt was off. As was my bra. And then the rest of my clothes.

After, I pulled a throw blanket off the back of the couch to cover us. We had somehow managed to get over to my super-comfy white couch, which was a lot more comfortable than the hallway. Actually, against the wall in the hallway had started off very, very good, but my coordination (or lack thereof) won over and after falling, we decided that moving to an alternate location would be a better idea. I laid there in O.K.'s arms, stroking his arm with my fingers.

"I thought you didn't want to stay."

"I didn't say that I didn't want to stay. I said that I should probably go to take care of stuff at home. I also said that I thought we'd be spending most nights together."

"I guess I can get on board with that."

From across the apartment, O.K.'s phone started chirping. He got up, retrieved his discarded boxer briefs from the floor and donned them, before walking a bit further to find his phone in the pocket of his blue jeans.

"Everything alright?"

"Yeah," he said distractedly, as he began texting. After a moment, he looked up. "This is not my weekend on, and I asked a colleague to take my shift earlier in the week so I could be off. That colleague is now asking me if I can take their shift tomorrow night. Is that alright with you?"

"I have to practice with The Rusty Buckets tomorrow, so I'm not going to be around for most of the night anyway."

He quickly texted back and returned the phone to his pocket. He pulled his jeans on and ran his fingers through his hair. "So I don't want you giving me shit about avoiding you tomorrow night when I have to work." He smiled.

"I won't. I promise. We're hanging out. No big deal. You don't owe me anything past this moment."

He looked hurt. "Esther, why do you keep doing this? Why do you keep selling us short? Obviously, I'm here. I want to be here. I saw the crazy family. I get it. It's not going to scare me away. I want you and I want to be with you. For real and for serious."

"I'm sorry I keep doing that. I don't mean to, and I don't mean to keep playing the pity card. Prior to six weeks ago, I was pretty normal. This whole Aster thing has turned my world on its axis. Funny, she's wreaking as much havoc in death as she did in life."

"Just don't keep doing it. I'm too old to keep having the same fights."

"Good, me too. I will do my very best not to keep acting like a psycho-hose beast. Now, sort of on the same subject, but somewhat different ..."

"I can't even begin to understand what you mean by that."

I laughed. I was up and walking around my apartment, collecting my clothing. I went into my room and pulled on clean underwear and a robe. "What started this whole—" I gestured between us "—thing was that comment about you having to work. I think you've been pretty upfront about how much you work. I'm fine with that. I take call periodically as well, and now I have this band thing. I don't know how much time that's going to take up."

"So what you're saying is that you don't have time for me?"

"So now you're giving me a hard time?" I picked up my shirt and threw it at him. He caught it midair and laughed.

"It's just so fun to rile you up."

"So where does this leave us?"

"We're busy people, but we like being together, so we're going to do what we can so that we can do what we just did."

"I'm not sure that makes sense, but I'm totally on board with it."

CHAPTER TWENTY-EIGHT

I was so freakin' nervous. Despite what reassurance Albert and the guys had given me, and the support from O.K. ("I listened to you sing for twenty hours in the car. You will be fine."), I was on the verge of panic. I felt like I was going to throw up. My stomach turned over. This morning, my outfit had seemed killer. Now that I was staring at myself in the mirror, I was second (and third and fourth) guessing myself. Tight skinny jeans. Black boots worn over the jeans with a high stiletto heel. A shiny metallic black knit tank top that had wide straps and a v-neck. The material inverted to a "v" along my lower rib line and chiffon cascaded down to my hips. It made it look like I was baring my midriff but without actually doing it. Now I was worried that it would be very apparent to everyone that I was in my thirties, and that I had no business buying my clothes from a store called Forever 21.

I left my hair down and worked the curl. I kept fussing with my hair. However, all the fussing was actually making my hair bigger and bigger. I put a ponytail holder on my wrist just in case. I put on a bit more eye shadow than normal, trying to go for a smoky eye. Glossy lips, large beaded hoop earrings and a leather wrist cuff completed my look.

I took another swig from my tumbler. All of the singing in the car, plus rehearsal last night, had left my vocal cords a little worn out. Albert swore by whiskey and honey mixed together. I was not a big fan of whiskey, and my mom had used honey as a cure-all when we were sick. Now, every time I tasted honey, it reminded me of being sick. I looked at the amber liquid. Perhaps my drink was the reason I felt like I was going to hurl.

I dumped the rest of the miracle cure down the drain and made myself a cup of tea instead. O.K. was going to meet me at the bar. He was bringing a few of his friends from work to see me. I wondered if Rob would be in that group and how that would go over. In all honesty, there was part of me that did not want O.K. to be there tonight. What if I was a colossal failure? What if I tripped on the mike wire and fell down? What if I threw up all over the place? I know that O.K. claimed to like me, but what if he realized what a hot mess I truly was, and this was a deal breaker for him?

I tried to do some deep breathing. After all, Cheryl had been into yoga for a while. I sat down on my living room floor, next to the coffee table, and did the best lotus position that my painted-on jeans would allow. Even unbuttoning the top button did not afford me the flexibility that a yogi needed. I tried to remember the meditation part. No sooner had I closed my eyes than my cell rang. I reached for it up on my coffee table. The caller I.D. said "restricted." I answered it anyway, not knowing if it was work related. "Esther Comely-Cox."

There was silence on the line. I waited a moment and then looked at the front of the phone. The call had ended. Alrighty, I guess they didn't want to talk to me. Back to my ohm-ing. The moment my eyes were closed again, my cell started ringing. Again, the caller I.D. said, "restricted." Again, I answered by saying, "Hello, Esther Comley-Cox." And again, the call immediately disconnected.

My moment for meditation was gone so I got up (which is no easy feat in skinny jeans, mind you). I was panting a bit by the time I was fully vertical and struggled to get the button fastened again. Knowing me, I would forget if I didn't do it now and end up on stage with my pants undone. And then the damn phone rang again. "YES?" I impatiently answered the "restricted" caller. Just as before, the caller hung up. What the fuck was going on? This was so not what I needed with my nerves already on edge. I threw the phone onto the couch and flopped down, covering my eyes with my hands.

Then I remembered that my makeup and hair had actually looked pretty decent, and I hoped I could get to the gig before I ruined them. I would get myself a drink as soon as I got to the bar. That would hopefully calm my nerves a bit. Either that or send me over the edge. That would be a short trip.

The damn phone rang again. Without even looking, I answered it with a "WHAT?"

"Damn Red, cool down. You're going to blow a gasket before you even get on stage."

"Oh, Jeez, sorry Albert. I keep getting hang ups."

"No big. You ready? I'm pulling into your lot."

"'K. Be downstairs in a minute."

Albert was picking me up, and O.K. was going to bring me home. I guess no one expected me to be sober enough to drive. I was ready. I put on my black leather (okay, faux leather) jacket and I was off to kick some singing ass. Yup. Totally gonna kick some ass by falling down my apartment stairs. Perfect. Just perfect.

"Dude, did you wipe out down your own stairs?" Albert said as soon as I opened the door to his white van. It kind of reminded me of the type of vans that creepy people who abducted kids drove. I tried to shrug off both my lack of grace and the fact that I was a teeny-tiny bit afraid of Albert at the moment.

"Maybe."

"Uh, does that happen to you a lot?"

"Maybe."

Albert looked at me. He looked worried. I could tell what he was thinking. I said it out loud before he could. "Yes, I'm a wee bit on the clumsy side. Yes, I'm afraid I'm going to trip over some wires and face plant off the front of the stage. Yes, I've thought about it, and no, there is nothing I can do to make up for the fact that I fall. A lot."

"Well, as long as we've got that covered." He paused. "I'll have Jules do the best she can to keep the wires out of your way."

Jules was Albert's wife. She also acted as the sound person for the band, running the sound board. I thought it was über cool that a woman did that job, when it was so often done by men. She did not find it cool and was not tolerant of being referred to as the sound guy. She wanted to be known as the sound engineer. I thought that sounded pretentious. Jules was not that pleased that The Rusty Buckets had taken on a female lead singer. I wondered if it was because she didn't want me moving in on her man (she needn't have worried about that one), or because she had wanted to be the lead singer for the band.

It was true, Albert and I had unbelievable chemistry when we sang. There was frankly a connection between us, and it was electric. It was like we'd known each other all our lives, but also had that electricity of a first kiss. But off the stage, I had no interest in him and I'm sure the feeling was mutual. Albert played lead guitar in addition to vocals. He would be stepping back from lead vocals now, letting me take over, although there were quite a few duets on the set list. Albert's brother, Drew, played the drums. Pauly played bass and Jugs completed the band with guitar and trumpet. I was guessing Jugs was not his real name, but had something more to do with his love of the female anatomy. At least that's what I hoped.

The Rusty Buckets had been looking to move in another direction when I joined. They had previously done a lot of classic rock, but Pauly and Albert wanted to move in a more current direction. You know, one in the current century. Drew had no opinion. Frankly, I wasn't sure if he actually spoke. He played a mean drum though. Jugs was the most reluctant to update the sound of the band and change the dynamics. I needed to be careful not to step on his toes. I think the fact that I had decent-sized breasts would help me sway him to agree with the change in direction.

The guys carried in the equipment while I tried to not be in the way. I helped Drew get the drums set up while Albert, Pauly and Jugs carried in the heavy stuff. The manager of the bar brought me a beer. While I wanted to chug it down, I tried to sip slowly, just enough to wet my whistle. I attempted some small talk with Jules while she set up the sound board, but she really wanted no part of it. Whatever. I went over the song list and the lyrics again. I had too much time and was starting to freak out a little bit. I needed to stop over thinking and get out of my head. The guys were used to getting things running before I joined, and they carried on as if I weren't there. I tried to figure out what they were doing and pitch in where I could. Sooner than I could believe, things were plugged in and instruments were being tuned.

I busied myself putting on the in-ear monitor and checking the sound. Of course, as soon as I did that, my nerves took over, and I really had to pee. I unclipped the pack from my waistband and made a quick trip to the ladies' room. As soon as that need was taken care of, I attached the earpiece to the back of my jeans and fitted it in my ear. Actually, Albert attached it to my jeans, which drew another slew of evil looks from Jules. I wish I could pull her aside and tell her she had nothing to worry about. I wasn't the type to swoop in and steal someone else's guy. Sure, Albert and I had good singing chemistry, but that was about it. Once plugged back in, I did a quick sound check with the guys.

The bar was starting to fill in. I thought that was a good sign. To me, it would be better to play to a full house than an empty bar. The bar certainly had its fair share of regulars. There was a guy sitting at the end of the bar who looked like Elvis. No shit, he had the black shoe polish pompadour, thick gold chains and the large sunglasses. He was dressed in regular street clothes, although his shirt was open a few buttons too many. I wondered if he was actually an Elvis impersonator or just a huge fan. We had an Elvis song in the playlist. I made a mental note to give that guy a shout-out if he was still sitting there when we started that song.

I started pacing, which is my usual behavior when I'm nervous. I felt like I had to pee again. I couldn't believe I was really going to do this. I needed to calm down, so I sat down at the bar, directly across from Elvis. The thoughts continued. I was the lead singer in a band. Never in a million years had I thought that this was something I would do. This was Aster's thing. As soon as her name passed through my mind, I got a pang in my chest. I missed her so much. Even though I had never pictured myself doing such I thing, I wanted nothing more than to be able to share it with her. I could picture myself saying, "Aster, can you believe it? They wanted me to sing with them. And I'm doing it! And it's so much fun! I love being up there. I now know why you loved doing it. I get it!"

I felt this wave of emotions start to crash over me. The emptiness that Aster's death had created in my world. My anger at her and the rest of my family. The loneliness and sadness started to envelope me like a weighted blanket.

"Red ... Red ... Earth to Red?"

I snapped to attention. "Oh sorry."

Albert looked at me. "You okay? You look a little spooked."

I pursed my lips together. "Yeah, sorry. Just thinking about my sister. She fronted a band before she died. I was wishing she was here to see this. Got me down for a moment."

"Well, snap out of it. We're about to start. I'm sure, in some sense of the cosmic flow, she's here."

"You think?"

"Yeah, man. I think those we love never really leave us. So channel that emotion into your singing, and you're going to rock it, Red."

I stood up from the barstool and started to head to the stage area.

CHAPTER TWENTY-NINE

I was absolutely killing it. The bar was pretty full. I was hoping it was because we were there, not just because of the excessively cheap (in more way than one) drinks. I was on fire. There had been a little feedback in my earpiece early on, so I took it out. We were about nine songs into the first set of twelve. The crowd was totally into it, and Albert and I were in synch. I was sure it was beginner's luck, but whatever mojo I had going, I hoped it was always like this. Even Elvis seemed to like the more current stuff we were debuting.

O.K. had shown up with a crew. He looked adorable in jeans and a fitted plaid button-down. He had on a blazer over it, and all I could think was he must be dying of heat. I know I was sweating something fierce up on stage. Between the lights, the adrenaline, and all the dancing around, I was profusely perspiring. I smiled at O.K. At a moment in a song when I was feeling saucy and could pull it off, I even winked at him. The grin that spread across his face was priceless. I was so getting some tonight. Even Jillian was there with a little posse. I had a following.

Albert and I moved into a current duet. It was an indie-folk alternative hit and was a bit outside the comfort zone for The Rusty Buckets. I loved it. We followed it by another current hit on which Albert took background vocals and Jugs was on the horn. It was a great, high-energy number and I gave it my all. We were ending the set after this number. I wasn't sure if I really wanted to break. I was afraid I would lose my momentum if we stopped. On the other hand, with all the jumping and sweating, my hair had grown in exponential proportions and needed to be tamed so Drew and the drums could be seen behind me.

As soon as we announced our brief break, O.K. pushed and shoved his way up to me. He handed me a beer.

"Esther, you were unbelievable!"

I took a long swig, hoping the ice-cold brew would lower my body temperature by a degree or ten. "Thanks." I took another drink. "And thanks for this. I'm so freakin' hot up there."

"I'll say," O.K. said, giving me a naughty glance.

"Are you being naughty?"

"Can I convince you to be?"

I smiled back. "Oh, you're going to have to wait for that."

He stuck out his lip in a mock-pout.

"Don't pout. That's my job. Trust me, the wait will be worth it."

He moved closer, with only an inch of space between his body and mine. "I don't do good with waiting."

"If we had more than ten minutes, I'd suggest we go in the bathroom or out to your car right now."

O.K. leaned in. He brushed my hair back away from my ear. Just his touch made me tingle all over. He whispered, his breath hot on my neck, "I'm pretty sure I don't even need ten minutes."

I licked my lips. "I'm pretty sure it wouldn't take that long either. On the other hand, shouldn't we want it to last longer?"

He kissed my neck. "Consider this round one."

"O.K., I can't. As much as I want to—and believe me I do—I can't right now."

He kissed me again. "How about now?"

Oh my God how I wanted to. With all the adrenaline pumping from being up on stage, there was part of me that wanted to throw O.K. against the juke box and take him right there. Especially with him kissing my neck like that. And his hands on my ass didn't hurt either.

"Hey, Red? You coming back to us?"

Albert distracted me from O.K. Jules was glaring at me again. What had I done now? I thought this should make her more comfortable, and show her that I had no interest in Albert. She probably thought I was a slut. Whatever. I was on fire tonight, and couldn't wait to start the second set.

I gave O.K. a quick kiss on the lips. "We'll definitely finish this later. I gotta go sing."

"You're doing awesome. See you out there!"

By the second set, the audience was even more packed. I was a little pitchy during the second song, but managed to pull it back together to nail our Elvis cover. I was worried that the King would not be pleased. I searched the crowd for him. Elvis was still at the bar and I could see him singing along with me. At one point, I even pointed to him. He stood up and took a bow. Albert smiled at me.

God, this was fun. I could do this forever.

But, before I knew it, all three sets were done. I had long since pulled my hair back and was helping the guys pack up. It was early, only midnight. I was so keyed up that I wondered if I'd ever be able to sleep again. I knew I didn't want to go home. The bar was still packed. Eventually, O.K. managed to work his way up to me. He grabbed me low around the waist and pulled my pelvis into his.

"Damn, you are so fucking hot!"

"I know, right?"

"You are also incredibly humble as well."

I laughed. "I usually am. I feel so incredible. Is this what it's like to be high? I've never done any drugs, but I feel like I'm totally high right now."

"You're probably on an endorphin rush."

"It's fucking awesome."

"I don't think I've ever heard you say 'fuck' before."

I gave him a kiss. "I don't just want to be *saying* it right now."

O.K. held up his hand. "Check please?"

At that moment, Rob came up. "Hey guys, you going somewhere?"

I shrugged. "Eventually, maybe."

O.K. released me and stood by my side. "Maybe?"

I elbowed him. "Definitely. Soon."

"That's better."

I turned my attention to Rob, worried that I was being rude. "Hey, Rob. Thanks for coming. I guess I owe this all to you."

"Oh, yeah, that's right. I guess you do." He sounded like he could barely remember the fact that we went on a date. I think my assessment that he was only after sex was probably correct. Somehow, it didn't bother me. He was attractive, no doubt, but I was honestly truly very happy with O.K.

"Are you here with people from the hospital?"

"Yeah, O.K. made us come out and see you."

"Gee, thanks for the support, I guess."

"No, it was a good show. You are really a good singer and you have an unexpected stage presence."

"Thank you, I think?" I asked with a question in my voice.

"No, I don't mean it like that—"

"Real suave Rob. Good thing you're attractive, otherwise you'd never get the ladies." O.K. chided him. Rob might be slightly more attractive than O.K., but O.K. had the personality in spades over Rob. "Speaking of which, where is your date?"

"Oh," he shrugged, "she went to the bathroom."

"Who's the lucky lady?" I surprised myself by asking this. Wow, singing had really empowered me. Normally, I would have sat and stewed that he was here with a date after he never called me. It didn't matter that I didn't want him to call. It didn't matter that I was with O.K. Normally, I would have felt rejected. But tonight, nothing could touch me. I felt almost generous, wishing my happiness and elation on all those around me.

"She's actually a patient's mother. Err, former patient, I guess. I've been treating the kid for a while, and we hit it off. Finally, she came in and told me she was leaving the practice so that she could take me out to dinner. That night. Who am I to say no to that?"

"You always did like them forceful and bossy," O.K. chided.

That would explain why Rob hadn't liked me.

"I thought I was over that after Melissa, but I guess I still want to be bossed around."

"Yeah, Melissa would have turned me off women altogether."

"I know how you feel about her. I think you'll like this one though. She's different. She has a magnetism about her. You can't help but get entranced by her."

"Does this mean your rebound player days are over?"

"O.K., I think that chapter may be closed."

I got distracted when a few people came up to congratulate me, including Elvis. I had a hard time keeping a straight face while talking to him, but think I managed. Someone bought me a shot. I didn't know how to turn it down. I was never really a big fan of them, so I opened up and downed the shot as quickly as possible. I tried not to immediately throw it back up on that person's shoes.

O.K. and Rob were behind me. Their friend group had migrated over to join them. I was standing back to back with O.K., while I talked with my new-found friends. Every so often, one of O.K.'s hands would migrate over and goose me. Finally, I was able to excuse myself from the well wishers and return to O.K. and Rob's group. I turned around and put my hands around O.K.'s waist. His hands clasped over mine and pulled me tighter against him.

"Before you two start doing it in the middle of the bar, I want Esther to meet my date. You'll love her. Here she comes." Rob looked across the crowded room with an expectant puppy-dog look on his face. God, he was already whipped. Anyone could see it.

O.K. pulled me around so I was standing in front of him. Rob had turned and started walking toward his date.

"Okay, quick, give me the 4-1-1 on this chick. What's she like?" And of course, by that I meant, "What does she have that I don't?"

O.K. shrugged. "I dunno. She seemed alright. She's pretty. She seemed pretty quiet, actually. She was really interested in the band. I swear her eyes never left ... you." He seemed puzzled as he said this, as if the words weren't making sense to him.

Rob stepped back up to us, his arm around his date. She was average height. 5'5" to be exact, but that looked short next to Rob's 6'4" frame. Everything about her was average. Her average length hair was pulled back in an average low ponytail. She wore average jeans and an average blue shirt.

He started the introductions. "You remember O.K.? This is his girlfriend—"

Before he could say my name, Rob's date said, "Hello, Esther."

Only one word escaped my lips.

"Aster."

CHAPTER THIRTY

Never in a million years had I ever pictured this scenario in my head. Through all the tears and disbelief, the anguish and grief, I had never ever thought I would see her again. So, my reaction was as much of a surprise to me as it was to everyone else as I drew my hand back and slapped Aster across the face.

Her hand flew to her cheek as she recoiled. Rob protectively put his arm around her. "Jesus Esther! What the hell was that? What are you doing?"

I was just standing there, paralyzed. I couldn't believe I had slapped her any more than I could believe she was standing there in front of me.

O.K. looked from me to Aster and then back to me. "Is it really her?"

We stood there staring at each other. After a moment, I said, "Oh yes, it's her. I need to go. Get me out of here. Now."

I turned to leave. It seemed I was always fleeing because of Aster. Dammit, how could this be happening? I needed fresh air. That would help. Everything started spinning. Pushing through the door, I tried to take a deep breath but could not seem to get air into my lungs. I gasped for air and gasped again. The periphery of my vision began to grow dark as I felt hot and cold all at the same time. My hands started sweating and I thought I was going to throw up. I felt my knees grow shaky before my world went black.

******

The next thing I heard was a man's voice. Somewhat familiar, but not really. He was speaking, but not to me. He was speaking in doctor-ese to someone. "If she doesn't wake up in the next few minutes, I want a CAT scan. Not only did she pass out unexpectedly, but she hit her head on the curb."

"O.K., you're not her doctor. You're her, I don't know what." The voice was familiar, female, but I couldn't place it. "I'm her doctor and will monitor her carefully."

"Melissa, you have to do something."

Melissa? Why did I know that name?

"We're waiting to get her blood work back and see if there is anything abnormal going on. It will be back in about ten minutes."

"Abnormal? What are your looking for?"

"O.K., you know the deal. We're looking at her CBC and Chem Seven, as well as a pregnancy test."

"Pregnancy?"

"I don't have to explain how that works, do I? I know you are in orthopedics, but you should remember basic biology. We need to know that before we continue with any kind of treatment."

"No, I don't think it is that at all. I think she was just in shock. I'm not as worried about the syncope. I'm more worried about the potential head injury."

"Okay, O.K. I understand. You have to trust that I will take proper care of her. No matter what I think of you."

What the hell was that supposed to mean? Who was this person? I didn't want some nasty sounding lady taking care of me.

I tried to force my eyes open, but they wouldn't move. It was so much effort to do that, and it made me tired. I decided I needed to rest a little bit more before I tried again. I would rest. Yeah. That was it. A little sleep and then I'd be able to get up and tell this Melissa person that I didn't want her to be my doctor.

******

"Esther, you need to open your eyes." Why was Charlie's voice in my head? It sounded so far away, like she was talking through a tin can. I must be dreaming. Man, what a weird dream.

"She's gonna hate this. Can you contact Cheryl and Dean? We need consent to operate." The voice speaking was tired and grave.

Operate? Who needed an operation? Was it Dean? Dammit, why wouldn't my eyes open? Maybe I could talk without opening my eyes. But for some reasons, the words wouldn't come either. What was going on?

******

I had never been so tired in all of my life. I just wanted to sleep. I just catch a few zzzzz's.

******

Why was there all of this beeping? Who was talking out there? Didn't these people know I was trying to sleep? Dammit, they're not being quiet. I wanted them to shut up. I needed them to shut up. All their yammering was giving me a headache. God, speaking of which, my head was killing me. For the love of God people, SHUT THE FUCK UP!

"Oh my God, what did she just say?"

"Esther, can you hear me? Esther, did you say something?"

"Somebody call the doctor!"

"I didn't hear anything."

"How could you not have heard that? I swear she said something."

All the voices grew louder in a barrage. It made my head hurt even more. I just needed them to stop. I knew yelling would make the headache even worse, but if it got them to be quiet, it would be worth it. Okay, I was gonna yell over all the voices with all my might.

"AARUGHUMPH!"

Wait—that was not what I was trying to say. I was trying to tell them to shut up. I needed to try again.

"AARUGHUMPH!"

The people in the room were rejoicing. But not me. I was terrified. Why weren't my words coming out the right way? I knew that I wanted to say, "SHUT UP!" but that did not come out of my mouth. I tried to open my eyes, but they felt glued shut. Trying with the effort that it would normally take to lift a refrigerator, I opened my eyes. Or eye, I should say, because my right eye did not really open. I looked around with my left eye. I could not see over far to the left. It was black. I tried to scan across the room. Cheryl and Dean were there. Charlie too. Man, she was looking old these days. I haven't seen her in about four years and time is not doing her any favors. Some guy I didn't know was there too. He was cute—dark brown hair and brown eyes. He looked concerned and as if he hadn't slept or shaved in weeks. Oh wait, he was wearing a white coat. I must be in the hospital, and he must be my doctor. Wow, they make doctors pretty cute these days. Lucky me. I continued looking. Gus was there and Aster too.

Wait ... Aster?

What the fuck was going on here?

CHAPTER THIRTY-ONE

The days were blurry. Not even the days, but the moments themselves. I was in and out of sleep constantly. I could not keep my eyes open most of the time. When I did, different people were there. Some of them I knew. Some of them, most of them, I didn't. I didn't know what had happened, but I knew it was bad. I could tell by the look on everyone's faces. They all had that serious look, like when someone has died. I was pretty sure that I hadn't died, but was fairly confident that I was in bad shape. I wish I knew what had happened.

The worst thing for me—I couldn't speak. Every time I tried to talk, garbage came out. It was so damn frustrating. I needed to ask what had happened. I couldn't remember much. The last thing that was very clear was being in my car. I had just chickened out of doing the speed dating thing that Jillian had talked me into signing up for. I was eating my Ho Hos, and then the car was rear-ended. Okay, so that would explain how I got here. A bad car accident.

Okay, one answer down. Now, I needed to know what was wrong with me. Other than the speech, of course. My head hurt, like all the time that I was awake. Now, it was morning. I was fairly certain by the amount of light pouring in through the window. There was no one in the room this time. I wondered if I had missed breakfast. I had a hard time focusing on things in the room, and I felt like there was something floating in my eyes. The sunlight was hurting them too. Maybe if I rubbed them, they would clear up. My left hand had an I.V. sticking out of the back of it, and a blood pressure cuff on the upper arm. My right arm was unencumbered, so I decided to use that one.

Except it weighed about eight hundred pounds. I looked at my right arm and willed it to leave the surface of the bed. After about six starts and stops, I was finally able to get it to my face. Except I missed the eye that I had intended to rub and smacked myself on the nose. I winced in pain and my arm fell back down to the bed as if an anchor was attached to it. It was so much effort to lift my arm, and then it didn't even work right. I needed to think about what could possibly be going on, but all of that work had exhausted me. I would think about it after a little nap.

Somehow it was now night. Was I sleeping around the clock? What was wrong with me? Why had it been so much work to lift my arm before? Shit, what *was* wrong with me? Was I a vegetable? No, I was thinking, and vegetables didn't think. Well, maybe the really smart ones, like broccoli do. Shit, what if people thought I was a vegetable and they turned my machines off because they didn't know that I was still in here? Dammit, I wish I'd had taken the time and effort to make one of those living will things.

Of course, therein was the problem. Who would I have put in charge of that? Certainly not my parents. They had no use for me, and I had no use for them. Were they here? Would they even be bothered to come and see me in the hospital? I thought maybe I had seen them in my room. I tried hard to focus for a moment on that thought. I had seen them here. They were with Aster. Aster. Oh, so it must have been a dream. As bad as I was, I still didn't matter enough to Cheryl and Dean to come and see me. Maybe Charlie would make decisions for me. How would someone get a hold of her? Jillian was really the only person I knew here in Columbus, and she didn't know anything about my family.

Okay, so there was probably no one here to speak up for me. I was alone. Did they even know my name? Did they consider me a Jane Doe? In the dark of my hospital room, I started to panic. At least the room wasn't totally dark. There was light from the monitors and seeping in from the hallway. Something attached to my left middle finger had a red light that glowed and made my fingertip glow. The buttons on my bed rail were illuminated by a soft green light. I tried to focus on the lights and do a little self-calming. There were buttons to move the head of the bed up and down, as well as my feet. It looked like there were volume controls as well, although I wasn't sure what volume they controlled. And there was a button that had a white cross on a red background. I wondered what that did. Very slowly, and with great effort, I lifted my right hand and managed to press it with the back of my index finger knuckle. Nothing happened. I pressed it again. Again nothing. Stupid button. It was broken.

I let my hand fall back down, tired from the effort, although not as tired as I had been this morning when I had tried to rub my eyes. Maybe I was improving. Before I could contemplate that any more, a heavy-set nurse in faded cartoon-printed scrubs came bustling into the room.

"What's up, Sugar?" she drawled. She was obviously a transplant to Columbus. But then again, so was I.

I tried to answer. The garbled garbage came out again. Fuck. Why couldn't I talk? The words were in my head. Why wouldn't they leave my mouth?

I tried again. Again the distorted speech. Tears of frustration welled up in my eyes and escaped down my cheeks.

"Sugar, don't get upset."

I tried to stop the tears and took a deep breath.

"Does something hurt?"

I nodded. She looked surprised that I had responded to her.

"Can you tell me what hurts?"

I tried to tell her that it was my head, but again, no go. I shook my head in anger, but that just made it worse. I started to lift my right hand, but let it drop. I looked at my left arm with all the crap attached and tried to lift that one. It came right up and I was able to point to my head. In fact, I touched the left side of my head, and it hurt a lot.

"Your head hurts?"

I nodded. I remembered that the sign in sign language for "yes" was a closed fist moving up and down in a nodding motion. I did that. Apparently, the nurse didn't understand sign though, because she missed it and asked me again, "Does your head hurt?"

I nodded and signed.

"Okay, Sugar. You sit tight. I, um, gotta go check on something. I'll be right back." She bustled out of the room as quickly as she had bustled in.

Damn, I was alone again. The speech thing was not happening, and my right arm was not right, but at least I could move my left arm. If only I could think of a way to get them to unhook all the crap from my left arm so it didn't hurt to move it. Speaking of which, something had been wrong when I had touched my head. I lifted my left arm and touched my head again.

I felt what had seemed so odd. Soft prickles where my hair used to be. Where my hair should be. Why did I have no hair? What the fuck happened to my hair? I touched my head again gingerly. I felt my scalp under the prickles of hair. Then I felt something metal. A little piece of metal, then another little one. Staples. Staples in my head. I counted. Twenty, traveling from the front left side of my head all the way to the back. Holy shit. Someone had cut my head open.

Before I totally lost it, I tried to piece together what I knew. I had been in a car accident. I couldn't speak and moving my right arm was difficult. It seemed as if I had had some kind of brain surgery. Shit, this was serious. I needed someone to come into the room and talk to me before I totally freaked out. I needed that Southern nurse to come back in and talk to me in her soft twang. I liked that she called me "Sugar." On the other hand, I wondered if she called me that because no one knew my name.

I made my right hand work again and pushed the call button. Then I waited. A few minutes later, I made the effort and pushed the button again. The nurse came in, this time looking frazzled. A bit breathless, she said, "I paged Dr. Cole. I'm waiting for him to come up to the floor."

I nodded. I made my right hand into a loose fist, which was the best I could manage, and kept my thumb up. I put my left hand flat under my right fist and lifted it up. It was the sign for "help." I let my fist drop and patted my chest with my left hand. "Me."

She stopped and frowned. "Are you trying to tell me something?"

I nodded. I repeated my signs. "Help me."

She looked apologetic. "I'm sorry, I don't speak sign. I'll put a note in your chart tomorrow and have the speech therapist come up and see you."

Okay. I wanted to laugh that she said she didn't "speak sign" but had no one to share that one with. I wondered how long it would be before the speech therapist would be in to see me. That made me realize I had no idea what time it even was. I used my left hand to point to my right wrist. It was the sign for 'time' but it was also a universally accepted gesture for "what time is it?" I hoped she would be able to figure this one out.

"Time?" She looked at her watch. "It's almost two in the morning."

Okay, that meant it would be a while before the speech person would be in to see me. I was glad that I had picked up some sign language along the way during my career as a social worker.

She went on. "I paged Dr. Cole, as ordered. He should be in soon."

I nodded again. I was getting tired. Perhaps I would close my eyes until Dr. Cole got here.

CHAPTER THIRTY-TWO

"Esther? Esther can you hear me?"

Someone was calling my name. That was a good sign. They weren't calling me Jane Doe. They knew who I was.

I opened my eyes. The person calling my name was a fairly attractive man. He seemed vaguely familiar. Brown eyes, messy brown hair. He needed a haircut. He was wearing a white coat. He was sitting in the blue chair next to my bed. Come to think of it, he looked pretty comfortable for a doctor. I thought the doctors came in, read the chart at the end of the bed, and then stood there looking down at you. He looked tired. Was he too tired to stand? Great, just my luck. I get a doctor who is exhausted. And I won't even be able to complain if he screws up because he is so tired. When I can talk again, I'm so gonna complain to the hospital administration about overworking their employees to the point of exhaustion.

I lifted my left hand and pointed to my head.

"You had an accident."

Yeah, duh. I may be brain damaged, but even I could figure that out. I rolled my eyes.

"Okay, don't give me shit."

Wow, pretty unprofessional language for a doctor. I pointed to my head again. I pointed to the staples, in case he couldn't understand what I meant.

"You had a closed head injury. You had to have a craniotomy to relieve the pressure on your brain. Do you remember what happened?"

I shook my head. I also signed "no" using my left hand. It felt unnatural to use my left hand, as I was a righty. Well, I had been a righty. I was guessing I'd be a lefty from here on out.

"You fell and hit your head on a curb. You hit it here—" he leaned over, and pointed to a spot on the left side of my head, about two inches above and just in front of my ear. "You were immediately unresponsive. You passed out, which is how you fell."

I frowned. How did I pass out? How did I hit the curb? Wasn't I in my car? I needed to be able to speak. I mimed writing with my left hand.

"Write?"

I nodded. He got up and left the room. He came back a few moments later with a pad of paper and a pen. He leaned over the bed rail to operate the controls. He moved the head of the bed into a more upright position and then moved the little table inward so I could use it. He lowered the table to the proper height and handed me the pen and paper. He was leaning close to me while making sure the bed and I were properly adjusted. He smelled really good. Familiar. I wondered if he wore a cologne that I knew somehow. Maybe it was something an ex-boyfriend of mine had worn.

With the incredibly poor penmanship of a person using their non-dominant hand, I wrote, "Car accident?"

He looked at my chicken scratch. "Car accident? No, you weren't in a car accident."

I frowned at him. I remembered getting rear-ended. I had been eating a Ho Ho. So I wrote, "Ho Ho."

"Ho Ho?" Man, this was going to get annoying if he read everything I wrote aloud. I could still read for Christ's sake.

"No, you didn't have a Ho Ho. You ... fainted and went down. You ..." he broke off. I could swear he was choking up. "Yes, you were in a car accident while eating a Ho Ho. That was over two months ago."

I looked at him. I was pretty sure my facial expression was something akin to Gary Coleman's, "Whatcha talkin' 'bout, Willis?" face.

He continued. "You've been in a coma for eighteen days."

Eighteen days? I had lost eighteen days. Check that. I had lost the last two months of my life. My eyes must have gotten pretty big and some of the machines started beeping. The blood pressure cuff on my left arm began to get tighter.

"Esther, you need to calm down. It's not good for your blood pressure to rise like this."

Okay, seriously Doctor? You tell me that I've been in a coma and can't remember the last two months of my life and you don't expect my blood pressure to rise. I kept getting more and more agitated. A few nurses came rushing in, followed by a different doctor. He must have been a more senior doctor, because he made my doctor leave pretty quickly. I heard him barking out orders, including for something called Ativan. A nurse whipped out a needle and pushed it into the I.V. in my left hand. Within moments, the world went dark and calm. Ahhh, peace.

******

The next time I opened my eyes, Charlie was sitting where the tired doctor had been. I wondered if he had gotten in trouble for making me upset. I hoped not. He was probably guilty of using poor judgment, but that was undoubtedly due to his fatigue. I was the one who freaked out. I needed to control myself better. On the other hand, whatever they gave me was pretty darn nice, and it totally chilled me out. I still felt a little Zen from it. I looked at my right hand, which Charlie was holding. I was going to do this. Coma or not, brain injury or not, I was going to get better. So, in order to do that, I knew I needed to get started moving. And the way to do it was to try, no matter how difficult it was. I looked at my hand

and thought about each bone and muscle curling in to squeeze. As I looked and thought, I was able to control my hand and make it contract, squeezing Charlie's hand.

Reflexively, she squeezed back. Then it occurred to her what had just happened. "Oh Esther! You squeezed my hand!"

I smiled at her and looked at my hand. I squeezed again, and she squeezed back.

"Esther, you're moving your right hand! They said they didn't know if you would be able to. They said you might be paralyzed on the right side."

That stopped me cold. I froze and let go of Charlie's hand. A panicked look crossed her face, and she started back tracking. "Don't freak out, okay? They said maybe, they weren't sure. They said it would be a 'wait and see' situation. But I knew you would persevere."

Of course what she was saying made sense. I knew my right side wasn't working. The doctor had said I'd had a closed head injury. It made sense that I could be paralyzed on one side of my body. Except I wasn't. It was so hard to move. But I could move. Okay, that thought calmed me down a bit. I was in the hospital and there were people here who would come in and help me. They would help me walk and talk, and I would be good as new.

CHAPTER THIRTY-THREE

Yeah, therapy sucked. I hated every single minute of every single session. Yeah, yeah, yeah, I know they were there to help. Yeah, yeah, yeah, I knew that it was good for me. But, man it sucked balls.

I hated everything about everything. I hated that someone had to wipe my ass. I hated that I had a tube in my nose and down my throat to help me eat. I hated that I had to use a bed pan and commode. I hated that they had shaved my head. I hated that I could not remember the last two months of my life.

I hated everyone and everything.

I was not making the progress that I wanted to be making. Of course, I wanted to go to sleep and wake up back to normal. I didn't want to admit that this was my new normal. My days were full of therapies: speech, physical, occupational, cognitive. They wiped me out. Apparently I was medically stable, which was why they moved me to a rehab facility where I would get to do therapy all day every day. Woo-fucking-hoo.

I wanted to hate my therapists, but there was still a quasi-rational part of me that realized this was not their fault. On the other hand, no one had bothered to fill me in on what exactly had happened. I knew from that doctor that I had fainted. That was unusual. I was not a fainter. Hmmm, that doctor. I wondered about him. He was pretty cute, and seemed pretty friendly. Too bad they had moved me to this rehab hospital. He wouldn't be my doctor anymore. None of the doctors that I had seen here so far were that cute.

Charlie had come to see me every day in the first hospital and even the first few days when I moved to the rehab hospital. That was a good part of the day. I looked forward to her visits. Apparently my dad had had a pretty serious heart attack and had to have a quadruple bypass. He was still recovering, although I guess Cheryl and Dean had been to see me when I was in my coma. I thought I remembered seeing them, but then again, I also remembered seeing Aster, so who knows what my brain had been doing.

The conversation with Charlie was pretty one-sided, what with me being aphasic and all. That was what Meghan, my speech therapist, called my inability to speak—aphasia. It was frustrating, because a lot of the time I knew what I wanted to say, but I just couldn't make my mouth move to form the words. Sometimes, I couldn't come up with a word that I knew I knew, so even writing or signing was difficult. Meghan was encouraged that I knew a little sign and was working with me using an app on the iPad to help me speak. Who knew iPads could be used for something more useful than Facebook and Candy Crush?

Anyway, that usually happened only when I was with Meghan, so I was forced to sit and listen to Charlie prattle on about inane stuff. She seemed nervous around me. I wondered if it was because I looked so bad. She didn't want to look at me. She would look at me when she thought I wasn't looking, but then when I looked, she refused to meet my eyes. I knew something was up. I wanted her to spit it out. I hated that seeing her, which was the best part of my day, was also like waiting for the other shoe to drop. Today would be the day I asked her what she was keeping from me. I was going to have to write it, and I hoped I would be able to think of the right words to ask her when she was here. Damn aphasia.

When I was in speech, I used the iPad to ask Meghan to help me write a note. It was slow and painstaking. Meghan did me one better, and I used the app to put together a series of words to make a sentence.

She saved it on the screen and told me that I could keep the iPad for the day. All I had to do when Charlie got there was touch the screen and activate the message that said, "What are you not telling me? I don't want you to keep things from me. I need to know what's going on."

I could not wait. It was the first ray of hope that I had felt since I woke up. I would be able to ask a question. I would have a voice and I would not have to search for words, since they were already there for me. Sometimes the words flowed in my head just like before. But it seemed whenever I needed to output the words, with sign or through writing, they just—poof—disappeared into thin air.

But Charlie never came.

Another day went by. No Charlie. She was gone and never even said good-bye.

I was mad. Furious, red rage mad. If I could have thrown something fragile, I would have, if only to get the satisfaction of watching it smash into a million pieces. There was nothing fragile in my room. There were no flowers in vases. There were no cards, no balloons. I was one of seven children and there was not anything in this room that was personalized to me, with the exception of a dry-erase board that listed my initials and my nurse for the shift. When Aster had gone missing and was presumed to have jumped off the bridge, my parents put flowers out on the bridge for two years.

I sat there all day again, waiting for my sister, but she never showed. It was the weekend, so there was very minimal therapy. It was over by eleven a.m., and I had nothing to do for the rest of the day. I got up and went for a walk. My physical therapist had told me to get up and move around. I was weak from being in the coma and lying around for almost three weeks. I was fortunate. My right arm was not functioning properly, but my legs seemed fine. My right arm could move, but it was effortful and I was clumsy. I seemed to have lost the dexterity in my hand, like I was wearing a big snow glove that weighed fifty pounds, all the time.

I was slowly walking down the hall, holding onto the rail with my left hand. My feet were in the hospital-issue socks with treads. I had on sweat pants and a t-shirt. They were not mine, and I had no idea where they had come from. They were too big and made me feel terrible. I wanted my own clothes. I wanted my own stuff. I wanted to be in my own bed again. Even though I had only been in my place for a few months, it would still be better than this hospital. Yes, it was rehab, but it was a hospital nonetheless. I wanted to get back to my own life, but I didn't know if it was a possibility. No one talked to me. They seemed to think that because I couldn't speak, I couldn't understand. I needed someone to tell me what the hell was going on.

As I approached the family room at the end of the corridor, I heard voices. Angry voices. People yelling at each other. I didn't want to eavesdrop on a personal conversation, so I turned around to head back towards my room. As I turned, I got a little dizzy and off balance. I fell into the wall a little bit but was actually able to grab onto the wide wooden rail with my right hand. It didn't feel right, and I wasn't sure I had a good grip. I guess I wasn't ready to be home yet. Dammit.

I stared hard at my hand, willing it to work. Somehow, it held on and held me up. I knew in that moment that even though I had a long road ahead of me, somehow I would be all right. I was standing there in the hall, dressed in clothes that were two sizes too big, and staring at my hand like an idiot when someone bumped into me from behind. He was yelling at someone as he was leaving the family room. He was one of those people with the angry voices that I had been trying to get away from. The bump was not that hard, but it forced me to hold on tighter with my right hand. Miraculously, my arm did the job and kept me from falling over as I took three small steps to regain my balance. I was so shocked by the bump and the stumble that the words, "Hey—watch out!" flew out of my mouth without me even thinking about it.

"Oh, sorry. Oh my God, Esther! Are you okay? I'm so sorry! What are you doing out of bed? Did you just talk to me? Are you all right?"

I slowly turned around to see who was barraging me with questions. Whoever it was was now grabbing my arm. I shrugged him off and turned to look. It was that cute doctor from the hospital. What the hell was he doing here? I went to ask him that, but the words wouldn't come. Gibberish came out instead. Dammit again.

"Esther, are you all right? I'm sorry, I didn't know you were out here. Speaking of which, what are you doing out here? Are you supposed to be out of bed? Were you coming into the family room? What did you hear? Are you all right?"

Even if I had been able to speak, this guy wouldn't let me get a word in edgewise. Sheesh.

He looked familiar, but I didn't know why. It seemed more than just my recollection of him as my doctor in the hospital. It seemed like a déjà vu or something, like I knew him from somewhere else. My brain was damaged and would not provide answers to me at the moment. It was busy keeping me from falling over. I couldn't answer his questions, so I turned around again and headed back to my room. I was getting tired anyway and was so incredibly frustrated that I couldn't speak when I wanted to. I knew I should have been encouraged that I had spoken a few words, but it was not enough. I wanted all my words back.

I shook my head, mostly because I was disgusted with myself. Suddenly, this guy put his arms around me, turning me back to face him, in a crushing hug. Whoa—what the hell? And then, he kissed me on the top of my head!

I jumped back, stumbling a little. "What the fuck?" came flying out of my mouth. There it was—I could speak again, sort of. Why was this guy kissing me? Wasn't that really crossing the line between doctor and patient?

"Esther you spoke again!" He still had me in his grip. I struggled to try and get away. "Esther, calm down. You're going to fall. Esther, listen to me."

Something in his tone was eerily soothing, so I stopped struggling for a moment. I did not like that this strange man had his hands on me and had kissed me, even if it was on top of my bald head.

"Esther, do you know who I am?"

I shook my head and gave him what I thought was a menacing look.

"So you have no memory of me?"

I remembered him from the hospital, but it seemed like he meant something more. I shook my head again.

His face crumpled and his shoulders sagged. Suddenly, he looked years older though just a moment had passed. "All right then, let's go back to your room."

He turned me around and guided me back down the hall to my room. There was no more touching, certainly no hugging and kissing. While his advances had been surprising and unsolicited, there was something that was comforting about his touch. It sounded corny, but somehow, when he was touching me, I felt better. Without his touch, I felt alone and sterile. I needed human warmth and companionship. I was too alone. And even though I didn't know this guy, when I was with him, I was not alone and I felt connected. I had even been able to speak some, with purpose. Granted, it was totally reactionary, but it was a step.

CHAPTER THIRTY-FOUR

My physical therapist, Chieko, was a lovely woman who exacted torture like no other. Day after day, she put me through my paces, strengthening my body and challenging my balance like a drill sergeant disguised as a delicate lotus flower. I could not figure out why I was so tired. Granted, I did have a brain injury, but other than my right hand not working so great, I was fine. Except I wasn't, as I found out in my twice daily sessions with Chieko. Because I couldn't speak, she often rambled on while we worked, telling me about the exploits of her kids. Many of the people who were working with me talked at me and obviously thought I was stupid. Or just brain damaged. It was amusing and entertaining and kept my mind off the fact that I was as weak as a newborn kitten. It was also refreshing because she talked *to* me.

To help build my endurance, Chieko put me on the elliptical machine. I occasionally used the elliptical at the gym but I preferred to run on the treadmill. Of course, I had no way to communicate that, so I sucked it up on the elliptical. Frankly, it felt good, in a weird sort of way. I was so weak and out of shape. I couldn't figure out how that had happened. They said I had been in a coma for eighteen days. That isn't that long. It didn't seem right that I was this weak. In my previous life, I had been good for a solid forty-five minutes of cardio. Here it was, set for six minutes, and I was sucking wind as if I had just climbed Mount Everest.

The gym where I did physical therapy was pretty impressive. It could put most upscale health clubs to shame. The people watching was totally different though.

Instead of watching meatheads hit on the hard bodies, I was watching people with broken bodies, broken minds and broken spirits. Go figure, I end up with a broken mouth. There was an innocuous radio station playing in the background. I wasn't a huge fan of the channel but it sure beat the silence that enveloped me most days. Finally, a song came on that I liked. It had been popular when I was little, and I remembered Veruca had wanted to be just like Debby Harry. Aster had sung this song in a high school show and it always made me think of her as well.

I was lost in the song and in my memories of my sisters. I felt so alone, so cut off from everyone and everything. At least my body was still working and I kept pumping away, taking out my frustration on the elliptical. The next thing I knew, Chieko was shaking my arm. I thought my time must be up. I broke my concentration and looked at the timer, but it still indicated that I had another minute. I looked at Chieko, who was obviously excited about something.

"Esther! I cannot believe it!"

I looked at her, not even trying to respond. I stepped off the elliptical, wiping my forehead. I made extra efforts to use my right hand. That sucker was gonna get back to normal. I might not be able to speak, but I sure as hell wasn't going to have a crippled hand too.

"Esther, you were singing!"

Huh. I hadn't even realized it. Maybe I was better? I opened my mouth to speak, but again gibberish came out. I sighed, shook my head, and stormed back to my room. By the time I got back there, the adrenaline of my workout and the thought of being cured had drained out of me as if someone had pulled the plug on a tub full of water. I sank down on the horrible hospital bed and wept.

I stayed in my room, refusing all therapy. After about two days, a bunch of doctors came in to see me. None was that cute doctor who kissed my forehead that time. Although I was slightly creeped out by his familiarity with me, I was actually a little disappointed that he wasn't in the group of white coats standing before me. They were there to give me a stern lecture. Apparently, I needed to attend therapy or I'd be discharged. And since I was brain damaged and all, and couldn't communicate, they would have to send me to a nursing home. They talked to me like I was an idiot child who didn't understand English.

Surprisingly, their pep talk did nothing to improve my mood. I started rummaging through the dresser drawers, looking for my stuff. I found my phone, but it was dead as a doornail. There was a flimsy, glittery black shirt. Well, what was left of it anyway. I must have been wearing it when I—whatever happened to me happened—because it had been cut off my body. I held it up and looked at it. It didn't look like anything I would normally wear. I wished I could remember that night.

Before my pity party could get any larger, I heard a commotion in the hallway. "I don't care who you are or what you say. I'm going in to see Esther. I can't believe you nincompoops have left her alone all this time! Of course she's not doing well. Who gave you imbeciles medical degrees?"

I dropped the unfamiliar shirt back in the drawer and rushed out to see Jillian. Finally, a familiar face. I practically ran (okay, it was more like a fast walk) to her. She turned to greet me, a huge smile on her face. Her arms were wide open and she took me in, embracing me and making me feel for the first time since I had woken up that it might all just be okay.

That was until she looked at me and said, "Damn girl, you look terrible. What have they done to you?"

Obviously, I was self-conscious about my head. As much as my hair had been my arch-nemesis, I hated that it had been shaved off. I did everything I could to avoid looking at myself. Not to mention the grotesque scar that was forming on the left side of my head. Also, I was in donated or borrowed clothing, which didn't fit right and was downright ugly. I dropped my head in response.

"Aww, honey, I didn't mean it like that. You are so skinny and pale and these clothes are terrible. Are they yours?"

I shook my head.

"Where are your clothes?"

I shrugged my shoulders.

A horrified look crossed her face. "Esther, has anyone gone to your apartment and gotten you your stuff?"

I shook my head again. How did I tell her there was no one here to do it? Charlie had been here at the beginning, but as soon as I figured out a way to ask her what was going on, she disappeared. I was guessing she had to go to New York to go back to work. I guess I should not have expected any less, but I was surprised that Cheryl and Dean hadn't at least stopped in once. I was pretty sure they had been to visit while I was in the first hospital, but who doesn't wait to see if their child comes out of a coma? My parents. I couldn't help but think bitterly, if it had been Aster lying in that bed, they never would have left her side.

"Is your family here?"

I shook my head again. Jillian put her arm around me and led me to some couches that were in a little alcove. I sat down next to her and put my head on her shoulder. I was not normally a touchy-feely kind of person, but I just needed some human contact. I needed to feel that I was not so alone and that someone in the universe cared about me.

"Esther, do you understand what I'm saying to you?"

I nodded. None of the doctors had asked me that. They were going under the assumption that I was functioning at a reduced mental capacity. I had so many questions to ask Jillian. I didn't know if she would have the answers, but I knew at least she would listen. If only I could speak.

"Esther, is your memory all right?"

I shook my head and looked around the room. I

needed a way to communicate. I felt like maybe I could write down something. Before I could even gesture, Jillian pulled her ever-trusty steno notebook out of the Mary Poppins satchel that she carried around. Never would I mock her carpet bag again.

I took the pen in my shaky right hand and willed it to write the correct words. In penmanship that made me cringe, I eeked out "Car accident last thing."

Jillian's lips moved as she deciphered my chicken-scratch. "The car accident is the last thing you remember?"

I nodded.

"That was two months before all this happened. That was three months ago."

I tightened my lips together.

"So you don't remember O.K. then?"

I gave her a confused look. What the hell did she mean by that? Her sentence didn't even make sense. How could I remember okay? I told her I didn't remember the two months from the car accident to the hospital at all. This was frustrating.

"I know he's been here to see you. He's been calling me and giving me updates."

What the hell was she talking about? I picked up the pen and scrawled "He who?"

"O.K. Your boyfriend."

What?!? I didn't have a boyfriend. And why did she keep saying okay? That was not a normal speech-tick that she had, like those people who say 'ahh' all the time. I wrote down, "Why do you keep saying ok?"

I looked at the sentence and was proud. It was a complete sentence, a complete thought. Maybe I was getting better. I was so busy patting myself on the back for writing a sentence that I almost forgot to pay attention to Jillian's answer.

"The guy you're dating—his name is O.K. It's short for something or other. He's a doctor. I know he's been here to see you, but he said you don't know who he is."

Holy shit, that cute doctor guy is my boyfriend?!?

CHAPTER THIRTY-FIVE

"Shut the front door!"

"Oh my God, Esther—you just talked!" Jillian jumped up off the couch, grabbed my hands and pulled me up to a standing position. She enveloped me in a huge hug and then released me. I knew the next time I opened my mouth, only gibberish would come out, and I knew it would wipe that expectant, hopeful look off her face. I didn't want to disappoint her. She was the only one who seemed to care. Well, I guess that doctor-guy cared. Now his hovering, inappropriateness and overall creepiness made sense.

I sat down and picked up the steno pad. "What happened to me?"

Her happy face faded into concern. "You don't remember?"

I shook my head.

"I never got the full story. You were great on stage and really killed it, all three sets. Then, you went outside after and passed out. I don't know why, but when you passed out, you hit your head on the curb, and that's what caused the brain injury."

Sets? What was she talking about? I knew about the passing out thing, but I wanted to know why I passed out. What was I doing?

I wrote down "sets?"

She nodded. "Yeah, you were singing at the bar."

I looked at her like she had three heads. That made no sense. I don't sing. Well, not outside the car or the shower anyway.

"Esther, do you remember that?"

I shook my head again.

She reached into her magical bag and pulled out her laptop. She adjusted her glasses and talked herself through starting it up. Her computer skills were actually pretty impressive, but her narration gave the impression that she had no idea what she was doing. After a few minutes, she pulled up You Tube and typed in "The Rusty Buckets." A few more clicks and there I was singing with some bald, tattooed guy. We sounded incredible, even on the poor quality video. She pushed the laptop to me and watched over my shoulder. I was wearing that black flimsy shirt that was in my drawer. Now I was sad that it had been cut, since I looked hot in it. Even though my hair was large, it looked fantastic and I missed it terribly. Never thought I would say that.

Wow, I was good. I never thought I was a particularly strong singer. That had been Aster. But in that video I think I sounded better than she did, especially in her last years. I had a stage presence that was unexpected as well. I had always thought Aster was the one with the charisma. I guess no one ever looked past her to see if I had any. But man, I did. I wondered if I would ever be able to sing again.

"Yeah, you were fantastic. I couldn't believe you were up there. I didn't know you had it in you."

Yeah, me neither. I was transfixed. She reached over and pulled up another video, and I watched myself, mesmerized.

"Oh my God, Esther!"

"What?" I said, snapping out of my reverie.

"ESTHER! You were singing along, and then you just answered me! Oh my God, Esther, you're cured!"

Jillian was now jumping up and down, arms flapping about. Her perfect black bob even dared to move out of place. She looked absolutely ridiculous. I started laughing. It was easy to laugh. I knew I wouldn't be able to speak, but I didn't want to disappoint her. It seemed to be my pattern. Apparently I could sing if I wasn't thinking about it. That shouldn't have surprised me. I was always singing in my car and in the shower. I think I probably sang and was not even aware of it. And it looked as though I could speak in response to something that didn't require an active thought. I could react when shocked or surprised. The act of thinking about what I wanted to say still had me tongue-tied.

I thought long and hard about what I wanted to say. I wanted to tell Jillian that I wasn't better. I wanted to tell her not to be too excited, that I was still broken. "No."

Jillian stopped flapping and flailing, and looked at me. "What did you say?"

"No."

"No what? Can you say something else?"

"No." Jesus Christ. I now had the vocabulary of a stubborn two-year-old. I'm not sure this was any better. I shook my head. Fuck. I handed her back her laptop and stood up. This was a lot to process. I was singing in a band. I had a boyfriend who was not only pretty cute, but he was a doctor. I was bald.

Oh God, this boyfriend guy—he's seen me all terrible looking and bald with bad clothes and stuff. I looked down at my clothes. No lie, it was a pink sweat suit. I had on white Keds that looked like something a little old lady in a nursing home would wear. My head had been cut open. I had not had makeup on my face since the accident. And I couldn't speak. Wow, I was bringing a lot to the table here. No wonder he didn't tell me who he was. I bet he was glad that I couldn't remember him. He now had an out.

Jillian was watching me carefully. She must have seen my despair when I was trying to figure out what I looked like.

She took on her nurturing, social-worker voice that soothed even the most irate of clients. "Oh, honey, it's not that bad."

I gave her the best dirty look I could muster, which must not have been that good, since it made her laugh.

"Okay, okay, it is that bad. Those clothes are terrible. We need to get you some of your clothes."

The thought of having my own stuff made me feel infinitely better and terribly worse all at the same time. I wanted my stuff. I wanted my apartment. I wanted to be out of this hospital, but I didn't know if any of that would even be a possibility. I couldn't work. I didn't know if I would ever be able to go back to work. I would have to go on disability. I didn't have a lot of savings, and I would be destitute soon. Where would I live? What would I do? Oh my God, I was going to be a homeless street person speaking in gibberish!

"Esther, Esther, calm down!"

I hadn't realized I was pacing like a caged tiger. I was on the verge of a massive panic attack. I looked at Jillian, begging her with my eyes to help me.

"Relax, we'll figure this all out. I'll help you get this straightened out, but you've got to calm down. I've been trying to see you, but they kept saying that you were not well enough for visitors. They said every time you had a visitor in the other hospital, your blood pressure would rise and they were afraid you would have a stroke. No one's really been allowed to see you, other than O.K., I guess."

Huh. Maybe that would explain why I hadn't had any visitors. I wondered if my family had tried to visit and had been turned away. Not that I could, but I was afraid to ask. If they hadn't come, I think it would break what little remained of my spirit. I tried to focus on an ugly painting of a warped bulldog on the wall and worked on evening out my breathing.

Jillian continued. "I'm going to go to your place and get some of your stuff, if that is all right with you."

I nodded.

"I'll track O.K. down and see if he has your keys. Or, I'll strong arm your super into letting me in." That made me laugh. Jillian was not quite five feet tall. I could not imagine her strong-arming anyone. But then again, I had heard her bully her way into the hospital.

"And don't worry. People have donated their sick time, so when yours runs out, you will still get paid.

We've taken up a collection too, to help you with your expenses."

I looked at her and started to cry. I hadn't even been there that long. Only about six months. Or was it eight? I had no idea when it was. Either way, I hadn't known these people that long and their generosity was touching.

"I'm gonna bring you your stuff and clothes and get you fixed up. All you have to do is focus on getting better. But that means you have to leave your room and do your therapies."

How did she know I had been refusing?

"They told me when I came in that you were depressed and were refusing to participate, and therefore you obviously were not well enough for visitors."

I shook my head. Seeing Jillian was exactly what I needed.

She pulled out a box of doughnuts from her bag. My eyes grew wide.

Jillian smiled. "See, I knew it. They've been starving you, haven't they?"

I smiled in return and took a Boston Cream. It was the best doughnut I have ever tasted. I licked my lips, enjoying the sweet thick cream. I could not remember the last time I'd had sex (did that doctor-guy and I have sex? Damn if we did and I couldn't remember!). But I'm pretty sure I was about to have an orgasm from this doughnut.

In about thirty seconds flat, I had housed the doughnut. I was licking my fingers when I realized that I had spilled the custard down the front of my rocking grammy-pink sweat suit. Damn it, I Berted.

Berted? What the hell did that mean? And why did I feel like it meant something sexual. Shit, why couldn't I remember?

CHAPTER THIRTY-SIX

"Hey Red, how's it shakin'?"

The bald, tattooed guy from the band was walking up to me. He looked like a badass Mr. Clean, carrying a guitar. I was in a large lounge for the rehab patients, where we could all hang out when we weren't being tortured by our therapists. I was reading a book since I couldn't really make small talk with anyone. I was having trouble concentrating on the book, so I welcomed the distraction. The distraction from being distracted, that is. I put the book down. I self-consciously smoothed the fuzz on my head. My hair was growing back in, and it seemed like it was going to be curlier than ever. I was happy that Jillian had come through for me, getting me some of my own clothes and personal items. I had a little makeup on and was at least in my own yoga pants and nice t-shirt.

I was glad I had seen the videos from the band performance, otherwise I would not have recognized this guy at all. At night, when all the rehab was done for the day, I snuck down to the lounge and watched the three videos of me singing over and over. I couldn't believe how well I sang and what great chemistry we had together.

"Do you remember me?"

I smiled and shook my head. I had made a little bit of progress in speech therapy during the week with Meghan, getting out a few words here and there. But it was in single-word utterances, and there was still a lot of garbage coming out of my mouth. We had figured out that I could sing along with music though. I didn't know the science behind it, but I figured it must be a different, uninjured part of my brain.

"How's it going?"

I shrugged and gestured helplessly. Somebody must have told him that I couldn't talk, right? I looked nervously around the room. When Jillian came to visit, she did all the talking. It was great. Mr. Clean just kind of sat there. He looked as nervous as I felt. I needed to do something to break the tension. I looked around again and then pointed to the guitar case by his feet.

"You wanna hear something?"

I nodded again. He busied himself taking his guitar out, turning the knobs and adjusting it. He played a few chords and then looked at me.

"Ready?"

I shifted forward on my seat and leaned in. I nodded for him to continue.

He started with one of my favorite Queen songs. It was the perfect duet for us, and without being able to understand how or why, I started singing along with Mr. Clean. He looked startled for a moment when I began singing but rolled with it and kept going. We did three songs, all of which I seemed to know. I was guessing that we had done them in our bar performance, but I couldn't be sure. For the first time since I'd woken up, I truly started to feel alive again.

"I wanna try something new. We did this one as a warm up. Before ..." He broke off. He swallowed hard and continued, "Not really bar material but I just think it fits now."

He strummed the opening chords and started singing. He had appropriately picked the song "Say Something" by A Great Big World. We were in tune and harmonizing, as if we had practiced this yesterday. I could not control the tears from streaming down my cheeks any more than I could control the fact that I now could sing. The song was emotional to begin with. Despite the fact that it was about a failed relationship, it had always reminded me of Aster. Looking for that explanation and then giving up when it doesn't appear. I had done that. I had given up on my sister and now my family had given up on me. The enormity of my solitude came crashing in on me as the song came to a close. My gentle tears took over and became an ugly sob.

Mr. Clean put down his guitar and awkwardly patted me on the back as I held my face in my hands. "Sorry, Red. Bad choice for a song," he stuttered. "I, um, I'm sorry. I just, I mean, I didn't think."

He was kind of cute stuttering and stammering. It was so incongruous with his outside appearance, which looked liked such a badass. I didn't really remember him, but I could tell he felt very awkward touching me. Frankly, I felt weird too. As much as I desired to be touched and held, I knew he was not the one I wanted to do it.

I straightened up. "That's okay. I'm fine."

He jumped back. "What?"

"I'll be fine. I'm sorry I broke down like that. My emotions are a little wonky right now."

"WHAT?"

"I said I'm sorry I started crying. Jeez, relax, would you?"

"Red, you're talking!"

I looked around. All of the people in the room, including a few nurses were staring. They had probably been watching us sing, but I hadn't noticed. My mouth was open and I shut it quickly. I was afraid the gibberish would come out again.

******

But it didn't. I could talk again. Sometimes, I couldn't come up with a word that I knew I knew. Sometimes, I meant to say one word but another came out. Like when I meant to say 'nutcracker' but said 'woodpecker' instead. Or when I wanted a Q-tip to clean out my ears but asked for a toothpick instead. The badass Mr. Clean had brought it out of me. I did find out his name was Albert, which was a good thing, because otherwise I was likely to call him Mr. Clean to his face. I somehow did not think it would go over that great. Meghan, my speech therapist, was amazed. My doctors were perplexed. Jillian was ecstatic. I was scared.

I was scared because I still couldn't remember the two months before my head injury. I wasn't sure I'd be able to work. I wouldn't be cleared to drive for a while, seeing as how I'd had my head cut open and all. I guess I was at high risk for seizures, although I wasn't sure if I'd had one or not. I knew that the people at work had taken a collection for me, but I wasn't sure how I was going to make ends meet. I couldn't turn to my family for help. Christ, they hadn't even been in to see me since my initial hospital stay. What was I going to do?

Apparently, I was going to answer question after question from therapist after therapist and doctor after doctor. It was determined that I had what was called retrograde amnesia, which is not uncommon with traumatic brain injuries. The doctor explained this to me as he was spouting on and on about something called the hippocampus, which made me think of a hippopotamus. Then I started thinking about the game Hungry, Hungry Hippos, which then led me to think about how hungry I was and how I really wanted a big fat burrito or something. I realized the doctor was still droning on, and I decided I'd better start paying attention again. I was having trouble concentrating, which I thought might also be a side effect of my brain injury. I focused in again. The doctor did not think my memory in general would be impaired and even thought there was a slight chance I could get my memory back. The whole return of speech thing had everyone a bit stymied, so I guess all bets were off with me. I meant to ask him about the attention thing, but I forgot until well after he was gone. I wrote it down on a piece of paper to ask him another time.

They also wanted to follow me for a while to possibly write a case study on me. They explained that my identity would be protected, yadda, yadda, yadda, and all that good stuff. Meghan was really excited about the use of music in my sudden return of speech. They were still trying to figure out how exactly that happened. One theory they were batting around was that my brain had simply been bruised rather than totally killed off. One doctor started talking about cortical versus subcortical skills and totally lost me. I couldn't wait for these guys to leave so I could think some more about food.

The herd of health care professionals had finally left me for the day. I was exhausted. I just wanted to sleep. It seemed like healing was hard work. My cell phone, which was again charged up (thanks to Jillian), beeped, indicating a text message. It was from a "Kingston Cole" which I guess was that cute doctor who was supposed to be my boyfriend. Damn I wish I could remember him from before the accident. I looked at the text.

"Can I come visit you tonight after my shift?"

I hesitated for a moment. This would be the first time that I would be able to talk to him. I was sure he knew that I didn't know who he was, and I thought it was nice that he was asking for permission to visit. I was also pretty sure he was coming to make sure that I knew we were over. I mean, who wants to date a person who doesn't even remember him?

"Sure."

"Want me to bring food?"

Oh my God, I didn't even know this man but I think I loved him. Hmm ... that was an interesting thought. Did I actually love him? I would have to ponder that one later. He was bringing me food.

"YES!!! PLEASE! The food here is terrible!"

"Any requests? Burgers? Pizza? Meat with a side of meat?"

I smiled. He must really know me and my penchant for meat.

"Would a burrito be possible?"

"Def. How?"

I sent him the specifics and he indicated that he would be over around eight. Then, I started to panic. I looked like shit. I was pale. I had no good makeup or jewelry. My hair was growing in, in tight fuzzy little curls. I did what any sane female would do. I called for reinforcements.

"Esther, you've lost a lot of weight, and you are thinner and taller than me to begin with."

"But Jillian, I don't know who else to call. You've got to have something, right?"

"I may have a dress that I wore a thousand years ago. Shave your legs while I'm on my way over."

We conferred and luckily shared the same shoe size. Jillian was going to hook me up so I could look like a human being. She was bringing the dress and shoes and even some more makeup. I hoped she would get here in time for me to get ready. I disconnected, went out to the nurses' station and requested a razor. It was a crappy one, and I nicked myself about ten times, but having smooth legs made me feel like a woman again. I couldn't wait to be able to dress in nice clothes and finally see my boyfriend.

CHAPTER THIRTY-SEVEN

"Oh, hell, NO!"

"What?"

"Jillian, is this seriously all you brought? I can't wear this!" This was a disaster of epic proportions. There was no way on God's green earth that I was stepping out of the bathroom wearing this. "Give me my yoga pants back."

"Come on Esther, it can't be that bad. I loved that dress. I bet it looks fantastic on you. Just come out and show me."

"I am not coming out."

I stared at myself in the mirror. I could not believe this was my life. Of course this was my life. This was total par for the course with me. But oh how I wished it weren't.

"C'mon Es, I think I hear him coming down the hall. You can't stay locked in the bathroom forever."

"Yes I can. Just watch."

Jillian was quiet for a minute. Then I heard her talking. I heard the male voice. Shit, he was here. I had to go out and face Kingston. Then I heard Jillian say, "I don't know. She won't come out of the bathroom. Do you think we need to call a nurse?"

"We'll give her a minute," I heard him say. Then he continued, "Was she all right before she went in there?"

There was a pause. Then Jillian said, "Do you think she's, you know, not right from the accident?"

Oh, hell no, they weren't gonna sit there and speculate that I'm not right in the head. I came barging out of the bathroom but skidded to a stop when I saw

Kingston standing there. His mouth fell open and hung there for a moment. He snapped it shut and pressed his lips together, obviously trying to hold the laughter back.

I shook my finger at him. "Don't. Don't you even dare."

He clenched his lips even tighter, every muscle in his body tensing.

Holding his gaze with my own death stare, I cautioned him. "I'm warning you. Don't."

Jillian interrupted, "Esther, are you okay?"

I turned on the stacked heel of the black Mary Jane that Jillian had brought. "No, I am not okay. I cannot believe you did this to me!"

Kingston could not hold it in any longer and burst out laughing. I glared at him, and then turned my death stare back to Jillian.

"What?" she asked helplessly. She honestly didn't see it.

The dress she brought me in theory was a cute dress. It was a fitted, mod style mini-dress with slightly full long sleeves. The problem was it was a red dress with a white pearled peter pan collar. There was a black-trimmed belt that hung low on my waist. And of course, Jillian had paired it with the heeled Mary Janes. On anyone else, it would have looked adorable. However, this was me. With my red curly hair that had been shaved but was now growing back in.

I shook my head and plopped down in the blue plastic chair right outside the bathroom. I buried my head in my hands.

"Oh, don't worry Esther," Kingston finally sputtered out, trying to catch his breath. "Just relax. I'm sure the sun will come out ... tomorrow."

I looked up. "You went there. I warned you, and I can't believe you actually went there."

"Went where?" Jillian looked back and forth between the two of us, completely and totally oblivious. Kingston had tears rolling down his cheeks. I couldn't help it. I started laughing too. Jillian kept looking back and forth at us laughing and asking "What? What?"

Kingston put down the bags with the food on the small dresser next to him and opened his arms. I stood up, smoothed down the skirt and walked into his arms. Even though I didn't remember him, I knew I knew him and I knew I felt comfortable with him. I laid my head on his chest while he enveloped me in his arms. In that moment, I felt safe and loved. I felt, in that moment, that maybe, just maybe everything would be fine.

I looked up at him and smiled. He looked down at me. I had a sudden, urgent need to kiss this man, even though I didn't remember him. My body seemed to, as I melted into him.

"Um guys? I'm still here. Will you *please* tell me what is going on?"

I broke from Kingston's embrace and turned to face Jillian. I gestured to the outfit. "Does it look at all familiar?"

"I think it looks cute on you. I do not see what the issue was."

"Look closely at the hair."

"Okay."

"Now look at the dress."

"Okay ... still not seeing it."

I sighed. "Never mind."

Kingston nudged me. "She can't see why it's such a hard-knock life."

I elbowed him back. "Stop it."

He couldn't let it go. "Maybe because you're never fully dressed without a smile."

I couldn't hold back, and whacked him.

Jillian, looking uncomfortable, picked up her purse. "Well, I know you two have a lot of catching up to do and a lot to discuss."

Jillian left in a huff and I just had to shake my head. Those not cursed with red curly hair would never understand the lengths to which us redheads went to avoid the dreaded Annie comparison. I wasn't sure what other embarrassing things I'd done in front of Kingston—knowing me there would have been a few—but this had to take the cake. Then I started to panic. I didn't know what embarrassing things I had done. I didn't know anything that I had done with this guy. All I knew was his name and that he knew I liked meat. Okay, so apparently we had eaten together. Crap, this was so not going to work. He was going to dump my ass when he realized what a basket case I was. Too bad, because he's really cute, too.

"Um, Kingston? Can I ask you a few things? I'm sorry but I don't really remember you at all."

He looked uncomfortable. Uh oh, here is comes. The great dumping.

"What did you call me?"

"Kingston. That's your name, right?" Oh sweet Jesus, please let that be his name. Please don't let me have called him by the wrong name.

He smiled. "Why did you call me that?"

Oh fuck me. I called him the wrong name.

"I'm so sorry. That's the name that came up in my phone when you texted me. I don't know why it would be in there. I'm so sorry. I just, I mean, I can't remember and, fuck, I can't believe I've fucked this up." I sank down on my bed in defeat. He was still standing by the door. I laid back and closed my eyes. "Thank you for stopping by. I'm sorry I'm such a basket case. I guess I'll see you around sometime." I covered my face with my hands and waited to hear him leave.

It was quiet for a moment, and then I felt him sit down on the edge of the bed. I couldn't bear to look at him. "No, seriously, why did you call me Kingston?"

"I told you, that was what was in my phone."

"Why was it in your phone that way?"

"I don't know. I don't remember putting it in there. How should it be? Is Kingston your last name? Did I put it in wrong?"

"No, but you never called me Kingston."

"What did I call you then?"

"O.K."

"Okay what? What did I call you?"

He sighed and laid down on the bed, snuggling into me. Holy shit, he was snuggling into me!

"You called me O.K. as in Capital-O-Period-K-Period."

"Why on earth would I call you O.K.?"

He explained the nickname thing. Even though I didn't know the story, I had a weird sense of déjà vu. If I were a betting person, and did not apparently have the worst luck in the world, I would bet that I would be experiencing sensations like this a whole lot from now on. I shifted slightly on the bed and we settled in, lying shoulder-to-shoulder, side-by-side.

"So, Esther, there's no way to beat around the bush on this one, so I'm going to jump into it. I need you to just hear me out before you get all riled up."

Uh oh, that didn't sound good. I continued staring at the ceiling, but I nodded so that he would know to continue.

"They are looking to discharge you in the next day or two. You can't drive, and I'm worried about you being on your own. They're still not sure how much long-term impact you will have, and you are still healing. Since you are not able to work right now, I think you should come stay with me."

I didn't say anything, just digested what he had said. I knew it was all true. I had very little money. I couldn't drive and I couldn't work. There was a part of me that wanted to be all indignant that this guy who I didn't remember was swooping in, trying to act like a knight in shining armor. On the other hand, there was an even larger part of me that was so terrified to be out in the world again that I was grateful he was making this offer.

Apparently my silence worried him, and he started rambling again. "You know, well maybe you don't know, but I have three bedrooms. You'd have your own room and we'd bring your furniture and stuff over. I work a lot, although I'll cut back if you want. I don't want you to worry about money or anything else. I just want you to get better."

"Okay."

"What? Am I rambling? Sorry, I tend to ramble when I get nervous. I don't know why I'm nervous. This isn't about me; it's about you. But here I am, the nervous one."

I elbowed him and he quieted. "No, I meant okay, I'll stay with you."

"Really?"

"Yes, really."

He was quiet for a moment. "That was a lot easier than I thought it would be."

CHAPTER THIRTY-EIGHT

The next day was my last day in rehab and it was a busy one. Everyone needed to do their final tests on me to see how far I'd come. My right hand was still weak and a bit clumsy, but it was worlds better, and I was determined to stay a righty. I could talk, but had occasional word-finding difficulties. I was having trouble staying focused. I was still tired. And, of course, there was still the amnesia. Kingston (I told him I wanted to call him that because the whole O.K.-okay thing was just too hard for my brain right now) was slowly filling me in on some details, but we hadn't had much time. I guess there would be time for that since I was going to be living with him.

Huh. I couldn't believe I'd agreed to move in with him. It seemed pretty impulsive for me. Other than marrying Dickie Cox, I did not usually fly by the seat of my pants, giving in to whatever whims I might have. Of course, that had been a unique time in my life, as was this. I could only hope that this had a better outcome.

I waved to the last nurse as Kingston walked me to the elevator. We were silent as we rode down to the parking garage. He carried my stuff and I let him. I followed him to his car and got in as he loaded my bags into the Maxima's trunk. He got in and smiled at me before turning the key in the ignition. I gave him a tense smile back.

"Don't worry, Esther. I'm having your stuff packed up and moved over this weekend. We can store things in the garage for now."

I smiled at him again, hoping it didn't appear as fake as it felt. He was a good guy, I was pretty sure. It was the total chaos of was my life that I was having trouble dealing with. My apartment, crappy as it was, at least had been mine. I would be homeless, jobless and virtually destitute. I was forced to move in with a guy I didn't remember because my own family members had turned their backs on me. That pissed me off more than anything. I had tried calling Charlie after my speech returned, but she never answered or even called back.

"What's wrong?" He could tell my smile was fake.

I could feel the tears welling up. I didn't want to do this. I didn't want to be this snively mess. What if he had never seen me cry before? What if he saw how ugly I looked when I cried and decided to dump me on the curb? I balled up my fists and tightened every muscle in my body to keep the tears back. I rocked my head back and forth, unable to speak.

"Are you okay?"

I shook my head again, burying my face in my hands.

"Esther, you've got to calm down. Look at me." His voice was firm and in control. I peeled my hands away from my face and looked at him.

"Is something hurting you?"

I shook my head.

"Are you scared?"

I nodded.

"Of me?" his voice cracked a bit, breaking through his calm demeanor.

I shook my head.

"Then of what?"

I took a deep breath. "Of everything. I have no home and no job. What am I going to do for money? I'm all alone. I have no one besides you, but I don't remember you." My voice was slowly rising into panic mode. "All my stuff is packed up. Everything is spinning out of control and it—" I broke off. I knew what I wanted to say, but couldn't come up with the right word.

"Esther," he said, drawing me into his arms, "you will be fine. This is temporary, I promise you."

"Control. No control."

"Yes, I get that. We'll help you to get back into control."

"No, that wasn't what I wanted to say." I sighed in frustration. "The lack of control makes me scared."

He released me and started driving. Without prompting, without questioning, Kingston told me the story of how we met. He told me of our chance encounters. He told me about how I went out with his friend, some doctor guy named Rob. That he was terrified that I would be another of the many women that Rob had gone through in his rebound phase. Kingston got a little funny when talking about this, but I chalked it up to jealously. I wondered if I had slept with this Rob guy. It seemed sort of out of character for pre-accident me, but hey, who knows? Kingston went on to tell me how we had dinner, I attacked him in my hallway and then threw him out. He said that had left his head spinning and he didn't know what to make of me, other than he was smitten.

Then he told me about Dean's heart attack and the trip up to Minnesota. I could not believe that this guy drove me all the way there. Actually, since he was moving me in with him to take care of me, I guess I sort of could believe it.

By this time, we were at his house. It was a cute little house in a subdivision where every third house looked the same. I was sort of relieved that I was not driving because I hadn't paid attention driving in, and I knew there was no way I'd ever find it in the subdivision again.

Kingston unloaded his stuff and showed me in. The house had obviously been freshly cleaned, and it looked like things may have just been moved around. I recognized some of my things—the blanket draped on the back of the couch. The vase on the dining room table. My coat rack full of coats.

I looked around and saw familiar objects next to unfamiliar ones. It was comforting and disconcerting all at the same time. He brought me upstairs to show me my bedroom. It was literally my bedroom. It was laid out exactly how my room in my apartment had been, right down to the cosmetics on the dresser and the books on the nightstand. I turned and looked at him, unable to articulate the immense swell of emotion that was overtaking me. "How ... why ... I don't ... how?"

"My family helped out and so did Jillian. I don't know how they got it so exact. I asked them to try and make it look similar. They told the movers where to put things, and just went from there."

"Kingston, I don't know what to say. Even if I could find all my words, I don't know which ones to use."

He smiled at me. "I want you to feel at home and comfortable so you can finish healing."

"I feel weird. I feel like me, but I don't. Things are different, and I don't know how or why they are. I mean, I guess ..." I trailed off, unsure if I didn't know what to say or if I didn't know how I wanted to say it.

"Why don't you settle in and make yourself at home. I'll be downstairs when you're ready. There are some things that we need to talk about."

That sounded ominous, but I was too distracted by being around my own stuff to think about what Kingston might be talking about. After he left, I closed the door and flopped on my bed. I wanted to sleep for about one hundred years. I wanted to wake up without a brain injury and with all my hair back. I was immensely grateful for Kingston and all he was doing for me. Without him, I'd probably be out on the street soon.

My thoughts were racing around in my head, rattling here and there, and I think I drifted off to sleep. When I woke up, it was dark outside the windows. It was November, so it did get dark earlier. I hoped I hadn't slept too long. I found and used the bathroom outside my room and headed downstairs to find Kingston.

He was working hard at looking relaxed sitting on the couch, but there was a tension about his neck and shoulders that betrayed him. I remembered sensing an ominous tone to his last comment to me, and wondered what could possibly be the matter.

I sat down on the couch next to him, and pulled my blanket off the back of the couch, wrapping it around my legs. "What's up?"

He sighed. He opened his mouth to start talking several times, but could not start. Finally, I said, "Kingston, I'm the one with the aphasia. You need to spit it out."

He smiled. "You're right. It's just that when you were in the hospital—"

"The first one?" I interrupted.

"Yes, at Riverside, when you were in the coma, there were times when people came to visit. It would cause a severe spike in your blood pressure and there was concern that it would cause you to have a hemorrhage. There was thought that you may have been having some seizure activity in response to this stimuli as well."

"I knew they were worried about me having a stroke. I didn't know that I was having seizures too. Does this mean I always will have seizures?"

"They never confirmed the seizures and did not record any on EEG. It was more of an observed thing, so I don't know. It is one of the reasons why I want you here, so I can monitor you and make sure you are okay."

I smiled. "I appreciate that."

His smile did not reach his eyes. Uh oh, wherever he was going with this, it did not seem good.

He took a deep breath and continued. "It was very obvious that your blood pressure spiked in response to specific stimuli."

"And what was that? Mary Hart's voice?"

He didn't laugh. "No, your family."

"My family? Were they even there?"

"Oh yes, at the beginning. The doctors finally decided that they needed to go, because you were agitated and in danger whenever they were around. You only started healing when they left. It was only when your parents left that you started becoming responsive again."

"Huh. I thought they had deserted me."

He shifted uncomfortably again. "Um, no, we asked them to leave."

This bothered me. A lot. "I know that you medical people thought you were doing a good thing, and I don't know what you know about my relationship with my family, but it isn't good. Usually they don't give a shit about me. I can't believe that for once they actually cared about me and you made them leave."

"Esther, we had to. It was detrimental to your health."

"But don't you know how lonely I was and how I wanted someone there for me?"

"I know Esther. I tried to be there for you, but you didn't know who I was. And it always made you upset."

"They left me all alone. I can't believe they didn't stay and fight to see me."

"They tried. We argued a lot. I was worried that you had heard some of it that day that I bumped into you in the hall."

"You were fighting with my family?"

"Yes."

I paused. I knew it was looking a gift horse in the mouth, but where did this guy get off telling my family to stay away from me? I said as much to him.

"Esther, I know how much you want your family to accept you. But you have to trust me. I mean, it was your sister's fault that you ended up with a brain injury in the first place!" His voice was rising, getting emotional and agitated.

My tone matched his. "What do you mean, my sister's fault?" I had remembered that Charlie had been to see me initially. "What does Charlie have to do with this?"

"Not Charlie."

"Not Charlie? Veruca wasn't there and I haven't talked to Violet in several years."

"No, not them."

"Jesus Kingston, just spit it out! What do you mean?" I was now yelling. Huh—maybe they were onto something about my blood pressure.

His hands were balled into fists and he looked like he was using every ounce of energy to appear calm. "No, this whole mess, your whole situation, is all because of Aster."

CHAPTER THIRTY-NINE

"Even though I like to blame Aster for a lot of the strife in my life, I don't see how this can be her fault." I very rarely even mentioned my twin sister to anyone. The fact that Kingston knew about her said something for our relationship, even if I couldn't remember it. When he mentioned her name, it made me remember that I thought she had been in the hospital room with my parents. "You know what's funny? When I was in the first hospital in the coma ... I woke up a few times and one of those times, I could have sworn I saw Aster there with Cheryl and Dean. Isn't that odd?"

He was quiet for a moment and appeared to be carefully choosing his words. "It isn't odd. She was there."

"I'm not that kind of person to believe in spirits and ghosts and shit. Oh—do you think I maybe died a little and saw her on the other side?"

His voice was too calm. It was freaking me out because it was very unnatural for him. "No, Esther. Aster was there. She is alive."

A thousand thoughts barraged my brain all at once, and I could not form a coherent statement out of one of them. My mouth hung agape, and the world started to get dark and hazy. Before I knew it, Kingston was right next to me, urging me to take slow deep breaths and focus on his eyes. I did as he instructed. His eyes were the gorgeous brown of liquid milk chocolate. The lines around his eyes betrayed a soul that laughed a lot, and there was no mistaking the concern and compassion pouring out of them. I could tell he really cared about me. He might even love me. I focused on this thought, and the dark retreated from my periphery, and the world stopped spinning. Gradually my breathing returned to normal, and I no longer had to think about breathing.

"Better?"

"Yes. Well, no, but I no longer feel like I'm going to pass out ..." I trailed off. He looked at me, knowing that my damaged brain was putting two and two together. "I passed out and hit my head?"

"Yes."

"Why did I pass out?"

"Because you saw Aster."

"How did I see her?"

"This is the funny thing. You had been hearing and seeing her, ever since your car accident. You had been worried that you were going crazy or had a brain tumor or something. She was at the club the first time you sang, when you were there with Rob."

"WHos Rob?" I interjected.

"Rob Olsson. You went out on a date with him before we got together."

The name sounded familiar. "Rob Olsson? Wait—is he a doctor?"

"Yup."

"I think I know him from a case at work?"

"Yeah, I think you did. Remember, he's the one who drove you home and you went out with him, before me." Kingston seemed uneasy.

"I don't remember going out with him, but yeah for me—he's hot! I can't believe I went out with him!" Apparently the brain injury and aphasia did nothing to help with my lack of internal filter.

"Um, yeah. You went out once, but you decided to date me instead." Kingston was obviously on the defensive.

"Oh, you're hot too. He just oozes sexiness. I don't even usually like blondes. Oh, wait, you're sexy too, but in a puppy dog kind of way. Like adorable. But he's just sex on a stick."

"Sex on a stick?" He looked at me, dumbfounded. He shook his head. "I reveal life-altering news to you, and you end up telling me I look like a dog and my best friend is sex on a stick. How did we get here?"

I blanched. Jesus, I was an idiot. "I'm sorry. I've always had an E-Z Pass mouth and I guess that hasn't changed. Plus, now I get distracted very easily and it is hard for me to stay focused. Okay, back on topic. I saw her some other time?" I was trying to pay attention to what came out of my mouth.

"Yes, you thought you saw her that night you were with Rob. And you did. Long story short, she started dating Rob, and he brought her to the show. He had no idea who she was. She approached you after the show. You hauled off and smacked her, and then you took off out the door. I was chasing after you and saw you buckle. I couldn't reach you to catch you before your head hit the curb. I am so sorry. I should have been quicker." He hung his head and his voice cracked.

I put my hand underneath his chin and lifted it up so I could look at him. I should not have been surprised to see the tears in his eyes, but I was. I leaned in and kissed him gently on the lips. That gesture startled him and he drew back slightly.

"Don't be sorry. This was not your fault. There was nothing you could have done. I wish I remembered us before all this happened. It seems like, from everything you've told me, you've done nothing but be there for me, right from the very beginning. I'm sorry that I'm such a train wreck."

He smiled. "It's what makes me love you."

I returned the smile. "You love me?"

He leaned in and kissed me ever so sweetly on the lips, drawing my body close to his. "Yes, of course I do. These past weeks have been hell. I didn't know if you were going to make it, and even if you did, what would be left. And then to realize that you didn't even know who I was ..."

I closed my eyes and rested my head on his shoulder. At this moment, with my life in such disarray, I didn't know how I could be feeling peaceful and content. I let those feelings wash over me for a moment, melting into Kingston's strong embrace. The moment was short lived as my mind darted back to the previous revelation.

"So, Aster's alive and she came to my show?"

Kingston pulled back and looked at me. "Yes." His grip remained firm, as if he expected me to pass out again.

I was quiet for a moment, searching his face for answers that were not his to give. Finally, I spoke. "I'm speechless. Again."

"I know you must have so many questions. I'll do the best I can."

"No."

"No?"

"No, I can't ask you. You won't have the answers I need."

"She's been asking to see you. I told her that she couldn't until you were medically stable. If you need more time, I can tell her you are not ready."

"You ... you're in contact with her?"

His arms dropped down. I suddenly felt cold and alone without his touch. He looked down at his hands, now in his lap.

"How much do you see her?" My voice was rising again.

"I don't see her that much."

I noticed his emphasis was on the word "I."

"If you don't see her, then who does?"

"Rob is dating her. He sees her. They're actually pretty serious, I guess."

Okay, so I didn't know what had happened between Rob and me. I didn't know if I had slept with him or not. But either way, he had gone from going out with me to being in love with Aster. Go figure. She had dominated my whole life growing up. Her disappearance and supposed death had cost me any relationship with my family. And now I was unemployed and brain damaged because of her. And yet, she still gets the guy. I mean, I had this wonderful guy too, but why did she have to be with someone that I had dated first?

I stood up abruptly.

"Esther, are you all right?"

"No," I started pacing. "No, I am not."

Kingston watched me pace. He was guarded, ready to spring into action if I started to fall.

I continued pacing, the thoughts racing and swirling.

"Esther, what do you need right now?"

I stopped and looked at him. "Honestly?"

"Honestly."

I considered for a moment. "I really, really need to break something right now."

Kingston looked at me and stood up. "Follow me."

I followed him into the kitchen. He opened up a cabinet to reveal plates and bowls. With a wave of his hand, he said, "Have at it."

Still pacing, I said, "You mean it?"

He nodded.

After I had broken almost every dinner plate, I finally met his eyes. Out of habit, I ran my fingers through my hair, or rather, where my hair should have been. Dammit, another reason to be mad. I was now virtually bald, and let's not forget the embarrassing Annie episode at the hospital. All because of Aster. I picked up the last plate, held it high above my head and threw it down with all the strength I had.

I looked at my mess. Slowly, I looked up at Kingston and said, "That last one was for my hair."

Without breaking my gaze, he reached into the cabinet and pulled out a serving bowl. He raised it over his head and smashed it down. I jumped, startled by his sudden and unexpected action.

"That was for your hair too."

CHAPTER FORTY

How was I going to do this? How was I supposed to sit down and have a logical, rational conversation with Aster? I was angry. So angry. My head was pounding all the time. And, as much as I had hated being alone in the hospital, I knew without a doubt that Kingston had made the right decision. I hated it, but he was right.

I had been stalling seeing Aster. I claimed to be too tired, which bought me several days. My therapies were now being done outpatient, although I was really doing pretty well, all things considered. And I was tired. I had no stamina. Chieko had mentioned early on in my physical therapy in the rehab hospital that for every day I spent in bed, it would take me a week to regain my strength. All told, I had been out of it for about twenty days. That meant it would take me about five months to be back to where I was the night I had my accident. It would be spring. Half a year lost.

Not to mention the previous seven years of heartbreak and anguish. I had never once prayed for Aster to be alive. That seemed too unreasonable—too much to hope for. I only prayed for her body to be found. The seven years of feeling dead on the inside. Seven years of not having a family. Seven years of isolation.

I think Kingston understood my anger. If I didn't know better, I would say he was angry on my behalf. Jillian was livid when I told her. It was odd, having people on my side. For so long, it had been me alone, standing against my family. Fighting for what I so believed was right.

But I was wrong. Dead wrong.

And they were right.

All along, I had been the wrong one. I had given up hope. I had believed her dead. I was wrong.

And that was all they would ever see. That was why no one contacted me. They were with her. Celebrating that their family was reunited. And I was still not a part of that family.

There had been a tiny part of me that had wanted to believe they were not all together, making up for lost time. Unfortunately, Rob had told Kingston otherwise. Apparently he was completely and totally head-over-heels for Aster. Go figure.

So I stewed in my anger. I stewed and stewed. I was sick to my stomach all the time and had terrible headaches. I was making slow progress in rehab, and I couldn't help but think that this negative cloud swirling around me and emanating from my pores was partly responsible. It didn't make sense to me that being angry could really have a physical effect on me. It really seemed to, though, so I brought it up in a therapy session. Kevin, my outpatient physical therapist, advised me to let it out and deal with it up front. He apparently had treated me after that car accident. While I remember the accident, I still didn't remember anything after, except for bits and flashes here and there. Since he had known me prior to this injury, he told me that he could see the big difference in me and how much this was weighing me down. He seemed to think that my emotional state would prevent me from making a full recovery.

I knew he was right. Kingston was not pushing me to see Aster or the rest of my family, but I could not put it off forever. I needed to bite the bullet and do it. I wished I could just hop in the car and drive myself to see her. I didn't want a big deal made about the fact that I was going. Frankly, I didn't even want to plan on going. I wanted to be able to get the impulse to go and then go. It was another thing Aster had taken from me—the freedom to be independent.

I was pissed and I was stubborn. Maybe a tad foolish too, but I decided to take matters into my own hands. I mapped out the bus route, cancelled my therapy sessions, and went to see my long-lost twin sister.

She had a place not far from mine. Huh. That was odd. What were the chances of that happening?

I steeled myself as I walked up to the town house's front door, pulling my coat around me to fight off the nip in the November air. I double checked the number that I had scrawled on a scrap of paper. If my information was correct, this was the house. I stopped and gathered my courage. For, behind this average-looking door with its average brown paint and average brass knocker, was the reason my life was in shambles.

Oh, and that's another thing. I really hate when people don't accept responsibility for themselves and their own actions. Here I was blaming Aster for all that had gone wrong in my life. I tried to step back and see where I could accept responsibility for my disaster of a life, but I couldn't see where any of it was my fault. Except maybe the passing out thing. I didn't know if I could control that or not. I would have to ask some medical person about that. I couldn't ever remember passing out before.

Before I could even knock, she opened the door. We stood there looking at each other. We were the same height. Her hair was a dull light brown and hung limply to her shoulders. It was parted down the middle and did nothing for her. We'd had a birthday while I was out of commission, but, to me, she looked older than thirty-two. Life had not been kind to her and it showed. Her posture was a bit slumped with her shoulders drawn forward, making her appear smaller and timid. Her effervescence was gone. She appeared to have had a very difficult life.

She stepped aside in a gesture for me to enter. I took a deep breath and did so.

"Can I take your coat?" she asked stiffly and formally.

I clumsily unbuttoned the tortoise shell buttons and slid the coat down my arms. I purposefully used my right arm to hold out the kelly green wool coat to her. It felt like it weighted about ninety pounds to my still weakened right arm. Aster accepted the coat and looked at it. "This green was always such a good color on you."

Instead of replying, I crossed my arms over my chest and raised an eyebrow. She had a lot of explaining to do. She owed me an explanation.

"Will you please come in and sit down?" Aster gestured down a narrow hall and to the kitchen at the back of the building. I nodded and then glanced around as I followed her. The place was relatively tidy, but lived in. Pictures of a red-headed boy hung all over the walls. Framed artwork of the highest preschool variety also filled the walls. There was some kind of video gaming system on the coffee table. It was pretty apparent. Aster had a child.

How could she possibly be anyone's mother? She couldn't care for herself, let alone a child. Where was the father? Did she even know who the father was? Obviously, he wasn't in the picture, or she wouldn't be dating Rob. Speaking of which, did she know that I had gone out with him? How could she do that to me?

She stopped dead and whirled around. Oops. Apparently I had been speaking those thoughts out loud. Dammit, I went from not being able to speak at all to speaking without knowing. The hurt on her face was apparent.

"Have a seat," she gestured to the beat-up, well-used kitchen table, pretending that I just hadn't completely and totally insulted her.

I did while she puttered about, making coffee. I very rarely drank coffee these days, but she didn't know that. She didn't know me anymore, any more than I knew her.

"Before you tear into me some more, I know I owe you an explanation."

"Leastmast. No, crap." I tried to pull myself together to get the correct words out. "At the very least." Better.

She turned and carried the coffee over. I envied the ease with which she moved and how both of her hands worked together at the same time. I took the mug in both of my hands and raised it, taking a sip.

"Esther, you out of everyone knew how sick I was. Frankly, you were the only one who even saw it."

"Did you intend on killing yourself that night?" I had to cut right to the point. I wanted my answers and I wanted to be out of here.

She nodded. Her emotions seemed shut off as she told me the story of that day, and the days that followed, sounding robotic and detached. "That night, I woke up after a little while, and I had this overwhelming sense of despair crushing down on me. I couldn't take it—not knowing if it was ever going to stop. I'd had feelings like this before, but this was way worse. You weren't there that night to talk me through it. I think that was why it was worse than it had ever been. Normally, you got me through. The quietness of the house only made it worse. I just knew I couldn't go on that way. I knew I had to end it all."

"So you were going to kill yourself?"

"Yes, of course. That was why I wrote the note. I knew I couldn't go on with that feeling any longer. There was no other way out. I figured the easiest way would be just to jump off the bridge."

"Had you thought about it before that night?"

She looked down at her hands. "Yes."

"Really? I hadn't pegged you for suicidal."

"It wasn't that I wanted to end my life, but I wanted the pain and despair to stop. That was the only way I could figure out of how to stop it." Aster paused for a minute and then continued. "By the time I got to the bridge, well, I guess the brisk night air cleared my head a little. I didn't feel quite so overwhelmed anymore. I stood there for a minute or two. Actually, it could have been hours, for all I know. My sense of time is skewed from that period. I started walking, and the longer I walked, the more the feeling of despair abated."

"So what did you do then?"

"I just kept walking and thinking. And thinking and walking. Like I said, the concept of time is distorted for me. If I got tired or hungry, I would try to find a homeless shelter. Sometimes, a lot of the time, I slept on the street. I was very disconnected from myself and reality. Eventually I reached California. I can't account for most of how I got there."

"So, it never occurred to you in all this time to contact us to let us know you were alive?"

Aster looked at her black coffee, as if it held the answers. She shook her head. "I ended up getting admitted to a mental hospital as a ward of the state for about nine months. They had to treat my addictions as well as the underlying mental illness, which was why I started using in the first place."

"I know that. I knew that when we were teenagers."

"You were the only one and I hated you for it."

"At times, I hated you for being sick, which is stupid because I know you couldn't help it."

"And I hated that you saw it, because I knew you were right. But also, in my messed up brain, I rationalized that I was helping you by staying away. I knew you were on the verge of dropping out of school because of me. I couldn't ruin your life too."

I burst out laughing a bitter, jaded laugh. "Oh, that's rich. Especially right now."

"What do you mean?" she seemed confused.

"Seriously?"

She nodded. Jesus Christ, she was serious. "Look at me Aster. Take a good look at me. I have no home. I can't do my job because I'm brain damaged. I had to have my head cut open and I'm still all messed up from it. I have absolutely no relationship with my family. The only person who seems to want anything to do with me—my boyfriend—I don't even remember. And it is all because of you."

Her eyes were wide. This had never occurred to her.

"What were you thinking showing up like that?"

"I had been trying to let you know that I was around. I didn't know how to do it. I've wanted so desperately to have you back in my life. I've missed you so much."

"I don't remember the few months before I was injured. Kingston told me that I thought I had been hearing you and seeing you, and that I thought I either had a brain tumor or was going crazy."

"Yeah, when I saw you in that car accident, I couldn't help myself. I yelled out to you and the first thing that popped out of my mouth was—"

"Avert your eyes."

She smiled through her tears at our private joke. "I was so worried that you were hurt and then I saw you get out of the car and I had to reach out to you. And I knew if I said it, you would know that it was me."

"And you were at the club the night I was there with Rob? Kingston told me I thought I saw you there."

"Yes. I saw you sing. You were amazing. You were about one hundred times better than I ever was. I wanted to talk to you after, but as soon as you saw me, I chickened out. I ran away."

I mulled this over for a minute. "Wait—why were you there in the first place? Do you follow me around?"

Aster shrugged. "Sort of, I guess. I've been in the last few cities that you were in. When you move, I move, just so I can be close to you. I've wanted you back in my life for so long, but I didn't know how to go about it."

"Well, you picked the wrong way."

She looked down, staring at her mug on the table. "I called you the night of the show, but every time you answered, I chickened out and hung up. I understand that you're angry. I know I messed things up. I've messed things up my whole life. I've often wished I was never born. I sometimes felt like disappearing was making it like that."

"But, Aster, Jesus, don't you understand that you can't just make it like you were never born? Do you understand what you left behind? That the family fractured because you disappeared?"

"Yeah, I heard" she mumbled.

"Oh, I'm sure you did. I'm sure they told you all about it." The look on her face painted the answer. "Yeah, I'm sure they told you all about how I insisted you were dead. How I never had any hope. How I refused to believe in you."

"Yes, Dean told me." Again, she looked hurt. Her hurt just fueled my righteous indignation. "I'm trying to get over it."

Okay, that was it. I was done. I stood up, spilling a bit of coffee out of the mug. I didn't care. "I'm done here. I'm so done. You people are unbelievable." I turned quickly and stumbled a bit. Aster jumped up and tried to steady me.

"Be careful, Esther. You can't move that quickly."

I screamed. It was primal and deep. The scream was of frustration and anger and years of hurt that had been locked away inside my heart. "DON'T YOU THINK I AM WELL AWARE OF WHAT I CAN AND CANNOT DO?"

She looked at me, her eyes wide. She looked to be on the verge of tears. Oh, no. She was not going to be the victim here. I lowered my voice to a cold, measured tone. "And don't ever forget that this is all your fault. Your choices, your decisions. You—you did this to me. Whatever you do for the rest of your life, I want you for once to own what you have done."

CHAPTER FORTY-ONE

I thought I would feel better. There was part of me that did. There was another part of me that was distraught to know that I had made my sister feel so bad. I had made her cry. I had said what I needed to say. I had let her know that she ruined my life. That I expected her to take responsibility for her actions. Not just the ones at the club which led to my injury, but the ones over seven years ago as well.

Aster was silent for a long time. Sitting there, tears running down her face, not moving. The clock chimed twice, and I figured I needed to get out of there before her son came home. That was a complication that I could not deal with. I knew if I met him, I would want to get to know him, and that would muddy the waters even further.

There was part of me that should have been happy, overjoyed, ecstatic that Aster was alive. I knew that was what my parents were feeling. They weren't mad at her in the least. I didn't know if I was too smart or too bitter to be able to feel that way. Finally, after watching her cry but not getting any response, I turned and went to grab my coat.

Without rising from the kitchen table, I heard her call out to me. "Esther, please don't go yet."

I faltered in my step, my arm falling back to my side without yet retrieving my coat. My bravado drained from me as if the sink plug had been pulled. Being angry was exhausting and I didn't have much fuel left. I didn't turn to look at her, but I didn't move further either.

"Esther, I know this is all my fault. Of course I know it. All of it. And it's killing me inside. Yes, I'm mad at you for believing I was dead. But not for the reason you think. I'm mad because you saw me, the real me. No one else saw it. You saw how messed up, how sick I was. I'm mad that you saw that I was weak enough to take my own life. You never questioned it. You knew it was plausible because you saw the real *me.* And I hated that you saw what I really was. You were the only one who called a spade a spade. There was part of me that wanted to believe that I was not as bad as I really was. But since you saw right through me, I was forced to admit it. And that's what made me mad. Why couldn't you fall for the act like everyone else?"

It made sense, in some sort of convoluted way. That was the thing—Aster and I had always understood each other on a deeper level than anyone else. And with her missing for the last seven, almost eight, years, I was alone without anyone who 'got' me the same way. I turned to look at her, as she was now standing behind me. She had been alone in the same way all this time. Why didn't she contact me? If she didn't want the family to know, I wouldn't have told them. I asked her as much.

"I don't know, Es. I was so sick for so long. It took years of therapy to even root through what thoughts were delusions versus reality. Sometimes, I'm still not sure what is what. I was angry with you for knowing how sick I was, but I missed you even more than that. I found you and then started relocating when you relocated, just so I could feel a little closer to you."

"Did you follow me around in my day-to-day life?"

She shook her head. "No, I would usually try to find a place to live close to yours so we would have the same neighborhood. Every so often, when I was very sad or lonely, I would drive by your place, hoping to see you. Once you bought car wash tickets outside the market from Willy. I had to duck down and tie my shoe so you wouldn't see me."

"That was in Florida." I paused. "How long have you been following me?"

"I caught up with you in Boston. You were a bit hard to find because of the name change. Thank God you hyphenated, or I never would have found you."

Great. Another thing to thank Cheryl for. If I had just taken Dickie Cox's name, none of this would have happened.

"Yeah, Cheryl made me hyphenate."

Aster started giggling. "Seriously, Dickie Cox? Who would do that to their kid? And have you ever noticed that Comely-Cox sounds just like—"

"—an internet porn spam name." I finished her sentence, like no time had passed. She smiled at me, love in her eyes. But I could not return it. "Aster, I don't know if I can do this right now. So much has happened."

Her smiled disappeared instantaneously and tears threatened her eyes again. "I guess I understand."

"There is a lot for me to take in and process here. I need some time."

"Okay, I can give you that. I have to go pick Willy up from school anyway."

"How old is he?"

"He's six. And no, I'm not sure who the father is. I have a pretty good idea, but not for certain. Getting pregnant with him was the best and worst thing that ever happened to me. I had to go off my meds, which I was not totally committed to in the first place. I was living in a halfway house and I relied on them totally for support while I was off my meds. My compulsion while I was off meds was to write over and over that I had a child I needed to be responsible for. By the time Willy was born, I had several hundred notebooks filled with such messages. As soon as I could, I got back on my meds and have never gone off since. I know I can never go off of them. I'm pretty functional when I'm on them. It's the best I can hope for. And I need to do it, for Willy."

"Willy?"

She smiled sheepishly. "I had to."

I shook my head at her. "Please at least tell me his middle name is not Wonka?"

She laughed. "No, I may be crazy, but I'm not that messed up."

"Well, that's good to know at least." I pulled my coat down and put it on. I was suddenly exhausted and wasn't sure I had the strength to get home. Kingston was working, so I didn't think he would be able to come and pick me up. If I could just get to the bus stop, I would be able to rest there.

"Es?"

I sighed, turning around again. My body felt like it was moving through quicksand.

Quietly, Aster said, "I'm sorry. For everything. I know things can never be the way they were, but I want to be part of your life again."

"I just don't know. I need time."

"How much time?" There was so much hope in her voice. It was killing me. I turned back toward the door, unable to look at her. Despite the fact that she had lost her sparkle, her personality still had that magnetism that could draw you right in. I knew if I looked at her for too long, I would forgive her and move on. I wasn't sure that I wanted to do that. "I can't say right now."

And with that, I left. I held my head high as I walked down the street and turned the corner. A few blocks down, I saw a small sandwich shop and went in. I collapsed into the nearest chair and put my head down on the table. I was so tired that I couldn't even keep my eyes open. Fatigue engulfed my whole body, and I slipped into darkness.

******

"Hey!"

A strange voice was invading my darkness. I didn't recognize it, and it was interrupting my peace. I chose to ignore it and let the darkness close in again.

"Hey! HEY!"

Dammit, there it was again. Whoever it was, he was determined not to let me sleep. I lifted my head and looked around. Oh, shit, I'd fallen asleep, like DEAD asleep in the sandwich shop. My hand was wet with drool and I wiped my mouth. "Oh, I'm so ..." crap, what was that word I needed to use? "Sorry. I'm sorry. I'm just so tired."

The hulking man stood there glaring at me. "Yeah? This ain't no hotel."

Okay, total aside here, but I have such a problem with people who use the word "ain't." Not to mention ain't combined with no to make it a double negative. He was basically telling me it was a hotel. Oh, shit, I need to focus on *what* he was saying, rather than *how* he was saying it. "Right, sir, I know. I'm sorry."

"Well, whatta you waiting for? You leavin' or do I've got to throw you out?"

I stood up, still weak and tired. It probably didn't help that I hadn't eaten in ages. My stomach grumbled. Loudly. The hulk looked at me and scowled even more, although I would not have thought his face could get any meaner. "Get out of here you bum!"

I moved as quickly as I could to the door and out into the brisk November air. The temperature had dropped precipitously and I was instantly chilled to the bone. I looked right and left and tried to decide where to go. Luckily, I was in a business district, and there was a pizza place a few doors down. I was immediately engulfed by the scent of garlic and baking cheese, and my stomach grumbled again. I ordered a two-slice-and-soda combo and virtually inhaled them as soon as they arrived. This inhalation, of course, resulted in a burned roof of my mouth, but I didn't care. I was actually surprised that I was able to eat both slices, as well as drink a twenty-ounce Dr. Pepper. My appetite had been so poor since the accident. I had lost a tremendous amount of weight, and now looked pretty anorexic. Combine that with skin that had gotten even pastier and the red geri-curls that were now growing in and I was mighty fine looking these days. No wonder that guy in the shop yelled at me. He probably thought I was some tweaked-out, homeless-druggie bum. I almost couldn't blame him for yelling at me to get out of his shop. Of course, I did have that *Pretty Woman* fantasy of being able to go back in some day and tell him what a big mistake it was for him to judge me so harshly and wrongly. I needed to make that possible. And, in order to do that, I needed to change something. I needed to let go of all the negativity. Right there in that moment, I knew I had to make myself be positive again.

My belly full, caffeine coursing through my veins, and my feathers in a ruff at being misjudged, I stood up quickly, determined to go back to Aster's. My life was a disaster, no doubt about it. I mean, that asshole in the sandwich shop was not far off. I was pretty much homeless, jobless, and was now relying on disability and welfare food stamps to make ends meet. Aw, hell, who was I kidding. Even with all that, I wouldn't be making ends meet if it weren't for Kingston. I needed some positive karma and quick. I knew deep down that this wasn't all Aster's fault. I mean, part of it was an accident. She didn't intend for me to end up with a head injury, right? I was going to tell Aster that I forgave her and just move on with my life. I could forgive her, but that did not mean that I had to let her back in. I would tell her that I needed more time, but that I was no longer going to be resentful at how my life was going these days. I could do this. I could be positive and move on. And then good things would finally come my way.

I made it back to Aster's in about half the time it had taken me to get to the sandwich shop. I was running on adrenaline. See, positivity was already working. I prepared myself to tell Aster what I had to say and then turn over a new leaf. I practically skipped up Aster's front path and rang the doorbell.

What I was *not* prepared for was for Cheryl to open the door.

CHAPTER FORTY-TWO

In my head, I had some witty zinger that did not betray my shock at seeing my mother in my sister's house. But, true to life, I just stood there with my mouth agape. My speechlessness for once had nothing to do with my aphasia.

I looked at my mother. She looked terrible. She looked much older than her sixty-five years. Her hair was a dull, non-descript color, somewhere between platinum blond and gray, and hung down, limp and stringy. Her face was weathered and leathered, having spent too much time out in the sun. Years of drug use were showing, as she looked gaunt and puffy at the same time.

Apparently, Cheryl had a touch of aphasia as well, because she stood there staring at me. Awesome. I wanted to turn and run. That's what I did with my family. I knew I could not win with them, so I ran away. Apparently, I had driven all the way up to Minnesota to see Dean and then never even went in his hospital room. Despite the fact that I had returned to Aster's to bury the hatchet with her, the past decade, no past three decades, of hurt came flooding over me.

She broke the silence contest and spoke first. "What do you want?"

"I'm here to see Aster." My hands were clenched at my sides. I hoped my voice did not betray the tension that my body felt.

"She's busy right now." Cheryl paused, looking me up and down. I felt like something the cat had dragged in. "You look like you're recovered."

225

"No, I'm recovering. They expect it to take a few more months, and there may be some residual deficits."

"Well, you look fine to me. Certainly better than when we were there and you had half of your head missing."

Her words cut, as they were meant to. Cheryl had always been flaky and out there, but when had she turned mean? Apparently, her ugliness wasn't just skin deep.

"I'm coming in. I need to sit down." I tried to push past her. She planted her feet and held her ground. "I don't think that is a good idea. Aster is still very fragile, and we don't want you riling things up, like you always do."

Then I knew, in that moment, that I would never be part of my family again. I didn't think it was that unusual to have tiffs and rifts, but this was an impassable schism. There was nothing that could repair that bridge.

"Fine. Can you at least give Aster a message for me?"

"I guess."

"Tell her that I forgive her." And with that, I turned away and started walking away for the last time.

"*You* forgive *her*? Well, you're really a piece of work, aren't you?" The acidity dripping in her voice made me pause and listen. One last barrage and then I would be forever done. "I cannot believe you think that Aster has done anything that you should be forgiving her for. If anything, you should be begging and groveling for her to forgive you."

I had to take the bait. I couldn't resist. Without even turning around I snapped, "What am *I* supposed to be asking for forgiveness for?"

She laughed bitterly. "That's so Esther. Going through life without a care in the world. Never thinking about anyone besides yourself."

What?!?

"What, you don't have a snappy comeback? What happened to that smart mouth of yours?"

The anger and, in that moment, the hatred poured out of me. I spun around and shouted, "I have a brain injury, in case you hadn't noticed."

Again, the vitriol flowed from Cheryl. "And what are we supposed to do, pity you? You brought this all on yourself."

To repeat myself, what?

"How *exactly* did I manage to bring this condition on myself?"

"You've done nothing but exude negativity for so long that it was bound to come crashing back on you. When you saw Aster again, her positive energy pushed all your negativity back onto you, and this is what you get."

Okay, that didn't even make sense. She certainly was grasping, wasn't she? It was pretty obvious that she hated me, but I didn't even know what I could have possibly done to deserve her treatment.

Quietly, making her strain to hear me I asked, "What did I ever do?"

"What do you mean?"

"What could I have possibly done to deserve your hate? Wasn't I a good enough child? I always did what I was supposed to. I watched out for Aster. You had to have known how much I took care of her. All those nights sitting up with her. Going to get her when she got herself into trouble. I worked hard in school. I did all my chores. I never asked anything from you, but you've never even loved me, have you?"

"You know how I feel about the numbers."

What?

"What are you talking about?"

"I need even numbers." She was always weird about things like that. I never really considered it, but she probably had some obsessive-compulsive disorder going on. Growing up, she always had to put things in pairs. Nothing could be asymmetrical in number, or Cheryl wasn't happy. "And you, you were odd."

Of course. There it was. She was blaming me for being born.

"I didn't ask to be born. That was all you and Dean."

"I just can't figure out why the universe would do that to me. It—you—were the ultimate punishment. Always making us odd. And then, you always stuck out even more. That hair that defied rule and order. You always were too perfect, making Aster look bad. You were the smart one and that made Aster feel badly about herself. And then you even made Aster sick, claiming that she was unstable. Of course, she was going to believe it. You drove her away and then you moved away, which kept her from us for even longer. If she hadn't been traipsing all over the country after you, she would have come home sooner."

How does one even respond to this? As we often said at work, there is no rationalizing with the irrational. And just when I thought it couldn't get any worse, Dean appeared behind Cheryl. His gray hair, even finer than before, was still in its trademark ponytail. He looked thin and old. His heart attack and surgery left him looking as frail as I felt. He looked at me and then at Cheryl. "What does *she* want?"

Christ, I was like she-who-cannot-be-named. "You know, Dean, I have a name and I am your daughter."

He looked at me blankly. "No, you are not. I told you that many years ago. Nothing has changed."

"What do you mean nothing has changed? You have your precious Aster back. I thought that would finally make you happy."

"Aster is back, but she is not the same. She is angry with us."

"And that's my fault because?"

Cheryl looked at Dean. "I told her that the universe is punishing her for her negativity towards Aster all these years."

I had enough. Once they started talking to each other it was like I didn't exist. And it hit me. I didn't exist to them. I had ceased to exist when Aster disappeared. I was fed up, so I let them know it.

"Well, MOM and DAD, I guess the universe got even with you as well by giving you me. Perhaps I am your punishment for all of your sins and transgressions. But don't worry, I'm done. You won't ever have to worry about me darkening your doorstep again."

I turned around, willing myself to walk away from her slowly. Dr. Olsson, I mean Rob, was standing there, having witnessed my verbal dressing down by the person who was supposed to love me most. Perfect. Just perfect.

But instead of hating me for being born like my own mother did, he closed the distance between us and took me in his arms. My adrenaline was rapidly draining from my body and I felt like I could barely stand. Again.

"C'mon, Esther. Let me get you home."

I nodded and willed the tears not to start, but they did anyway. Rob deposited me in the front seat of his BMW and ran up the front walk to the house. I saw him talk to Aster, who was now standing in the doorway where Cheryl had been. He gave her a quick but tender kiss on the lips and my heart wrenched in my chest. I didn't want to see her loved and happy. She didn't deserve it. She deserved to be alone like I was.

My whole life, I had been passed over for Aster. It never really bothered me because I was just as infatuated with her as everyone else. Rob was certainly not the first guy I had been interested in to choose Aster over me. It bothered me nonetheless. I mean, I didn't want Rob. Not really. I knew that. Rather, I didn't want yet another person picking Aster over me. That was what it was about. I had Kingston who loved me and cared for me. But he was separate from all of this. Rob was in the middle now, and it seemed that he was choosing Aster and my parents. No one ever chose me. Why was I never good enough? I guess because, when push came to shove, I was never wanted. By anyone. Now it at least made sense why nothing I ever did was good enough for my parents and why it was so easy for them to let me go. I could never figure out how they could not let go of

Aster, but could let me go incommunicado and never attempt to get me back.

I was not wanted. I was never wanted. I was blamed for stealing Aster's place in the sun and the easy scapegoat for Aster's illness. I guess I had always felt this way, but there was something earth shattering about finally hearing it confirmed.

Rob opened the car door and quickly got back in. I was going numb, from the inside out. "Esther, are you all right?"

I shook my head a little. How could I possibly be all right?

"Esther, look at me."

I turned my head only, the rest of my body limp against the black leather seats.

"Esther, you ..." he faltered. I shook my head and turned it to stare out the window. Now, granted I didn't actually remember our date, but it was no wonder that he never called me. My own mother didn't want me. My father didn't want me. Why would anyone else?

"Oh no, Esther, you've got it all wrong."

Shit, was I speaking my thoughts again? Dammit, I really had to get a handle on that.

"Okay, then tell me why—how—you ended up with Aster instead of me?"

He sucked in a deep breath and let it out slowly. "Okay, but it is going to be bad."

Sarcastically, I said, "And just when I didn't think I could feel any lower. Thanks for kicking me when I'm down."

"No, no, no. I didn't mean it like that! I meant, this is going to make me look bad. Okay, here goes. I know you have some memory gaps, but do you remember anything about our date or how it came about?"

Turning a bit pink, which is a disastrous color on me because of the hair, I sheepishly admitted, "Um, no, not really. I remember working with you on the Children's Services case, but that is about it."

"Okay, then you don't remember Melissa ."

"Nope, who's Melissa?"

"Lucky you to be able to forget her. Melissa is my ex-fiancée. She's also a doctor at the hospital, and the night that we met up again, she had been working with O.K. on a grand rounds presentation, which is how you ended up stranded in the first place."

I was totally clueless about this, and made him tell me the story. "So, I was still basically trying to piss Melissa off by screwing every attractive girl that I met, and I was trying to do that with you."

"Gee, thanks, I think."

"I was pretty confident that you were a sure thing when we went out. And you were so hot up there singing. I couldn't wait, but then you kind of got all weird. Even back at your apartment, you were still off. I knew you were into it before, but then I felt like I would have been taking advantage of you, so I stopped."

"So, it wasn't me?"

"Well, you were definitely shaken up, and I thought it was about the singing thing. Now it all makes sense. I felt guilty about taking advantage of you while you were obviously—"

"—going crazy?"

"No, you, well—something seemed off."

"So that was it then? You didn't think I was worth going back for since I didn't put out the first time around?"

He was quiet for a minute. "No, Aster asked me out right after that. I said yes, and that was it. We've been together ever since."

"Did she put out for you on the first date?"

"I don't really think that's any of your business, but I will tell you this. I really liked you. I did. I thought you were cool and funny and smart and pretty. And so incredibly sexy when you sang. I was attracted to Aster as well, and it wasn't until I found out that you are sisters that it made sense. In some ways you two are alike and those are the qualities that I liked in both of you."

"But still you chose her over me, just like everyone does." I couldn't help pouting, but I think this situation totally justified it. Again, I knew it wasn't really about Rob. He was more a symbol of what our family had done—picking Aster over me. Rob didn't say anything in response. We were pulling up in Kingston's driveway. I wanted to get out of this car and run away and hide forever. In this moment, I could not ever picture feeling good about myself again.

As I fumbled to unbuckle the seatbelt, Rob put his hand on mine. It was warm and made me feel a bit tingly inside. Figures. He's off limits to me. "Esther, I liked you. I do like you. By the time I went out with Aster once or twice, O.K. had asked you out and basically told me to stay away from you. So I did. Things just happened that way. It wasn't because I didn't like you or find you attractive. Because I did. You're a super cool girl. Don't forget that."

"Thanks, I guess." I mumbled. Rob was not only easy on the eyes but a pretty good guy, too. It was a shame that he had to be dating my sister. I hoped she didn't hurt him like she hurt me.

CHAPTER FORTY-THREE

"I cannot believe you did this!" Kingston was furious and fuming. He was always so laid back and easy going that I honestly could not believe he was capable of getting this worked up.

"Calm down, jeez."

"Calm down? CALM DOWN? You want me to calm down? Do you even know what you put me through this afternoon?"

"I doubt your day could have been any worse than mine. And I don't have to sit here and take this shit."

"Esther, I thought you were missing. I was getting ready to file a missing person report on you."

"Kingston, I was only gone a few hours. Simmer down."

Oh, boy that did it. He had been angrily stacking and restacking magazines on the glass-top coffee table. Now he jumped up and was pacing back and forth. He was waving his hands as he spoke. If the day hadn't been such a colossal disaster, his performance would have been a bit comical. He sort of looked like a chicken being electrocuted. And the more he flapped and flailed, the more I found it funny. There he is, totally losing his shit at me, and I couldn't hold it in any longer—I burst out laughing. I knew it was inappropriate, but the more I tried to stop, the more I couldn't. This whole thing—him acting out, me, my family, my supposedly dead sister, it was all utterly ridiculous.

Finally, I looked through the tears that my laughter had produced to see Kingston just staring at me. He was so not amused. That sobered me up quickly.

"Esther, this is serious."

I nodded, wiping the tears off my cheeks. "I know it is."

"No, I don't think you do." His tone was condescending and it immediately got under my skin.

"Yes, Kingston, I am acutely aware of how serious this situation is." I couldn't keep the smirk off my face when I said it. There was that smart-alecky mouth that Cheryl so hated.

His rage continued to build. Wow, he was really angry with me. "Really?" he shouted.

I stood up and stepped close to him, so I was only about three inches from him. "Really. Because I feel that I am very aware that I am brain damaged with possibly no hope of any further recovery. I cannot do my job and as such I'm living on public assistance, living with a boyfriend that I don't remember. I am aware of how tired I am all the time. So tired in fact that I fell asleep in a sandwich shop today until I was thrown out after being mistaken for a drug-addicted, homeless bum. Which, I appear to be, even though I'm not. But this was *after* I confronted my sister, but *before* I was confronted by my mother who basically said that she hated the fact that I had ever been born and as such, deserved all that had happened to me. And then my father came out and reiterated that I was dead to him. And all of this was witnessed by my sister's boyfriend, who I had actually dated first, but he passed me over because I freaked out on our date because I thought I saw my dead sister who wasn't really dead, but was just pretending to be, just to apparently fuck me over some more. Which she did, which brings me full circle to the brain injury thing. So yes, Kingston, I am very aware that I cannot even go anywhere by myself without help. I am aware that I have lost absolutely everything in my life, including my family, who never wanted me from the moment I entered this earth. So, to answer you, yes, I know how serious this is."

We stood there, virtually nose to nose, staring each other down. My chest has heaving up and down from the tirade. The moment stretched out, but dammit, I would not be the first to turn away. And then before I knew it, Kingston's hands were on my cheeks and his mouth was crashing down on mine. It was intense and frenetic and so powerful. My arms circled around his back as our bodies pressed together. Oh my God, I literally felt weak in the knees. I tightened my grasp on him to hold myself up, pushing my breasts against his chest. My mind may not have known Kingston, but my body certainly did. Oh God, I needed this. I needed him. A soft moan escaped my mouth. That was all the encouragement he needed. His mouth traveled down to my chin and then my neck as his hands found the hem of my shirt. He made quick work of taking it off and then I eagerly tugged at his sweater. In that moment, my body was humming with anticipation, and I hoped it was going to be good. His hands trailed down my sides, easily encircling my thinned frame. His hands could now span my back. Feeling his hands there, all I could think of was how all of my vertebrae were now sticking out. Dread washed over me like a cold shower. How could he like feeling that?

And with that, I lost it. My hands had been on his firm chest, and I used them to push him back. "Stop, no."

His molten chocolate eyes showed his confusion. "Stop, no, what?"

I was out of breath from all that kissing. Panting, I gestured with a circular motion between our two bodies. "This."

Kingston tried to close the gap between us, but I took a step backward and held my arm out to maintain some space. "Esther, what's wrong? Don't you want this?"

I bent down and grabbed my shirt. "No," I said as I fumbled with the cloth, trying but failing to right it. I clutched the useless fabric, trying to cover my breasts. "I don't ... I can't ..."

"You can't what?" he closed the distance between us and engulfed me in his arms, pinning my arms to my chest and in between us. He bent in to kiss me again and I turned my head. "Kingston, please don't."

He released me and stepped back. "Esther, why not?"

I shook my head. "I can't be your pity fuck. I know I've sunk pretty low, but I can't sink that low. I need to hold onto that tiny scrap of dignity."

He angrily bent down and in a swift movement, put his shirt back on. "How can you honestly even think that, let alone say that out loud to me?"

I had finally managed to get my shirt back on, and I sank wearily down on the couch. All of the adrenaline rushes today were really taking it out of me. Without being able to control it, my eyes started leaking. Dammit, I did not want to cry in front of Kingston.

"Esther, I asked you a question. Answer me!" Shit he was now madder than before the whole almost-sex thing.

I swallowed, wishing I had some water. But the kitchen seemed too far away to get up and get a drink.

Quietly, I finally started. "Kingston, how can you want me? How can you want this?" I asked as I gestured up and down my body. "I'm a bag of bones right now. I look like I'm wearing a Bozo the Clown Afro wig. I bring all the appealing things that come with brain damage. I'm pretty much penniless. I have utterly no redeeming value. My own mother doesn't want or love me. How can you?"

Wearily, he sank down next to me on the couch. I played with the hunter green fabric while I waited for his answer, partially wishing the couch would swallow me whole.

"Esther, I know how you can think all those things. I get it. But it's not real."

"What do you mean, it's not real?"

"None of those things are *who* you are, Esther. Yes, you've been ill and are recovering. I don't think you understand what I've been through since the night of the accident. I watched you go down. I watched your head bounce off that curb and I couldn't get to you in time. I thought over and over that I was going to lose you. I had just found you, and I was going to lose you. I've been looking for you my whole life, and then you woke up and didn't know who I was. I tried to stay away but I couldn't. I don't care if I have to take care of you every single day for the rest of your life. I just need to be with you. I almost lost you once and I will not do it again."

After letting his words sink in I said, "That's why you got so upset today."

He swallowed hard. "I went to pick you up at therapy and they said you had cancelled all your sessions today. I had no idea where you were or if anything had happened to you."

"I forgot you were supposed to pick me up." Stupid attention deficit disorder. I was still staring straight ahead, but I could feel him looking at me. Slowly, I turned to look at him. He looked as tired as I felt. "I didn't mean to worry you. I'm sorry. I'm not used to anyone looking after me or missing me when I'm gone."

"I can't go through losing you again."

His chocolate eyes were melting my heart. God, what had I done to deserve this man? "Why?"

"What do you mean?"

"Kingston, why do you want me? Why can't you lose me again?" I was not trying to be dense. I was trying to process what he was saying.

He grabbed my hands and held them tightly. "Because I love you."

"You do?"

"Of course I do. I've told you that. I think I fell in love with you when I pulled you out of your car. I've been such a basket case without you. You bring purpose to my days. I know you don't know how you feel about me, and that is okay. I can wait. But you need to know that I love you. And that you are lovable and deserving of love. And there is no pity in any way shape or form."

That was all it took. This time, I lunged onto him, pushing him back on the couch and claiming his mouth with mine, as he had claimed my heart.

CHAPTER FORTY-FOUR

We were lying on the living room floor, partially covered in my blanket from the back of the couch. I had purchased it because it was so soft and plush. Now it felt sensual against my bare skin that was still on fire from Kingston's touch. I was resting my head on Kingston's chest, basking in the afterglow. He was lazily running his fingers up and down my bony spine. I hated that I was practically skeletal, but if it didn't bother him, then it shouldn't bother me.

"I'm glad we got that all straightened out," he said while kissing the top of my head.

"Yeah, once again, I'm sorry. Up until just now, the day was so colossally bad. I just can't even believe my parents were at Aster's. That was so unexpected, but then again so was all this."

"I agree that when I spent the afternoon looking for you, this was not exactly what I had in mind. But on the other hand, it has been a bit challenging having you here, not sleeping in my bed and not being able to make love to you."

"I didn't know you wanted to. I mean, I guess I figured that we had done ... it ... before, but I didn't see any way that you could still possibly want me."

"Esther, why wouldn't I want you? You're beautiful and funny. You are without a doubt the strongest woman, no, person, I know. You are caring and compassionate. You are sexy and smart and resilient."

"I am none of those things. Just ask my mother."

"You're every single one of those things and more."

I was silent. I propped myself up on my elbow and looked at him. "How can a person's own mother not love them. I mean, I always knew that she loved Aster more, but it was okay because everyone loved Aster more. I always thought she loved me, at least a little. I honestly had no idea that she hated me that much. I don't know where it came from. It's new for her. Of course, I haven't talked to her in several years."

Kingston was silent. I mean, even when you're in the midst of post-coital bliss, it's hard to find words for that one.

"Know what's funny? The whole time she was going off on me, all I could think was, 'Man, she looks terrible.' I mean, she does. And she was ranting and raving like a crazy person. About how my negative energy was repelled back on me by Aster's positive energy and that is what caused my head injury. Crazy. Just crazy."

"Yes, she probably is. Didn't you say she has done a lot of drugs?"

"Yeah, she has. I don't think she ever stopped smoking weed, but I think she's off the hard stuff."

"What kind of hard stuff?"

"Oh, I think she did a fair amount of acid and quaaludes back in the day."

"That would explain it."

"Explain what?"

"Long-term cannabis use can definitely cause brain damage. LSD not so much, unless she's schizophrenic, and then it can exacerbate the symptoms tremendously."

"You think she might be schizophrenic?"

"Who knows at this point, because long-term marijuana use can cause brain changes that mimic schizophrenia. Either way, she's not right in the head."

"You say that with a high degree of certainty."

"I met her, Esther. When you were in the hospital."

"Oh, that's right. They were still there when I was in rehab too, right? You were fighting with them? Did we talk about this before? Sorry if I'm repeating myself."

"Yeah, we did talk about it. It was that day I ran into you."

"So, you weren't overly impressed with them then, huh?"

"Not so much. Charlie really stood up for you and fought to keep Cheryl and Dean from getting power of attorney."

A shiver ran through me. Kingston pulled the blanket up to cover more of me. "That would have been terrible."

"Yes it would have." His voice was grave.

"You know, I've called Charlie, but she hasn't called me back."

"I can't justify her actions, but I do know it was very hard on her taking your side. She took it because it was the right thing to do, but Cheryl and Dean were vicious in their treatment of her as a result."

"I don't think she's going to stand up to them."

"Probably not."

"So I might never actually talk to her again." Saying it aloud made it real and was a bit shocking to me.

"Esther, I think you need to think that way. She crumbled when they started attacking her. I don't think she can stand up to them. She's not strong enough. Not like you."

"Wow, they really don't want me to have any family, do they?"

"You have me, and my family. You have Jillian. We'll take care of you."

"I don't want to be taken care of." I stuck my lip out, perhaps a little bit.

"I know you don't, and you may not believe this, but you are truly very lucky. This could have been so much worse. You could have died or been so much more incapacitated."

"I could have been a vegetable."

"Yes, you could have."

"But I'm not. I mean, sometimes I can't find words or the wrong ones come out. Sometimes, I don't even realize I'm speaking my thoughts. I'm very distracted, which kills me because I used to be very organized and able to focus. Okay, well not very organized, but somewhat at least. And now I'm always so tired."

"Well, we've got to fatten you up." He started to get up. I rolled over and let him up. "Why don't you go take a shower while I make you something to eat?"

"You can cook?"

"I can make eggs, so that's what we're going to have."

I laughed. Surprisingly, breakfast for dinner sounded great. My stomach growled in anticipation. "Sounds great." I got to my feet, slowly, because that's how I did everything these days. "I'll be back in a few."

The shower made me feel slightly better, but I was still exhausted. I put on my favorite pink penguin pajamas, ran my fingers through my short damp curls and went back downstairs. I have to say, the shorter hair was definitely easier to take care of, and I never had to worry what it looked like, since it was always equally bad. When my hair was longer, I never knew on any given day what the curl was going to do and just had to go with it. I promised myself that when my hair grew in, I would never, ever curse it again. I would love every single wild and unruly strand.

"Smells good in here."

Kingston stopped and froze, spatula mid-air. A wide smile broke out on his face.

"What's so amusing?"

"Your pajamas."

I looked down. I knew they were childish, but I loved them.

"It's a good thing we already, um, did what we did."

I crinkled my brow. I had no idea where he was going with this. "Me too, but why, and what on earth do my pajamas have to do with that?"

His smile turned sad. "You don't remember, of course. When we were on our way home from Minnesota, in the hotel in Madison, was when we first, um ..."

"Had sex?"

"I was going to say made love, but it sounded corny, even in my own head. So yeah, you were wearing those pajamas, but not for long."

"This is so weird, hearing about things that we did, but that I don't remember. It is very disconcerting, frankly." I paused. I guess there was no other way to say it. "Was it good?"

He walked over and kissed me. "Yes, Esther, it was always good and it will always be good. Tonight was just the beginning."

"I think my eggs are burning."

A brief look of discomfort crossed his face. Dammit. A girl should never mention eggs right after having sex. "I meant my eggs, as in dinner, are burning."

He laughed, a deep throaty laugh and darted back to the stove. With a flash and a flourish, he deposited my omelet on a paper plate and slid it onto the island towards me. I corralled the plate and smiled. "You know, I still owe you a set of dishes. Tell me what you want and I'll get your replacements."

"You don't have to do that. We can get yours out of storage."

"Oh, that's right. I have some too." I wrinkled my brow in thought. "Why, then, have we been eating off paper plates for two weeks?"

He walked around and sat down next to me. "Because there are more important things than our plates." He reached over and tapped my nose. "Like your well being."

I had just shoveled another forkful of the light and fluffy omelet into my mouth. Without any couth or manners, I spoke, "I think things are starting to look up." And then I winked at him.

Kingston smiled at me. "This is the most relaxed I've seen you since the accident."

"A good orgasm will do that to a girl."

Kingston choked on the drink of milk that he had just taken. I don't think I had ever seen a grown man drink milk before. With his bed head and the big glass of milk, he looked like a little kid. And totally adorable. I started laughing at him spluttering and coughing, knowing that he wasn't really choking.

"No, seriously, I think confronting everyone today really helped. And now I can move on. I'm still not sure if Aster will be in my life. I know she is the one person in my family who actually wants me, but I just don't know if I can do it. I now know that I have nothing to do with the rest of my family, but I'm okay with that. Well, except Charlie, but I'll deal with it."

"Are you really okay?"

I considered for a moment while I took another bite and chewed. "You know, I think I am. I still have a lot of work to do to get back my life."

"Do you want your old life back?"

"Why wouldn't I?" I looked at him. "What are you saying? What was wrong with my life?"

"No, nothing, and I know you were very good at your job. But you worked so very hard and, well, frankly the pay sucks. And you know you were doing that to make amends to Aster, but you don't really need to do that anymore."

"No, I did the job to help families that were messed up, like I wish someone had been there to help my family. Today, more than ever, shows me that I'm in the right field. Maybe not the right job, but the right field."

"Okay, valid points."

I smiled at him. "I know you want to take care of me, and I appreciate that. It is difficult for me, because I am used to being the caregiver. So, bear with me when I'm a bear."

"Only if I can see you bare."

CHAPTER FORTY-FIVE

"So, you're sure you're up to this?" The concern was apparent in Albert's eyes.

"Yeah, I'm fine. I mean, I get tired still, but I think I'm up to it."

"The gig is New Year's Eve. That gives us three weeks to practice. But, we'd probably need to practice two to three times a week. Is that too much?"

"Albert, I'm going stir crazy here. I'm still not back to work, and most of my therapy is done. I sit around all day, just thinking. I need to get out of my own head. Rehearsing for a gig would be the perfect distraction."

"Cool, Red. Glad you're back." He gave me a firm pat on the shoulder. I threw my arms around him and hugged him tightly. After a moment, I released him.

"Al, I never said thank you."

"What for?"

"That day, when you came to visit me in rehab. The music—the singing. That is what unlocked my speech. I don't know how or why, but you gave me back my ability to speak. So, thank you."

He blushed. "Anything for you, Red."

"Am I making you uncomfortable?"

He laughed. "Yeah, I'm terrible at emotional crap. Ask Jules. That's why I sing—so I can get it all out that way."

"Sounds reasonable." I paused. "You ever think about writing your own songs?"

Albert looked down, and rubbed his chin. He seemed a million miles away. "Yeah, I've been working on some new material."

"I'd love to hear it someday." I said hopefully.

"When it's ready, I'll let you hear it."

"I'm holding you to it." I playfully hit him on the shoulder.

Pauly and Jugs banged into the room, a clichéd repurposed garage, ready for rehearsal. I tried to help them set up the equipment, but they all shooed me away, insisting I sit on the old worn flowered couch that had probably seen its best days around 1982.

Jules came in and barely glanced at me. I had tried to be friendly to her when I first arrived but got the distinct impression that she did not like me. This was something I couldn't deal with. There was too much other shit I was going through right now. "Hey, Jules, how's it going?"

She glanced at me and sort of grunted in my general direction. Okay, time to try another approach.

"Jules, can I speak to you inside the house for a minute?"

She rolled her eyes, but followed me into the house. The temperature was about fifteen degrees warmer in the kitchen. Drew had installed some portable heaters in the garage, but it was still December. I rubbed my hands together and tried to get them warm. I opened up a cabinet, found the glasses and poured myself some water from the tap. I drank it down, feeling parched at the thought of confronting Jules.

"What?"

Okay, so I guess we could skip all the pleasantries and formalities.

I swallowed the rest of the water and put the cup in the sink. I turned to face Jules, who was leaning on the counter at the opposite end of the kitchen. "I know you don't like me, but I don't know why. I don't know what I ever did to you. Did something happen that I don't remember? If so, I'm sorry."

She just looked at me. "You really don't see it, do you?"

"See what?"

245

"You and Albert."

"You know there is no 'me and Albert.' We are in a band together. We sing together. That is it. That is all."

"But I see how he is with you." Her fingernails flicked the laminated edges of the counter. Drumming impatiently, waiting for my reply.

"Jules, I know that the two of you are married. I respect that. Not to mention that I'm in a relationship myself."

She looked down at her shoes. "It's hard, you know? Watching the two of you together on stage."

"But on stage is all it is. Yes, we have an incredible connection when we're singing. And, I do feel very close to Albert. He's the one who really helped me get talking again." She looked at me blankly. Obviously she didn't know about his visit. "He came to see me in rehab. I couldn't really speak, and it was killing me. He brought his guitar and we sang a few songs together. Then, it was like someone flipped a switch and I could speak again, for the most part. And for that, I will be forever grateful. And forever bonded."

"That makes me even more nervous."

"Jules, I know you don't know me, but you have to know that I would never ever come between the two of you. I have the utmost respect for marriage. And I would not do anything to jeopardize my relationship with Kingston. He is all I have in this world."

"I guess."

"You guess what?"

"I guess what you're saying makes sense. It's just, I, uh, I see the two of you on stage together and I'm just so jealous. And after, he always wants to ... you know ... and I can't help but wonder if he's thinking about you, not me."

"I don't know. I can't say. I don't remember my one and only gig. I wish I did. I heard it was great."

"It pains me to say it, but it was."

"I don't know if this will make you feel any better or not, but I have no memory from about two months before my head injury. When Albert came to visit me, I only knew who he was because my friend Jillian had shown me the videos of our show. I didn't know his name and was referring to him in my head as Mr. Clean."

Jules laughed. "Oh, I would have paid to see his reaction when you called him that."

"I couldn't speak, which was a good thing. Now, since my speech has returned, I sometimes say my thoughts out loud. Gets pretty embarrassing."

"I can imagine."

"So, we good?"

She sighed. "I guess. At least now I know that you won't make a move on Albert. I guess you can't control his reaction toward you."

The door between the kitchen and the garage opened and Drew stuck his head in. "Are you ladies planning on joining us at some point this evening?"

As we returned to the garage and started practice, I felt finally that another part of my life was clicking into place. I knew Jules and I would never be besties, and I could be okay with that. I would have to ask Kingston at some point if he got a similar vibe from Albert and me. I couldn't help the chemistry we had on stage. I just knew I needed to be singing right now as part of my recovery. It gave me a purpose and inspiration. Singing empowered me. It was the one time when I felt confident and powerful. It was the only time that I felt like I fit in and belonged, since I never even felt that way with my own family. I needed this to reclaim my life.

Wiping the sweat from my brow, I finished the last note of the last song. There had been some rough songs and some stuff that definitely needed work, but we'd be ready for the New Year's Eve gig. We were trying to really mix up the set list, with a variety of music to reach the most people. Being New Year's, we added some slower stuff, in case people wanted to dance. Somehow, having the mike in my hand, my world felt balanced. And not saying that there was anything to Jules' concerns, but singing with Albert did make me feel sexy. If I wasn't so tired, I'd plan on jumping Kingston's bones as soon as we got home.

I texted Kingston that we were all done, and then helped the guys pack everything up. Twenty minutes later, I still hadn't heard from Kingston. Shit, how was I going to get home? It was after eleven, so I didn't feel right calling Jillian. Albert and Jules were the first to take off, and hell would have frozen over before I asked for a ride from them. Pauly and Jugs drifted off and Drew opened his sixth beer of the night. Shit. What was I going to do?

I was sitting on Drew's front step, freezing my tail off in the clear, cold December night. I should go back inside and call a taxi. I couldn't believe that Kingston let me down like this. He was always there, coming through for me when I needed him. I guess it shouldn't surprise me though. Everyone else in my life eventually let me down. I don't know why I was surprised that Kingston was following suit. The cold from the cement was seeping though my jeans and acted as a catalyst for my anger.

Lost in my own pity reverie, I didn't notice the black BMW pull up. "Hey! What are you doing sitting outside? Aren't you freezing?"

Seriously?

"You gonna sit there all night or get in the car?"

"Do I have a choice?" I said through gritted teeth.

I could see Rob smiling at me through the rolled-down window. Damn, he was hot when he smiled like that. Shit, I couldn't think about that. He was in love with my sister who I hated. Oh, yeah and I had a boyfriend. Speaking of which, where the hell is he? Why didn't he come to pick me up like we'd planned? Oh no, maybe he was sick of me. Maybe he was tired of me being so needy. I mean, I'd be sick of carting my brain-damaged ass around by now too. Maybe he was over me and was going to disappear from my life, just like Aster did.

"Esther, you look like you're doing advanced calculus in your head right now. You gonna get in or what?"

"I guess," I mumbled, making my way slowly off the concrete steps and towards Rob's car. The car was nice and toasty and the seat warmers had the soft leather a welcoming temperature on my tushy. I couldn't help but melt into the leather like butter. "Aaahhh. That feels so good. I think I'm in love with your seats and seat warmers a bit."

I heard Rob laughing. "Aster is the same way. I swear, I think if we ever break up, she's going to fight me for the car."

The mention of Aster's name had me instantly tensed up again. Even though Rob had bailed me out at least twice (although I think there was another time during the time that I couldn't remember), I couldn't let my guard down with him. After all, he was in love with Aster and therefore the enemy. I sat up stiffly and said, "Thank you for the ride. I was not expecting to see you."

"Yeah, O.K. called me, frantic. He got called into surgery. I guess his mom's best friend broke her hip or something, and he felt he had to do the surgery. He called me from the O.R. to see if I would come and get you. He didn't want you to think he'd abandoned you."

I am such a shit, because that is exactly what I thought.

"Well, thank you for coming to my rescue. Yet again." Why did my boyfriend's best friend have to be in love with my sister? Why couldn't he just be my boyfriend's best friend? Why did he have to be in love with Aster? It made the whole dynamic more intense.

"Esther, for you, anything, anytime." His smile was genuine, but I felt like there was more on his mind. More he wanted to say to me. I was not sure I wanted to hear it. I just wanted to go home and put my head under the covers and come out in about five years. But since that wasn't really an option, I guess I needed to find out what was on Rob's mind.

CHAPTER FORTY-SIX

"Rob, can I ask you something?"

"Sure, Es. Like I said, anything for you."

"What's on your mind?"

He stuttered and spluttered, trying to come up with something because I'd caught him off guard, and he didn't want to tell me what he was actually thinking about.

"Rob, I can tell you want to say something, which I assume has to do with Aster, so just spit it all out."

"How did you know?"

"Because I'm good like that. Now stop stalling and spit it out."

He smiled for a brief moment, and then the smiled faded as he started speaking. "She wants to be a part of your life."

"And I want my hair back the way it was and not to have a brain injury. Doesn't mean it's going to happen."

"Esther, listen, she's changed. She's not the irresponsible person she used to be. She really has gotten herself straightened out."

"Well, that's fantastic that she finally got her shit together."

"Esther—"

"No, Rob, don't 'Esther' me. You have no idea what I went through. First, taking care of her, and then mourning and grieving for her when I thought she was dead. Then comes the whole fucked-up-family thing where mine deserts me. And that is before you even get to the brain damage part."

"You're right. I can't possibly know. But she has changed. She wants her sister back."

"Even though I grew up in a family of seven children, I have no siblings and no parents. Can you even imagine what that's like for me?"

There was silence in the car and it hung, thick enough to cut.

"We went there—to Minnesota—for Thanksgiving." Rob said quietly.

Why in God's name would he tell me this? My mouth dropped open in shock. After a moment I recovered and slammed my jaw shut, clenching my teeth so tightly that I thought my teeth might break.

"It was terrible. The most terrible thing I've ever seen."

"Yeah, tell me about it," I muttered bitterly. "No, wait, don't. I had a very pleasant Thanksgiving with Kingston's family. They were nice and civil and didn't treat me like I had the plague. Mrs. C. actually appeared concerned about my health and well being, and sent the most delicious leftovers home with us." That was all true. It was the best Thanksgiving I'd ever had. I loved Kingston's family immediately. They were wacky and eclectic and perfect. Not perfect in the sense of making no mistakes, but full of love and humor and understanding. Just like a family should be.

"I wish I could have been anywhere but with your family."

"The sad thing was part of me missed my family. Not my parents exactly, but talking to Charlie and Veru. I usually at least call them on the holidays."

"Veruca and her family were there. Holy cow. Those kids are wild."

"I know, but Veruca has never even called me since my accident. Charlie flew all the way out here from New York, but I haven't heard from Veru since, gosh, I don't even know when."

"You were talking to her the night we went out."

"I was? Shit, that means I won't remember the last time I ever spoke to her." I paused. "Amnesia sucks."

"Yeah, it does."

I couldn't resist any longer. "So why was dinner so bad? Did Cheryl make the Tofurkey again?"

He shook his head. "No. I wish that was the problem. Aster and your parents got into it. In the middle of Thanksgiving dinner. We ended up walking out."

"Don't tell me they finally realized that their precious Aster is flawed and should be held accountable for her actions?"

He was silent for a minute. We had now reached Kingston's house and were sitting in his driveway. He turned the car off, but still stared straight ahead.

"No, actually it was the opposite. They made this big deal about how their family was complete now that Aster was home. Aster was furious. She called them out on it. On disowning you. On not blaming her. She said that the family was not complete without you."

"And what did they say?"

"Nothing. Cheryl started weeping, begging Aster not to leave. Dean was yelling that this was your fault and that you were no longer welcome."

"Typical. They hate me for being born."

"Aster said that she couldn't believe that they would treat you like this. Aster did say that you were the only one who saw her for who and what she was, and that you were the only one worth coming back for. She said if you weren't part of the family, then neither was she."

You could have knocked me over with a feather. When I was finally able to speak I said quietly, "Really?"

Rob seemed offended. "Yes, really, Esther. I don't know why you are always looking to think the worst of her."

I raised my eyebrow and gave him my best 'Whatcha talkin' 'bout, Willis?' look.

"Okay, okay," he raised his hands in mock defense. "I mean I know about the past, but why can't you believe that she's different? That Aster wants to be different. I wish you knew how hard she works. She takes care of herself. She takes care of Willy. She works at a shelter for women who are just like she was. All she wants to do is make it up to you. She is wracked with guilt over what happened to you. I mean, we were all there. It was sort of a freak accident."

"But I never would have passed out if it had not been for her showing up like that and sending me into shock."

"No, I know. And she knows. She was so scared you were going to die. She kept crying, saying that she had missed her chance with you. That she waited too long to get in touch with you."

"I know. Why did she wait so long?"

"See, Esther, that is something you could ask her."

I thought about it for a minute. Could I? Could I open myself back up and let her in? What about all the times she let me down before? What about her pretending to be dead for seven years? Well, the rational part of me knew that I really couldn't hold against her things she did when her illness was uncontrolled. And, given my reaction when she reappeared, I guess I could understand why she lived by me but never made her presence known.

"I know I gave you a lot to think about tonight, but, um, are you going to get out of the car?"

"Oh, yeah. Jeez, sorry Rob. I guess I just started thinking and forgot that I needed to get out of the car."
I unbuckled my seatbelt and opened the door, letting the brisk December air wake me up and clear my head.

Rob waited as I fumbled my way into the house before he pulled out of the driveway. The house was too quiet, and tired as I was, I doubted I would be able to sleep. I wanted to have a glass of wine, but I was still on lots of medication, so that was a no-no. I wished Kingston were here. He always made me feel better. I had no idea how long he would be in surgery. I couldn't hold it against him for caring about his mom's friend. It was his caring and compassion that I so loved about him. But still, without him, I felt like a caged tiger. I needed him to soothe me. Just being around him had that effect.

I paced around, wandering in and out of rooms before I ended up in the master bath. I decided to draw a bath in the large tub. Maybe that would relax me. While I waited for the water to fill, I went to the room where all my belongings were and pulled out a photo album. I carried it back to Kingston's bedroom and sat on the bed, flipping though the pictures. It was the album I had put together of Aster and me after she disappeared.

I flipped through page after page of Aster and me, smiling, posing awkwardly, laughing. There were the heinous school pictures, where my hair resembled Roseanne Roseannadanna. Even Aster went through a terribly awkward and ugly phase. Of course, the secondhand thrift shop clothes that Cheryl made us wear really didn't help. But we always looked happy together.

I put the album down and went into the bathroom. The bath was ready now, so I stripped down and let myself sink into the water. I put my head back on the cool porcelain and closed my eyes. Images from the album danced through my mind. Aster and I had been together since conception. When she disappeared, it was as if part of my soul had been torn away. It was a raw, open wound that would never heal, no matter how much time had passed. We were two parts of one being. When Aster started getting sick, I felt so helpless. I would have done anything for her. I did everything I could. When she left that note and left, I knew I had failed her. But I hoped she was at peace. She wasn't. She had years of torment still ahead.

I wondered if she felt just as helpless when I was in the hospital. She had, indeed, been in my hospital room. Kingston told me she was there for days initially, until my blood pressure became unstable and they thought I was going to stroke out.

But even that crisis didn't cause her to relapse. She held it together. So, it seemed now she was at peace. She had a stable job and her illness was controlled. She had a son and apparently took good care of him. And she had renounced our parents. Because of me. Because they didn't accept me. She loved me more than she loved them. She loved me. Period. And I loved her. Aster couldn't stay away from me, any more than I could stay away from her.

CHAPTER FORTY-SEVEN

I stepped on the stage and walked with confidence. The pants were painted-on leather. The shirt gold sequins. The hair, well, shit, it was still too short for my liking, but I no longer looked like a boy. I could do this. I could so do this. I was gonna send this year out rockin' and rollin' like a badass. Good bye and good riddance.

Three weeks ago, I could never have imagined the turn my life would take. After the heart-to-heart with Rob got me thinking, I decided that the only way my life would be complete was with Aster in it. When Kingston arrived home in the wee hours of the morning, tired but wired, I was still pruney from my extended bath. I told him about my decision, looking for his approval. Of course he granted it. He really was the perfect man for me. That is not to say he is perfect. Just perfect for me.

Anyway, I reunited with Aster a few days later amid copious amounts of tears and laughter. And laughter and tears. Within moments it was as if we had never been separated. As if her terrible disease had never torn us apart. I knew that my head injury was a freak accident and I apologized for blaming her for ruining my life. I forgave her for leaving me and she forgave me for being so mad at something she had no control over. I knew she was right. She was sick. And now she was better and so was I.

We had almost eight years to catch up on, plus I had a nephew to get to know. Seeing Aster with Willy was awe inspiring. She was so in her niche as a mother. I never, ever would have believed it and told her as much. Aster then reminded me about providing for me by giving me the better hair products. My response of, "Yeah, but you stole them!" dissolved us into another round of laughter that turned into tears and apologies. After about three boxes of tissues, and four pounds of chocolate, we emerged from the room where we had holed up, arms around each other and ready to take on the world. Apart, we had been two lost souls, adrift. Together, we were invincible.

Christmas was challenging for me, since I had little in the way of funds, and I wanted to be able to give back to those who had done so much for me over the past three months. Living with Kingston was a godsend, and I had sold my car, since there was no use in paying the insurance when I had no idea how long it would be before I could drive again. Of course, because I lived with a boyfriend who could technically kick me out at any time (not that he ever would), I was deemed, in the eyes of the government, homeless. Still, disability didn't go that far, and it was going to be expiring soon when I started back to work part time. I was collecting food stamps, so I decided to work the system a bit. Hell, I had seen people do it for years. I baked for my Christmas gifts and let the system pay for it. It felt lame. Especially since I had never been a good baker before. I felt even worse when Aster gave me the most kickass outfit to wear at our New Year's Eve gig. It was a gold sequined tank, black leather leggings (!!!) and the most awesome leopard print ankle boots. The colors worked perfectly for me, as she had known they would. I was starting to put some weight and muscle tone back on, so the leggings were just right. She shrugged off my embarrassment, telling me that my acceptance of her was more of a gift than anything purchased in a store.

Kingston gave me the most unusual bracelet. It was a hand-crafted bracelet in titanium and copper. It was one large cuff in copper, showing off beautiful oxidized colors, with a titanium band wrapped around it. Of course, I loved it immediately but even more so when Kingston told me that he purposely got me titanium to reflect that I was the strongest person he knew. It was a well-thought-out, symbolic gift. Not to mention that it looked great with the outfit from Aster. I will never figure out how I ended up with him. How in the midst of a run of terrible luck, I was so lucky.

Christmas Eve and Christmas Day were whirlwinds of activity. We went to Rob's house for Christmas Eve. His parents were visiting from North Dakota and they put on a huge traditional Swedish feast, which included all sorts of dried and cold fish, pickled pigs' feet (blech!), sausages, ham, red cabbage, potatoes, these delightful traditional ginger snap biscuits, and more types of pastries than one could imagine. Mr. and Mrs. Olsson were immediately enraptured with Aster and Willy, who seemed to possess his mother's charm and natural charisma. I already loved my nephew and for the first time ever, wished I had a child of my own.

Christmas Day was spent with Kingston's family. All nine billion of them. His parents were there, along with his siblings and their families. I loved that he considered his stepsiblings his siblings. They were his family and that was all that mattered to him. There were aunts and uncles and cousins and friends who were like family, including Mrs. Pascale, the woman who had broken her hip the night Rob picked me up. Rob, his parents, Aster and Willy were there too. It was loud and chaotic and crazy and perfect. There were arguments. There were spills. A platter was dropped on the floor and broken. The potatoes were a little undercooked and the roast was little overcooked. And you know what? Not a damn bit of it mattered. The house was filled with people who loved each other and wanted to be together. It was filled with family, even though not many of them were blood related.

At some point during the day, I finally realized that I was part of *that* family. Kingston's family. I did not need to grieve for the family that had abandoned me and that did not want me. I had a family right here. True, Kingston and I had not been together that long (and the first part of it I didn't even remember). That didn't seem to matter. Sitting on the floor in his parents' house, twirling my new bracelet around my wrist, I knew I loved him and he loved me. I couldn't see either of us wanting to go anywhere. It wasn't ideal that I had nowhere else to go, but it seemed somewhat fortuitous actually. I had found the love of my life, my twin sister had found me, and I was now part of a family that loved and accepted me for me.

So, now here it was, New Year's Eve. I would say goodbye to this year which had brought me to Columbus, introduced me to my boyfriend, showed me my sister was still alive, and left me a coma and brain-injury survivor. And I was gonna send the year out singing. Literally.

I wished I remembered if I had been this nervous the last time I took the stage. From what Albert said, we had rehearsed significantly more for this gig, so I should feel prepared. Right? Nope. I felt like I had to pee. Again and again. I had already gone twice (once before my earpiece was hooked up and once after), and felt the urge again as I took the stage in one of the ballrooms in the Hyatt Regency. We were playing in one of the rooms as part of the "The City is Yours Tonight" celebration. There were DJs and other bands playing. It was mass mobs of people and our room was packed. Holy shit, I've got to pee again.

I didn't have time to pee though, because Pauly and Jugs were starting to play. I took a deep breath, rolled my shoulders back and strutted onto the stage. "Are you ready to rock, Columbus?" I shouted and was met with a deafening roar. Damn. This was going to be good. I hope. "We are The Rusty Buckets and we're going to be rocking you into 2014!"

We had planned and prepped for this. We had rehearsed and rehearsed. We had revised our set list over and over, looking for the perfect balance for the diverse crowd that would hear us. We were in the party room, so we would be rocking. And rocking we were. Right from the first song, Albert and I were in synch and playing off each other. The crowd was electric and I felt it too. I easily found Rob in the audience—I guess being 6'4" has that advantage. With him were Aster and Kingston. I gave Kingston a little wink for which I was rewarded with one of his heart-melting, stunning white-tooth grins. It was almost enough to make me lose my place in the song.

I guess maybe Jules had not been that far off in her assessment of Albert post performance. Being on stage gave me a heady rush, made me feel powerful and was definitely a turn-on. Kingston was so in for it when this night was over. But I needed to focus on what I was doing at the moment, which was singing. I turned my attention back to Albert and he smiled at me. It was like he knew what I was thinking. I'm fairly certain that I blushed, although I hoped most people would attribute it to being hot up on stage under the lights. I scanned the packed audience again, this time avoiding Kingston.

The crowd was mixed, ranging from young party goers in their mid-twenties to more established couples in their fifties. Most of the women were in cocktail dresses and many of the men wore suits of some sort. There was a fair amount of foil-and-cardboard New Year's tiaras adorning heads, and every so often I heard a noise maker at a quiet point. I spotted Jillian and her husband, Bruce. She was wearing a bright red dress, which marked a stark contrast to her raven hair. I couldn't believe she came out to see me! When I looked around her, I realized it was pretty much my entire office. From what I could remember, most of us in the office didn't socialize outside of work. I thought it was odd that they were all there together. Then it dawned on me. Holy shit—they were all there for me!

And for some reason, that made me nervous all of a sudden. It was one thing to sing to a bunch of anonymous people, but these were people I knew. I looked anxiously at their faces. Even Tom, my crotchety old boss, and his wife seemed to be enjoying themselves. For the second time in a week it hit me. I had family. I had a lot of family. True, we shared no genetics, but I had people who were there for me when I needed them. I had people who cared about me and loved me for me. I had people who accepted me and my red hair. This was what I had been searching for ever since I lost Aster. This was what the quickie marriage to Dickie Cox was about. This was what the moving from city to city was about. Trying to find someplace where I belonged and fit in. Trying to find people who would listen to me. People who would not force me to be incommunicado. And here, in Columbus, Ohio, on the last day of 2013, I found it. As I belted out tune after tune, I realized that I had found my voice and would never lose it again.

CHAPTER FORTY-EIGHT

We finished up the first set and took a quick break. The timing was such that midnight would strike at the beginning of our third set. There was less than an hour left in this year. I couldn't wait for 2014 to bring a new, fresh start. I didn't know what would happen, but it had to be better than this year, right? Making my way off the stage, I looked around for a chair and some water. While on stage, with the adrenaline rushing, I felt fine. Now that the singing had stopped, I could feel a bit of fatigue creeping in.

Jules, looking stunning herself in red leather pants with a black Flashdance-inspired top, appeared before me with a glass of ice water. I took it and gave her an appreciative smile. "Jules, thanks. I need to sit. Where can I sit down?" She held up her finger to signal me to wait a moment, and before I could finish my next drink, had appeared with a folding chair.

"You guys are on fire up there. How do you feel?"

"I feel like the set was great. I'm tired now that I'm not up there, so I want to conserve a little energy before the next set." I took another drink, relishing the ice cold liquid as it ran down my throat. "You think we sound good?"

"I think we're going to have a lot more gigs after this."

Before she could say more, Kingston, Aster and Rob were there. I knew I should stand up, but I needed to sit and rest. I went to lift myself out of the chair.

"No, Es, stay down. You were fabulous up there. How are you feeling?" Of course Kingston was worried.

"I feel fine. I mean, I feel great up there, but I need to sit for a bit before the next set. The crowd gives me energy that I feed off of. I totally understand why people always want to be on stage."

Aster smiled. "I know. For me, it was just another one of my addictions. It gave me a high just like speed did."

"Never having tried speed, other than what is prescribed for me, I'll take your word for it." I smiled at her and she laughed. "Where's Willy tonight?"

"Rob's parents have him. They stayed purposely through to New Year's to watch him for tonight."

"Oh, that's good. That was nice of them." I had been so busy with rehearsal that it had never occurred to me to ask before.

I drank my entire glass of water and another magically appeared. I really wanted a beer, but the water was cold and wet and would hopefully replace some of the moisture I was sweating out up on stage. I wasn't sure of how long I had before the next set started. I wasn't wearing a watch, and no matter how many times I looked at my titanium bracelet, it never told me the time. I chit chatted with Aster and Kingston for a few minutes. I figured when they needed me back on stage Jules would tell me to head up there. I probably should have gone to the bathroom, but I didn't feel like fighting the crowds to get into the lobby and then wait in line. I was pretty sure I could hold it. I hoped I could anyway.

Figuring that it had to be almost time to go back on, I stood up. I pulled out my purse, which had been stashed behind stage with the equipment. I fluffed what little hair I had, put a little more powder on, and re-applied my lipstick. As I was double-checking to make sure that I didn't have any lipstick on my teeth, I heard the guys start tuning their instruments and Albert on the mike. What the hell? They were starting without me? What was this shit? Angrily, I stuffed my purse under the table and stormed towards the stage stairs. I was stopped cold when I heard what Albert was saying to the crowd.

"The Rusty Buckets want to thank you all for coming out tonight for our very special cause. We want to thank the sponsors of this event for allowing us to make this special night about a very special lady."

What the hell is he doing? And what is he talking about?

He continued. "As many of you know, in September, our lead singer, the lovely and talented Esther Comely-Cox was injured in an accident just following her debut performance. Esther was in a coma for three weeks and since then has spent every moment of every day working toward recovery. Outside of her commitment to The Rusty Buckets, Esther is a dedicated social worker with Franklin County Children's Services. Her injury has left her unable to return to work yet. Initially, her injury robbed our beautiful singer of her ability to speak. Music returned that gift to her."

The crowd erupted into applause as I stood on the steps to the stage, frozen in horror. What was Albert doing? I looked frantically around, from Pauly to Jugs to Drew to Jules. They were all smiling at Albert.

"Esther, can you please come up here?"

I swallowed hard, as there was not enough moisture in the ocean to wet my suddenly dry mouth. Feeling like a newborn calf, and about as sturdy, I made my way up onto the stage. I gave Albert a look that clearly said, "What the hell are you doing?"

Jules was suddenly there behind me with a stool for me to sit on. Albert had a similar one. Not trusting my legs to continue supporting me, I sat down, never taking my eyes off Albert.

"Red, you've been through a lot this year. As a band, we were pretty selfish. We were devastated that we might have lost our voice, just when we had finally found you. But as we started asking around, we realized that you are so much more than a voice. You are a loyal friend and a dedicated social worker. You are a sister and a girlfriend and will drop everything in the blink of an eye

264

to help someone else. Your whole life has been dedicated to serving others."

I swallowed again, this time scanning the crowd for Kingston. Did he know about this? I spotted him right down front. The shit-eating grin on his face told me he did. They all did. It explained why my entire office was here.

Albert continued, "The generous sponsors of this event have let us charge an extra admission fee to the show to be made as a donation to you. We have also done a fundraiser for the Esther's Voice Foundation to help defray some of your medical costs and expenses until you can return to work."

In a supremely attractive manner, my mouth fell open and I almost fell off my stool.

"I can see that this is a bit of a surprise. Good, that's how we wanted it." The crowd roared with laughter. "We know that this won't cover everything, but we hope it helps a bit. So, the guys, Jules and I would like to present you with this check for $11,000." The approval from the crowd was deafening.

That did it. I fell off the stool. Just a little, but enough that Jugs had to rush forward and catch me. I saw Kingston get concerned and shook my head at him. He was worried that it was a medical issue, like I was finally having that stroke they always thought I was due to have. It wasn't. I was barely seated on my stool again when Jules thrust a mike into my hands. My voice shaky and my hands shaking even more, I cleared my throat before speaking. "I am literally bowled over by this. I cannot even begin to thank you, Albert, Pauly, Jugs, Drew and Jules for this. I, um ... I—wow." I took a deep breath and started again. "Obviously this is not what I expected when I came out for this gig tonight. I wanted to put this past year behind me and look toward the future. I ... wow, I can still not even ... wow." I wasn't sure if this was my aphasia or what, but simply no words would come.

Albert was chuckling. "I think she's officially speechless. But this time in a good way." The crowd clapped again and I smiled out to the throng. It was then that I noticed Chieko, Meghan and Janet, my therapists from the rehab hospital, were there. So were Kevin, Dawn and Beth, my therapists from outpatient rehab. They all knew and were here for me. Me!

"So, Esther, before we continue on with our celebration, we have one more thing for you."

Holy crap, what else could there be? They just surprised me with a fundraiser and a check that was going to make a huge difference in my life. Then I saw Albert pick up his acoustic guitar. As he strummed the first few chords he said, "Red, I wrote this song for you. I hope you know that your home is here with us and that we, us, all of us—" he gestured to the crowd, "are your family. And that, no matter what, you will always be loved and will always have a voice with us."

My mouth was open again, as I heard him sing beautiful lyric after beautiful lyric, entwined with a melody that I knew would run through my brain for days and days.

Your lips are still and silent, but your eyes do all the talkin'.
They speak volumes, and make your voice so loud and clear.
Don't you worry 'bout a thing now darlin',
You've got the strength to persevere.
You're loved, you're home, and baby you're still here.

As he finished, I wiped the tears away from my eyes. Then Albert announced that the song was available for sale on iTunes, with a portion of the proceeds going to the Esther's Voice Foundation.

I took a sip of water from the glass that Jules had handed me and put the glass down by the chair. I stood up and hugged her and then Albert and each of the guys. I think Jugs may have touched my ass when I leaned into him, but hey, who was I to deny him anything at a time like this? I picked up my mike again as I sat down. "I don't know how you all expect me to sing after something like that. I am truly speechless. How do I even begin to thank all the people who have helped me? How do I thank each and every one of you for supporting me by being here tonight? Ho—"

I was interrupted by a voice from the crowd. "Enough with the touchy-feely crap. Get back to playing before the year ends!" boomed Tom, my boss.

"Well, that was my boss, so I'd better do as he says." The crowd laughed. "I won't delay much longer, but thank you everyone for everything."

Somehow, I made it through the next two sets, rang in the New Year and lived to tell about it. After the show, we went back to Albert and Jules' house to wind down. Kingston, Aster and Rob were there, of course, and Jillian and Bruce joined us as well. This was it. This was my family. So, since I could not toast the New Year with champagne, I did the next best thing. We toasted with Ho Hos and Fritos. And this time, I made it through the whole night without getting any in my eyebrows. It seemed like 2014 would be my year after all.

THE END

KATHRYN R. BIEL

AUTHOR'S NOTE

One has to look no further than the news to see the impact that mental illness has on today's world. Treatment facilities are few and far between and grossly underfunded. One of the largest barriers to proper treatment for individuals with mental illness is the stigma that it still carries. As long as this stigma exists, efficient and effective treatments will never exist. Help end the stigma by asking for help. Now is the time to start talking about it. #itstime.
More information is available through the National Alliance on Mental Illness: www.nami.org.

For Amanda King and Anna Kroup; you are not forgotten.

ABOUT THE AUTHOR

Telling stories of resilient women, Kathryn Biel hails from upstate New York and is a spouse and mother of two wonderful and energetic kids. In between being Chief Home Officer and Director of Child Development of the Biel household, she works as a school-based physical therapist. She attended Boston University and received her Doctorate in Physical Therapy from The Sage Colleges. After years of writing countless letters of medical necessity for wheelchairs, finding increasingly creative ways to encourage the government and insurance companies to fund her clients' needs, and writing entertaining annual Christmas letters, she decided to take a shot at writing the kind of novel that she likes to read. Her musings and rants can be found on her personal blog, Biel Blather (kathrynbiel.blogspot.com). She is the author of *Good Intentions* (2013) and *Hold Her Down* (2014). Please feel free to follow on Twitter (@KRBiel) or on Facebook (Kathryn R. Biel: Author).

If you've enjoyed this book, please help the author out by leaving a review on Amazon and Goodreads. A few minutes of your time makes a huge difference to an indie author!

32607183R00169

Made in the USA
Charleston, SC
22 August 2014